Boc

THE CODED MESSAGE TRILOGY

F-S-H-S

Book Two of
The Coded Message Trilogy

F-S-H-S

Randy C. Dockens

Carpenter's Son Publishing

F-S-H-S

Published by Carpenter's Son Publishing, Franklin, Tennessee

'ublished in association with Larry Carpenter of Christian Book Services, LLC
'w.christianbookservices.com

and Interior Design by Suzanne Lawing

Robert Irvin

United States of America

-5

CONTENTS

ONE

F-S-H-S

Luke opened his eyes. *A dream?* Surely, a dream. It had to have been a dream. The next thing he realized was he had a terrific headache. He rubbed the back of his head. He winced. It still felt tender. No dream. The guard who had knocked him out was definitely real enough. He looked to the side, and a sense of déjà vu came over him. He had smelled that same acrid odor before. He looked over and saw a latrine and bars. He plopped back down on the cot. *Jail.*

Deep discouragement filled Luke. Despair was not far behind. Where was he, exactly, and how would he get out? Did Oliver and Viktoria know where he was?

He sat up, wincing as he did. This jail looked different, larger. The first jail had been in a Houston precinct. Now he resided somewhere in Paris. Or he did before being knocked out. He went and stood at the bars. He could see more than one level to this jail, and the number of cells looked numerous. *Where am I?*

He sat back down on the cot and leaned against the wall. He put his hands over his forehead and ran them down his face. He thought back to the previous night and his unexpected find under the foam in the case holding the mini drive. It held a book he thought had been destroyed. Those three words on the book burned into his mind's eye. While glad no one else had been caught, he felt betrayed. He now knew why this . . . this *T-H-B* had been so protected and hidden. He had uncovered one of the most outlawed books that existed. Hadn't Oracle Tatum stated anyone caught with it would be considered in the same category as a terrorist? If he had known *T-H-B* stood for *The Holy Bible*, he would not have agreed to be a part of this . . . this quest. He ran his hands through his hair. Was it really supposed to be the answer to life? If so, wouldn't it be the most sought-after book in the world? Would it really be sequestered from anyone and everyone? Why would it be so demonized—unless it really was an evil book?

What would happen to him now? He certainly hoped Oliver's reprogramming for all those involved the night before worked. Otherwise, he would be in jail for the rest of his life. He couldn't imagine never seeing Sarah again—her golden blonde hair, amber-colored eyes, luscious smile, and intoxicating laugh. What about his career? He couldn't just lose that. He had worked so hard to become an astrophysicist. He just couldn't lose everything for . . . for a book no one was supposed to read in the first place.

Luke laid back down on the cot. He closed his eyes but couldn't sleep. His mind spun with thoughts and questions. He gave a half laugh. Viktoria, the Ice Lady, the one who worked for the Illumi-Alliance, knew about *The Holy Bible* all along. No wonder she accused him of terrorism that first unforgettable day he picked up that piece of confetti with the letters T-H-B on it. Yet the kind Viktoria, the wife of Oliver, had no knowledge of it. Oliver helped her each day get her memories back—but apparently not all of them.

Luke put his hands to his head and shook it. He felt like he had entered a nightmare. He had watched a few episodes of the old show *The Twilight Zone.* One episode showed a man whose family began stringing random words together to make sentences. They seemed to understand each other, but to him it sounded like gibberish. The man's world had turned upside down; yet, to everyone else, the world seemed normal and hadn't changed. This is how Luke now felt. His whole world had turned upside down, and he would never get it back.

His mind switched to another thought. Now that he had stolen it, would he read it? *What would make it such an evil book? Is it some kind of manifesto against life?* But then, why would Oliver say it held the meaning to life? Luke shook his head. The inconsistency here didn't seem to make sense.

Was this book tied to all the reprogrammed memories? To the Mars mission? Maybe it was the key—to everything. And what about all of his teachers, who stated that any book written before 2030 couldn't be trusted? Had that been to protect . . . or to ensure control? Had this Illumi-Alliance controlled everyone for the past fifty-nine years? He put his hands to his head again. All this just made his head hurt even more.

He had to keep himself from going into conspiracy theories. Maybe that was the reason the book had been classified as dangerous. It made people think irrationally. But all the reprogramming was also irrational. He let out a loud "Uggghh." Thinking about it proved too confusing. Maybe he would have to read the book to find out. He shook his head. One should not have to disobey the law to understand the law.

As he laid there thinking, something caught his eye. Another déjà vu moment. It looked like a piece of confetti floating down in a twisting, turning fashion. Someone from one of the upper cells must have dropped it. Once again, one side, apparently metallic, caught the sunlight as it passed through a section where the sun came pouring through a window. As it descended through this section of light, it seemed to twinkle. Luke kept glancing at the confetti. He found he couldn't keep his eyes off it as it descended and landed at the edge of his bed—nonmetallic side up. Once again, there seemed to be something written on it. He leaned over to look more closely and saw four letters, but couldn't quite make them out. He reached to pick it up . . .

. . . He heard the familiar *click, click, click* of someone approaching. Luke smiled, then frowned. Of course. Viktoria. Would she come as the Ice Lady, or as the friend who helped him so greatly last night? The sound got closer and closer. Then, there she stood, outside his cell. As usual, she looked quite attractive with her jet-black hair in ringlets throughout, yet she had no expression, except for her penetrating hazel eyes. She wore the same crimson-red dress with Chinese characters all over it that she had the first time they met. A bead of sweat ran down Luke's temple. This didn't seem like a good sign.

Luke slowly sat up. His and Viktoria's eyes met for several seconds with no change in her disposition. He swallowed hard. Had she come to gloat—or release him? A smile slowly came across her face. Luke breathed a sigh of relief. A warm smile greeted him, not the threatening smile the Ice Lady was so capable of delivering.

Luke spoke first. "What's the verdict? Did Oliver's reprogramming work?"

Viktoria nodded. "Seems to." She unlocked the cell and slid the door open. "No one knows you're in here, so you're free to go."

"Has anyone looked at what we took?"

"Not yet. We've had a few other things to worry about first, like getting you out of here. Ready to go?"

Luke nodded. He bent down and picked up the piece of paper and walked from the cell. He looked up. There were three layers of cells above his. He looked down. Another layer spread out below him.

"Where are we?"

"We're still in Paris. Or, rather, just outside Paris."

"So, what is this place?"

"I'm not entirely sure. I learned just enough to get you out of here. Let's go before someone changes their mind about letting you go."

"Sounds good to me."

Finally, Luke looked at the piece of paper: *F-S-H-S.* He shook his head. *What does that even mean?* Should he throw it away?

Would it lead to another forbidden text somewhere?

Luke realized he had not finished the quest.

This had been only the first part of the journey.

TWO

THE ANSWER?

Viktoria opened the door of the black sedan. Luke climbed in. He breathed a sigh of relief. No one else was in the car. Viktoria entered from the other side. She announced their destination. A female mechanical voice replied, "Time of arrival: sixty-five minutes."

The car pulled off and Viktoria sat back. Luke could see her muscles visibly relax. He guessed her day had been just as bad as his. Well, he actually didn't believe it had been as bad, but it was likely stressful nonetheless.

Viktoria turned to him. "So, what happened? Oliver said you ran into guards and shortly after the earwig went dead."

The memory from the night before started to flood back to Luke. "Philippe Mauchard happened."

Viktoria's eyes went wide, but she quickly recovered. It seemed she used her training to hide her true feelings. "Sarah stated he had stepped down and Professor Mercure took his place."

Luke shook his head. "He gave Simone, 'Professor Mercure,' his position because he moved up."

Viktoria raised an eyebrow and brought her hand to her chin. "Hmm."

"What?" Luke stared at her expression; she was already deep in thought. "You know something. What is it?"

She blinked a couple of times and glanced at him. She shook her head. "No, not really. But there is a feeling that I should know something." She talked slowly as she retrieved memories that had been suppressed. "I know Mr. Rosencrantz periodically got memos from a Philippe Mauchard, but I saw no clear indication he was connected to the Illumi-Alliance." She turned more toward Luke. "So, this would put Mauchard at the same level as Rosencrantz."

Luke cocked his head and gave a mild shoulder shrug. "Or higher."

"Higher?" She looked ahead, in thought. "I guess the six we targeted would have to report to someone."

"Just how high does this Illumi-Alliance go? Who's the real top dog?"

Viktoria slowly shook her head. "Probably only Mauchard knows."

"Well, I'm pretty sure he was the one in Professor Mercure's lab when Sarah and I got trapped there. We overheard the two of them talking. We didn't see his face then, but I recognized the voice of Philippe Mauchard as the one I encountered last night."

Viktoria nodded but didn't say anything. He wondered what she thought. *It must be weird to be in her shoes. She wakes up every morning an Illumi-Alliance agent and stays that way until Oliver can get to her and reprogram her memory.* Oliver had worked out a code word to make the process shorter. When he said "Coconut River," it would trigger the reprogramming and Viktoria would become the person she was at this moment. He thought about the times he had encountered her as an Illumi-Alliance agent and as she currently was. He definitely preferred her this way. Bottom line: she was one beautiful, scary lady. Yet, Oliver absolutely adored her—the light of his life. How he dealt with her every day . . . Luke shook his head. He didn't think he could handle that. Yet if it was true love, then likely nothing would seem too difficult.

"So, I know you encountered guards. You couldn't find an escape route?"

"Well, if I had your catlike ninja skills, maybe I could have."

She gave a half smile. "Or a toilet seat."

Luke laughed out loud in spite of himself as the memory of his fight in the Invocation Center restroom began coming back. "Yes, unfortunately, I had left that behind."

"So, what happened?"

"Like I said, Philippe Mauchard happened. He was dressed in a suit, but wasn't sweating, so I knew he had to have just entered the facility. Oliver had the thermostat in the place cranked up to turn the compound into a vapor in hopes the guards and security would inhale it. He could then reprogram their memories." Luke shook his head. "I knew then that getting the compound into Mauchard's system was top priority."

Viktoria nodded. "Thinking like a true soldier. I'm impressed." In her seat, she again turned toward Luke. "So, how did you manage it?"

Luke gave a slight smile. "Well, Oliver told me if I could close a door it would give me a five-second head start before it unlocked again by itself."

Viktoria nodded.

"I asked to shake his hand. When I did, I pulled him into a couple of guards and ran through the door and shut it."

Viktoria smiled. "Good thinking. Then, what happened?"

Luke's smile broadened. "Thanks. I put the contents of the last vial of compound in my mouth and destroyed my earwig.

The guards rushed in, pinned me against the wall, and forced me back into the other level through the door. Mauchard came up to me. I waited until he had his mouth open and then spewed the compound into his mouth and eyes. I hoped he would breathe in any that had vaporized."

Viktoria's eyes went wide. She didn't try to hide her emotions this time. She laughed and put her hand on his shoulder. "Luke, I must say, I'm very impressed. That was quick thinking. But . . . " She laughed again. "He must have been livid."

Luke nodded. "Yeah, and I've got the bump on the back of my head to prove it."

She patted his arm. "Suffering for the cause."

He smiled, but turned somber quickly. He looked out the car window. They were now in Paris proper. *What was the cause?* The feeling of betrayal came back. He wasn't sure what to expect to find, but a forbidden text wasn't what he had envisioned. He propped his elbow on the car door's armrest and stared out the window, not really looking at anything in particular.

Silence remained between the two of them for several minutes.

Viktoria reached over and touched Luke's arm. "Hey, are you OK?"

He nodded, but didn't initially look at her. After a few seconds, he turned with a weak smile. "I guess the adrenaline surge is wearing off."

She returned the weak smile and nodded. He could tell she didn't believe his reply. Yet, he turned back and mindlessly stared out the window again. He stuck his hand in his pocket and found the piece of confetti. He took it out and looked at it.

He turned to Viktoria and held it out to her.

Her eyes widened slightly. "What's this?" she asked.

"You tell me."

She looked at the piece of paper again and then back to him. *"F-S-H-S?"* She shook her head. "I have no idea." She handed it back. "Looks like you're on another quest."

He rolled his eyes. "Yeah. Just what I need."

He turned back to the window and mumbled. "I wasn't thrilled with the ending of the first one."

"What did you say?"

He shook his head, but didn't answer. After another minute, he turned to her. "Viktoria, what do you think we accomplished yesterday?"

Viktoria blinked a few times before responding. "What do you mean?"

"Do you think we found the answer you were looking for?"

She scrunched her face. "*I* was looking for? Weren't we all looking for the same thing?"

He shrugged. "I wasn't looking for something that would get me classified as a terrorist."

She shook her head slightly. "What are you talking about?"

"Viktoria, it was *The Holy Bible.* That's what *T-H-B* was—*The Holy Bible*."

"And what is that?"

Luke opened his mouth to answer, but then closed it. Did he know what it was? Not really. All he knew was this: it was a religious book banned back in 2030. "I . . . I'm not really sure. But I do know Oracle Tatum stated it was a religious book, and anyone caught with it would be in the same category as a terrorist."

Viktoria shrugged. "Doesn't matter."

Luke's eyes widened. *Why would she say that?* Maybe she didn't care. But it really mattered to him. "What do you mean, 'It doesn't matter'?"

She turned back to him and locked eyes. "Luke, it wouldn't matter what was in that room. It could have been a piece of pottery, a painting . . . anything."

Luke shook his head. "Of course what it is matters."

Viktoria nodded. "Yes, of course. But not what it *makes us*."

Luke still shook his head.

Viktoria gave a sympathetic sigh. "Luke, just us being there makes us terrorists in their eyes. Something they deemed to be secluded from the rest of the population was taken. That alone makes us terrorists."

Luke rubbed his hand across his mouth. He had not thought of it that way. "But . . . but it's a religious book."

Viktoria shrugged. "I don't care what it is. It must be important if they kept it so secluded from the general population."

"Maybe it was to protect us."

Viktoria gave a smirk followed by a half-laugh. "If that was the case, the best way to protect someone from it would be to destroy it." She shook her head. "No, they likely *fear* it. If they revered it, they would want everyone to do the same. No, there's something about that book that's important. I want to know what that is. I would think you would, too."

Luke thought about this. He wasn't sure. He needed more time to think.

The mechanical voice chimed out: "Destination achieved."

Viktoria looked at him. "Let's go meet the others." She smiled. "Sarah's dying to be sure you're OK."

THREE

Reunion

As soon as the door to Jeremy and Natalia's hotel room opened, Sarah fell into his arms, squeezing him in a tight hug. She gave him a lingering kiss. Luke reciprocated, just not to the extent with which she supplied it. He felt heat rush to his cheeks.

Once their lips parted, Sarah smiled. "Sorry. I got carried away." She ran her fingers through his hair, trying to put it in order. "I just had no idea if, or when, I'd see you again."

He looked at himself in the wall mirror. His brown hair did look pretty disheveled. But his blue eyes were the same—although bloodshot from the poor overnight sleep and trip.

She squeezed his arm and whispered, "I really missed you."

Luke smiled. Jeremy gave Luke a wink when no one else was looking.

Sarah pulled on his arm. "Come. Tell us all about it."

Oliver nodded. "Yes. I'm dying to hear what happened after you killed the earwig."

Luke spent the next half-hour going over everything he had already told Viktoria, but in even more detail. Everyone seemed riveted. Every so often, Sarah squeezed his hand, especially when he mentioned a part where he was in danger—which was most of the time.

Once finished, he looked at Oliver. "Please tell me your memory reprogramming worked and we're all out of danger."

Oliver shrugged. "As best as I can tell, the answer is yes. Otherwise, I think we would be joining you—rather than you, us."

Luke nodded. He had a point. That made him feel a little better.

Oliver held up his phone. "I have sent each of you an app to your phone. Download it and the document will be there. It is encrypted so it will look like gibberish until you enter your decryption password. I have sent that to you separately. Each person has a different one. Whatever I sent you, go higher by two letters or two numbers. For example, if I sent A12B, you'll use C34D. An 8 is a 0 and a Y is an A. Understand?"

Everyone nodded.

"I suggest you memorize it and delete the e-mail. I have a virus embedded in the e-mail which will delete the record from your phone once you delete it." He sat up in his seat and leaned forward. "Now, if you feel compromised in any way, hold the app down and then tap it. It will delete itself. I can always send you another copy, so better safe than sorry."

Luke downloaded the app, then looked up. "There's one more thing that happened I need to tell you."

He took out the piece of confetti and handed it to Oliver, who raised an eyebrow and passed it along to the others. "Where did you get this and what does it mean?"

"It drifted down to me while I was in the prison. I have no idea what it means." He looked at the others. "Anyone else?"

Everyone shook their heads.

Sarah patted his arm. "Another mystery to add to all the others." She stared at him for a few seconds. By this point in their relationship, Luke knew she could read him very well. "That's not your real concern, is it? What's really bothering you, Luke?"

Luke shook his head. "So, no one else has second thoughts about all of this? I mean, after all, we've stolen a religious document—something that's been banned for fifty-nine years. We've committed treason in the eyes of the government, and we're sitting here casually talking about it." He opened his arms slightly. "I don't know, I just feel like I've been caught with my hand in the cookie jar." He looked at each of them. "No one else feels this way?"

Oliver sat back and stared at Luke. "So, what exactly did you expect? You said you understood the risks."

Luke stood and walked behind the sofa he had been sitting on. He leaned in, putting his hands on the back of it. "I understood the risks of what we were doing. I just didn't expect the so-called answer to be some religious book."

Sarah took his hand. He looked into her eyes. He saw concern. "What were you expecting, Luke?"

He shook his head and now started pacing behind the sofa. He threw his hands up. "I don't know, but certainly not this. Maybe some manual that explained the plans behind the memory reprogramming, the reason for the Mars mission . . . " He threw his hands up again. "Anything!"

"Luke." It was Jeremy. Luke turned toward his friend. "What has you so bent out of shape about this just because it's a religious book? Maybe it's not the book itself but something in it that's the key which the Illumi-Alliance wants to keep away from us. Isn't it worth reading to find out?"

Luke cocked his head and gave a slight shrug. "Maybe." He shook his head. "But what good has ever come from a book on religion? Remember what Oracle Tatum said? It's caused all sorts of damage and hurt."

Jeremy squinted. "But isn't that just *his* take, or what he's been told? I mean, how do we even know *he's* read it? Maybe it's all hearsay."

Natalia leaned forward. "Lukey, I'm not sure why this has you so upset, but if it's been kept so well guarded all these years and not destroyed, the Illumi-Alliance must have some respect for it." She glanced at the others. "I, for one, would like to find out why, or find out what they're afraid of."

It was hard to get upset with Natalia when she called him Lukey, a name she first gave him when they were both in college. They took an astronomy class together that had two Lukes in it. His middle initial being E, she took to calling him Lukey. She had never stopped calling him that.

Luke sighed. "Maybe you're right, Natalia. Perhaps I'm losing focus, or maybe I'm just tired. All I know is, I feel very uneasy about this."

His phone beeped. He looked at it: a text from Larry, his supervisor.

Sarah touched his arm. "What is it?"

"It's a text from Larry. There's a big meeting the end of this week. He wants me there in person." He looked up at all of them. "I . . . I have to get back to work. I'll fly out tomorrow evening."

"I'll go back with you."

He looked at Sarah and smiled. "I hoped you'd say that."

She patted his hand. "We've been through too much together to do otherwise."

Oliver slapped his knees. "Well, it's for the best anyway, I think. The quicker we get back to our daily routines, the less reason for others to think we're doing anything but."

Jeremy nodded. "I should have my obligations wrapped up here by the middle of next week. What if we meet next Friday at our Mars City penthouse, and then see where to go from there?"

Everyone nodded. Luke felt himself anxious to get back to normalcy, to some type of routine. He hoped the uneasy feeling he had was only that. Yet he couldn't fully convince himself that this was all there was to his unsettled feeling.

FOUR

PLOTTING

Luke opened the portal to the Aerospace Engineering Center and gave a contented sigh. It felt good to be back at work in Mars City, just outside of Houston. He noted the large atrium, the palatial marble steps leading to the second floor—even though they were more for public display than utility—and the large fountain next to it. He felt like he had come home. He looked forward to some normalcy. He entered the elevator and pressed the button for the fifteenth floor. Arriving at his floor, he stepped off the elevator into the soon-to-be-hubbub of preparation for the Mars mission. He had arrived early, so it was relatively quiet. That allowed him to get in the zone at his open-space desk and tune others out. At the same time, his colleagues would be there for him if he had a question, just as he would for them.

Luke sat down, fired up his holo-computer, and got to work. Its transparent screen allowed him either to focus on things in the distance or to focus on his work on the screen. Even though he had worked while in Europe, the amount of work Larry had for him on his return surprised him. Maybe all of this was to prepare for whatever the big meeting announcement would be in two days. He prepared several simulations, did gravimetric and gravitational calculations, observed the simulations in the pod rooms along the interior wall, and made tweaks as necessary. Before he knew it, lunch arrived.

Luke grabbed a prepared salad and protein bar at the cafeteria and looked to see if Sarah was in the seating area. They usually sat along the outside lower tier which overlooked a large pond out front. They would often sit and observe the swans swimming; the large birds looked quite majestic as they moved across the water. In truth, it was all only a hologram—the true outside was a busy city street—but it helped engender a sense of calm while everyone ate.

Luke finally spotted her. Or, rather, Sarah spotted him and waved. He nodded and headed over. Someone was sitting with her. As he walked closer, he recognized it was Jason. He grimaced. He hadn't spoken to Jason since the boysenberry tart incident that started the whole spy mission to Paris.

Luke sat next to Sarah and smiled at Jason. "Hey, Jason. Good to see you again."

Jason smiled back. He opened his coat and showed his white shirt. "See, no stain remaining."

Luke raised his eyebrows. "Oh, is that the infamous boysenberry tart shirt?"

Jason chuckled and nodded. "I told you I'd get the stain out."

Luke took a bite of salad and pointed his fork toward Jason. "Well, I'd never be able to tell. I'm sure your clients can't either." Luke knew Jason, as the site's event planner, always wore a suit since he had to meet many clients throughout the day and present a professional image. "So, what's new?"

"Funny you should ask." He nodded toward Sarah.

Luke looked at Sarah and then back to Jason. "What?"

Sarah smiled and patted his hand. "Remember the 5K we talked about but never entered?"

Luke nodded. "And?"

"Well, there's another one this weekend. Jason and Jared are entering, and they want us to enter with them."

Luke's eyebrows raised. "Oh?" He looked at Jason. "No offense intended, but it's not a team sport, so why?"

Jason smiled. "Well, Sarah and I were talking. Neither of us feel we can keep up with either you or Jared."

Luke tried to follow, but was evidently missing something. Confused, he looked at Sarah.

"Luke, rather than me slowing you down and Jason slowing Jared down, we thought we'd run together and the two of you could run together."

Jason leaned in. "Yes, Jared is pretty fast. So the two of you could challenge each other to keep improving." He nodded toward Sarah. "She and I will take a long time before we could match your speed."

Sarah smiled. "That way, we all continue to improve without holding each other back. We can then meet after the race and have smoothies or something."

Luke looked from one to the other, then back. He shrugged. "Sure. I guess. What's his normal time for a 5K?"

Jason gave a grimace. "Oh, I'm not sure. Somewhere around eighteen to twenty minutes, I guess."

Luke nodded. "Well, that will definitely give me a challenge considering I haven't run in quite some time."

Jason smiled. "It's a date, then? Uh, I mean the race, not that you and he . . . " His face turned red.

Luke laughed. "Relax, Jason. Yes, it's a definite . . . whatever you want to call it."

"OK. Great. We look forward to seeing you there." Jason looked at his watch. "I have to run. I have to see a client in ten minutes."

He left. Luke looked to Sarah. "This was all your plan, wasn't it?"

She shrugged. "Well, sort of. You said you wanted some normalcy. I thought you getting back into running would be good."

"But I thought we would run together."

"We will. But you also need to be challenged sometimes as well." She cocked her head. "I saw it as an opportunity, and I took it."

He smiled and reached over and kissed her on her cheek. "Thanks. You're always looking out for me. Yet . . . "

She gave him a *What?* look.

"I think you want to find out something from Jason."

Sarah's head bobbed. "Well, killing two birds with one stone isn't a bad idea, is it?"

He smiled. "No. No, it isn't." He looked at his watch. "Oh, I have to get back to work too. I may need to work late, so it may be lunch tomorrow before I see you."

She nodded. "OK. I'll walk to the elevator with you. I should get back to work as well."

Back at his desk, Luke became engrossed in his work again. After a few hours, he looked up for a breather. He looked around and saw that everyone was doing their thing. He smiled. It felt good to be back.

FIVE

RENÉ MAUCHARD

The big day arrived. Luke went in early to get some finishing touches completed before the meeting would be held. He felt a tap on his shoulder.

"OK, Luke. It's time." It was Larry. "Head down to the large amphitheater on the first floor."

Luke's eyes widened. He had not expected that. "This must be a really big announcement."

Larry smiled, but didn't elaborate. "Just get there pronto."

Luke nodded. He walked to the elevator with Scott and Brian. "Either of you know what's going on?"

Both shook their heads.

"Whatever it is, I bet it leads to more work."

Scott looked at Brian. "You're always the skeptic."

Brian shrugged. "I'm just telling it as I see it."

Luke laughed. "More work, less pay. Count me in."

Both rolled their eyes. Scott smirked. "OK. I'll give you mine."

Luke smiled at that. He felt like cattle as they were compressed into the elevator by several people around them.

Brian leaned over and whispered, "I'm glad this is a short ride. I could faint and stay standing."

Luke nodded and smiled. These two guys were great to work with. They complained, but when push came to shove, they worked hard, just like Luke did. All three had each other's backs when deadlines were due. Larry often referred to them as his "dynamic Neapolitan," since Scott had blondish-colored hair and Brian darker hair with reddish highlights.

By the time they reached the amphitheater and found three seats, they were five rows from the back. The place was packed.

Luke noticed Larry and a few other managers on the front row. Rosencrantz stood at the front talking with someone Luke didn't recognize. He leaned over to Brian. "Who is Rosencrantz talking to?"

Brian shook his head and shrugged.

Scott leaned over. "I think that's Mr. Mauchard, from Paris."

Luke jerked his head back slightly. Couldn't be. "*That's* Mauchard?"

Scott nodded. "Yeah, a René Mauchard, I believe. I heard his father was some big uppity-up who recently passed away. Now his son René seems to be the big shot to the big shots."

Luke thought that interesting. *Is Philippe his brother?* Maybe the two of them were the top dogs, so to speak. He studied the man's features. If he squinted, he could see some facial similarities, but it was also hard to tell.

Mr. Rosencrantz approached the podium. The crowd noise died. He smiled. "Welcome, ladies and gentlemen. Thanks for coming. I have some really exciting news to share. I know you all have been working tirelessly on getting us ready for the Mars mission. And I'm happy to report, all is so far on schedule."

A round of applause exploded throughout the room.

"And I know the success for that goes to all of you. We

may think we are responsible, but I know we can do nothing without you." He pointed to the front row. "Managers, shall we stand and give our great employees the round of applause they deserve?"

The front row stood and turned, clapping toward the audience.

Brian leaned over. "That Mr. Rosencrantz has quite the PR shtick, doesn't he?" He smiled. "I like it, though."

Scott leaned in. "That's the most appreciation I've received from Larry this whole month."

Luke jabbed Scott's shoulder. "Oh, please. He sang your praises just yesterday."

Scott beamed. "Just wanted to be sure you boys were paying attention."

Luke shook his head.

Once the clapping died down, Rosencrantz stepped back to the podium. "Now, I get the pleasure to announce the surprise. I know some of you have heard the rumor, but I'm here to put the record straight." He left a dramatic pause, then delivered his next line. "There is more than one Mars mission."

Luke heard rumblings all around him. It went from minor to a major rumbling in a matter of seconds.

Rosencrantz held up his hands. "Now, now. Let me finish."

The large room went silent.

"In addition, there will be a worldwide lottery for individuals to go on the Mars mission."

The noise shot up to a high decibel level in a matter of seconds.

Rosencrantz raised his hands again. "I know. I know. You have a lot of questions. Unfortunately, I don't have a lot of answers right now. Some of you will be asked to work with colleagues from various places around the world as this has now turned into a global effort." He smiled. "More information will be coming about the lottery. Yet, this turns our efforts—your efforts—into global recognition."

He gestured for Mauchard to step to the podium. "Many of you don't know this gentleman, but his father was the one with the vision and chutzpah to get this ball rolling. Yet, this man, Mr. René Mauchard, is the one who has turned his father's vision into a global mission. René, please come and address our employees."

Mauchard had youthful-looking tanned skin even though he was bald. Luke couldn't judge his age. He looked pretty spry, however, and even in his suit he looked muscular. Luke assumed Mauchard couldn't be much older than he was.

"Thank you, Jerome. It's my pleasure to be with you today. I don't often get to be here in the States with you. I am happy to carry out my father's vision. He wanted mankind to reach the stars with Mars as the first stop. This is too much of a historic moment to share with only one country. We must share it with the world. Don't you agree?"

The crowd erupted into more applause and even a few whistles.

Mauchard gave a brief history of his father's dream and his vision for going forward. Luke noticed he left out a great deal of detail and made it much more of a rah-rah type of speech. He ended his talk. "I hope you will work with us and be willing to step up when called upon. It's no longer a job. It's making history."

More applause erupted.

Rosencrantz returned to the podium. "Thanks for coming so we could share this important and wonderful news. Have a great rest of your day."

The buzz in the room increased as everyone stood to exit. Luke could hear various people saying they wanted to be in the lottery; others said they wanted to stay on terra firma.

Luke heard one man put it this way: "I work here so others can go into space and I can just go home."

In spite of what Rosencrantz and Mauchard had said, just the opposite occurred—for this day at least. Very little work got done. Everyone talked about the lottery and what they would or wouldn't do if selected. Others speculated as to where and in what stages of development the other missions were in at the various workplaces around the globe, and where they might hope to be temporarily assigned to help.

Luke listened and laughed along with the others. Yet he wondered what this was really all about. He couldn't help but feel this was another smoke screen for something the Illumi-Alliance had up its sleeve.

On the way home, Luke remembered Jeremy and Natalia would be back next week. He wondered if they would have any further insights into all of this. Perhaps Viktoria would.

And there was one other thing that worried Luke: now there were not one, but two, Mauchards to contend with.

SIX

5K

"Do you see them?" Luke turned a 360 while looking in all directions.

Sarah shook her head. "Not yet."

"I guess we should have designated a spot to meet. There are hundreds of people here."

"Well, I didn't realize . . . oh, there they are." She held up her hand and waved.

Luke looked in the direction Sarah was waving. At first he didn't see Jason and Jared. He looked for something flamboyant, but found their clothes no different than his. There were handshakes and hugs all around.

"Thanks for agreeing to do this, guys. It's going to be fun." Jason smiled. "Right, Jared?"

Jared returned a weak smile and nodded. Luke had a feeling that Jared, like himself, wasn't necessarily thrilled with the idea. They both knew Sarah and Jason had concocted the whole thing.

An awkward silence fell. Luke looked around and then at his watch. He wanted this to get started. Once they started running, they didn't necessarily have to talk. They would just keep pace with each other.

"Uh, shall we find our places?" Luke offered.

The others nodded and headed toward the race's start line.

Sarah gave Luke a quick kiss. "Have fun."

He smiled and nodded. "You too." He turned to Jared. "Ready?"

Jared nodded.

Luke wondered how fast Jared would be and if he could keep up with him. No, he *was* going to keep up with him. Luke would never say it out loud, but his machismo was on the line—and he was determined to keep it.

The runners lowered into their starting stances, the gun went off, and the race began. At first, Luke and Jared were side by side as they tore past most of the crowd. There were a few who flew past them. Luke was OK with that. He wasn't here to win the race—just not to lose to Jared.

After a while, Jared sped up to take the lead between the two of them. Luke let him do that for a few minutes and then caught him. Jared looked over and smiled. Luke smiled back and ran a little faster to take the lead. Luke smiled to himself. He saw the look of surprise on Jared's face. There was no way he was going to let Jared win this.

But shortly after, Jared caught up with him. They ran neck and neck for several minutes. Jared then pulled ahead. Luke realized this was going to be tough. He already felt fatigued, but he plowed through it and caught up with Jared once more. They jockeyed back and forth for the lead many times throughout the race. Luke began to wonder if he could hold out at this pace. He looked over. Jared seemed to be in the same boat as he, but Jared also had determination on his face.

Once Luke saw the finish line in the distance, he picked up his pace. He wanted to actually beat Jared. As soon as Jared sped up and matched his stride, he would speed up just a little more. The finish line was now looming closer. Luke put all he had into it. Apparently, Jared did the same. Luke felt his energy draining. He started to question if he had enough to finish the race at this pace. Now Jared was pouring it on. They were a few meters from the finish line when Jared came up even with Luke and matched him stride for stride. Luke realized he couldn't put any more into it, even though he tried. He no longer tried to win—his only goal now was to not let Jared get ahead of him. Better to tie than lose.

They crossed the finish line side by side. Luke careened to the sideline, put his hands on his knees, and sucked in air like it was in extremely short supply. He glanced over at Jared, who was doing the same. After a couple of minutes, Luke went over to a grassy spot and sat down. Sweat poured off of him. He kept wiping his eyes as the sweat stung them and made them water.

Jared came over and sat near him. Sweat was pouring off of him as well. They didn't say anything and didn't look at each other for a few minutes. Still breathing hard, Luke finally looked over at Jared, who glanced at him. They locked eyes and looked at each other for a few seconds. Luke couldn't help but smile. Jared did the same, and then they both broke into laughter. Luke—and likely Jared as well—realized he had been a fool to run so hard to prove a foolish point.

Jared stuck out his hand. Luke grabbed his forearm. "Good race, Jared."

Jared laughed. "You too. You turned into quite the competitor."

Luke laughed. "Well, I could tell you were thinking, 'I'm not letting a scientist take me down.'"

Jared leaned back on his hands and gave a hearty laugh. "Yeah, and you were saying, 'I'm not going to let a gay guy get the best of me.'"

Luke smiled. "I guess we were both idiots."

Jared nodded. "Yet, I think I did my best time ever."

Luke laughed even harder, but stopped to get more breath. He patted Jared's shoulder. "Glad I could be of service."

Jared smiled. "I think since I lost my job, I haven't had a chance to work out regularly."

"You lost your job? What happened?"

Jared shrugged. "Cutbacks, I guess. Anyway, I've tried starting my own business, but it hasn't gone anywhere yet."

Luke lightly smacked his own head. "Oh, wait. I just saw something at work about the gym needing another assistant. Why don't you apply?"

Jared's eyes went wide. "Really? I . . . I'd love that."

Luke nodded. "I'll e-mail you the information. Give Jason your résumé and he can drop it off for you."

"I appreciate that, man."

Sarah and Jason came over. They were sweaty and breathing heavily, but not out of breath.

"You two look like you ran a marathon." Sarah laughed. "There's not a dry stitch on you."

Luke stood. He held out his arms. "Give me a big hug for finishing."

"Eew, eew. No." She held up her palms. "Not until you take a shower and get cleaned up."

"But if you loved me . . . "

"Yeah, and if you loved me, you wouldn't ask."

All four of them laughed.

Jason gestured toward Sarah. "Thanks for the jog and walk. Want to meet at Earth's Garden in about an hour for a light bite or a drink?"

Sarah looked at Luke. He nodded. "Sure. I think that's only two blocks from us. We'll see you there."

They all shook hands and went their ways.

As they headed back to their apartment complex, Sarah said, "It looks like you and Jared hit it off OK."

Luke laughed. He told her about their conversation. She rolled her eyes. "You guys are ridiculous."

"So, what did you find out from Jason?"

Sarah smiled. "More than I thought I would. Let me do some more thinking about things and I'll tell everyone on Friday."

Luke nodded. "OK. I think now that the worldwide approach is out in the open, Jason can likely help us know what's going on—at least at a higher level."

"That's the plan." She kissed her fingers and placed them on his cheek. "Now go get your shower and we'll meet them at the restaurant."

SEVEN

MR. MANCINI

Friday came much faster than Luke expected. The buzz at work continued. Yet, toward the end of the week, everyone began to get back to their routines. Luke picked up Sarah after work at her apartment and they headed to Jeremy and Natalia's place.

The taxi dropped them off at Continental Drift, the namesake seven-story restaurant owned by Jeremy Pangea; it was designed by his architect wife, Natalia. They entered through the bar on the first floor, went to the back, and took the elevator, using Luke's specific numerical code, which allowed him and Sarah access to the penthouse.

Natalia answered the door. Her bright smiled greeted them. She gave each of them a hug and Luke a kiss on the cheek. "Good to see you again, Lukey."

Luke smiled. "Same here."

She gestured toward the seating area. "Please come in. Oliver and Viktoria are here."

There were handshakes and hugs. Jeremy had drinks and hors d'oeuvres ready. Everyone prepared a plate and found a place to sit.

Luke looked toward Jeremy. "I guess you heard the news. Rosencrantz and Mauchard announced more than one Mars mission."

Jeremy's eyebrows shot up. "Really? So, they're not trying to hide it anymore?"

Sarah shook her head. "No, and they announced a world-wide lottery will be instituted for people to be part of a mission."

Oliver sat his glass down. He was blunt: "That's a smoke screen."

Sarah nodded. "That's what I think, also. I think they plan to target immunes." She looked at the others and shrugged. "It's the perfect cover story. I mean, who's going to know they were not the ones who drew the . . . "—she did air quotes—" . . . lucky numbers?"

Oliver leaned in. "Let's summarize all we know. Maybe that will give us some perspective as to what the Illumi-Alliance has planned."

Everyone nodded, then Luke spoke up. "We now know there is more than one Mars mission. It wasn't announced how many, but we know, based on what we've discovered, there is one per continent."

Sarah nodded. "And we know Professor Simone Mercure, with the help of Philippe Mauchard, plans to find a compound that will help reprogram the memories of those currently immune."

"Let's not forget . . . " Natalia jumped in. "We now have a copy of their well-protected *T-H-B* and, as far as we know, they are still unaware we have it."

"Has anyone read their copy?" Oliver glanced at each of them. "I've started, but haven't made a lot of progress yet."

Luke sat down his plate. "What have you read so far?"

Oliver gave a half-shrug. "I started at the beginning. It talks about how God created the world."

Luke sat back. "Really? How does that help us?"

Oliver held up his palm. "I'm not saying I've discovered any answers yet. There's still a lot to read. And there must be something there somewhere."

"I've been reading also." All eyes turned to Natalia. "I started reading what is called the Gospel of John. I find it very interesting. I think there may be something there."

Luke scrunched his face. "What made you start there?"

Natalia shrugged. "I'm not sure. I have this vague memory of my father talking about it."

Jeremy turned to her. "I didn't know your father was religious."

She gave a slight smile. "I didn't really remember that until I started looking at this book."

Sarah patted Natalia's knee. "What happened to your father?"

Natalia shook her head. "I don't know. I haven't really seen him since 2071, when I was taken to government boarding school when I reached the age of ten." She thought for a moment. "He would be 78 if still alive." She gave a weak smile. "I've had strange dreams since I started reading this book."

Jeremy had a look of concern. "What kind of dreams?"

"About my father." She shook her head. "Odd, I know. I mean, after all, we're taught that parents give their children for the betterment of the community. Yet, I found a verse in . . . in . . . what was it? E— . . . E-phesians. Yes, that's it. A book in *T-H-B* called Ephesians. It said to 'honor your father and mother.' For some reason, that verse has stuck with me. I've considered looking up my parents."

Luke turned to Viktoria. "Not to change the subject, but that jail you found me in seemed to have a lot of elderly people in it. Any idea what type of prison that was?"

Viktoria nodded. "I was wondering when to bring this up. Well, I think these are the immunes you stated Professor Mercure suggested using as test subjects."

"What?" Sarah looked from Viktoria to Luke. "They're testing old people?"

Viktoria gave a slight shrug. "Well, not all of them are old. But many are."

Luke nodded. "Makes sense."

Sarah gave him an incredulous stare.

Luke held up his palm. "I'm not saying I agree with it. I'm just saying it makes sense from their agenda and point of view."

Viktoria threw three folders on the table. "I found these in Mercure's lab. She had a whole stack, so she probably won't miss these."

Jeremy picked up one and opened it. "Wow. You mean this guy has been in prison for fifty-nine years?"

Sarah's eyes widened. "Why? Just because he was an immune?"

Jeremy scanned the document. "Apparently. This doesn't list any crime."

Sarah shook her head. "They're the ones who are the criminals."

Jeremy picked up the second one. "Well, I can't argue with . . ."

Natalia put her hand on his back and rubbed. "What's wrong?"

He glanced at her. "Your maiden name was Mancini. Your father Italian and your mother Chinese, right?"

Natalia turned up a brow. "Yeah, but you already know that. Jeremy, why . . . why are you asking me that?"

He slowly laid the file—turned open—on the table. "I . . . I think I've found your father."

"What?" She looked at the file and then at Jeremy. She

slowly picked it up and looked more closely. Her hand went to her mouth with a slight gasp. "That's . . . that's him." She slowly ran her fingers over the photo.

Luke put his hands to his temples. "Wait a minute. Your father is in the prison in Paris? The one Viktoria pulled me out of?"

Natalia nodded. She looked ashen at this news. She handed the file to Luke. He looked at the photo. He flipped the page. It had a picture of the man when he was apparently first arrested. He glanced from the photo to Natalia. He could see she had her father's skin tone, lips, and nose.

Sarah looked over Luke's shoulder. "We have to do something." She looked at Viktoria. "Surely we can do something. Can you break him out?"

Viktoria nodded, and yet had a quite serious look. "But it won't be easy."

EIGHT

THE ARGUMENT

For some reason, Luke felt himself getting more anxious over the next week. He had a hard time understanding why. He had empathy for Natalia. As kids, all are taught parents are just a part of the journey into Community. Yet, knowing Natalia's father had been in prison for all these years was unconscionable. Maybe part of it was waiting to hear back from Viktoria to see what she had planned for breaking Mr. Mancini out.

He still couldn't force himself to read his copy of *The Holy Bible.* He still felt betrayed that he had risked everything for something others purported to be the answer to everything. He couldn't articulate what he expected, but he had expected something more. Then he felt guilty; it seemed everyone else was really getting into this Bible and he hadn't even started his reading.

As Luke sat on his sofa trying to figure himself out, he realized what bothered him the most. He almost didn't want to see Sarah because she now always talked about something new she had read in her copy of the Bible. Until now, the very thought of seeing her would send tingles through his being.

Now he felt like he was competing for her attention.

He had almost convinced himself to sink further into his funk by ordering a pizza and watching an old movie when his doorbell rang. He looked through the peephole. His pulse quickened; it was Sarah. He was glad to know seeing her, as usual, put a little zing through him. This proved he still cared a great deal about her. His adrenaline rush turned into a sigh. He realized that her coming by at this hour likely meant she wanted to tell him about something else she had read.

Luke opened the door and smiled. "What brings my favorite person by at this hour?" He gave her a kiss and invited her in.

She smiled, but seemed reserved. "Are you OK?"

He gave a slight shrug. "Yeah, I'm fine. Just feeling a little anxious and unsettled."

She cocked her head. "Want to talk about it?"

He shook his head. "Not really. I just need to work through it." He gestured to the sofa, offering her a seat. "So what brings you by?"

She scooted closer. "Well, two things. First, you've missed several lunches."

He held up his palm. "I'm really sorry. Larry has gone ballistic with extra work lately."

She held his arm and squeezed. "I know. I'm not complaining. I just missed you." She smiled. "But it has allowed me to pump Jason a couple of times for more information."

Luke laughed. "Has he been forthcoming?"

"Well, he is a little reluctant to give information, but he's hinted there's likely a big meeting occurring in Paris soon."

"He didn't say when?"

She chuckled. "I think it will take more prodding to get all the information out of him. I'm not sure if he doesn't know, or if he's just reluctant to give it out. Probably the latter."

Luke nodded and smiled. "And the second reason you came by?"

She gave a sheepish smile. "I wanted to read you something."

Luke rolled his eyes. "I was afraid of that."

"Luke, I don't understand your reluctance to read this book. I think I've discovered its power is to change people from the inside."

Luke's head jerked back slightly. "What is that supposed to mean?"

"It's starting to make me think about things differently."

"Like what?"

"I started reading in the section called John based on what Natalia said. It's made me start to think about God."

"God?"

She nodded. "God loves us and wants us to be with him once we die."

Luke shook his head. "Sarah, do you hear yourself?" He stood. "That's why I haven't started reading. It messes with your mind." He started pacing. "That's why I was disappointed in finding it. I think that's why they sequestered it."

Sarah turned on the sofa to look at him. "Luke, do you hear *yourself*?"

He shook his head and scrunched an eyebrow.

"That's what these people are already doing. They're already messing with our minds. If that's what this book does, then they would use it to their advantage." Sarah shook her head. "No. They're afraid of this book. And I think I'm beginning to see why."

"Why?"

"It makes us look at the world differently. Our life is supposed to be something more than just about ourselves."

"Well, yeah. We are to serve Community. That's what all the

oracles have always told us."

Sarah gave a sigh. "It's more, Luke. I haven't gotten it figured out yet, but if you would just read it, you'll see: there is just something about this that is so intriguing."

Luke could feel his frustration rising. "But Sarah, I didn't risk my life to find something intriguing. I wanted something with answers."

She got up on her knees on the sofa and faced him, a more intense look on her face. "It does have answers. We just have to read to find them."

"But if it has answers, why are they so hidden? I just don't see how a religious book can have the kind of answers we need with the issues we're facing."

"I think I'm seeing that no outward change occurs without an inward change first. We talk about Community, but we're just a manipulated community. Our leaders don't really care about us as individuals." She threw up her hands. "Do we even care about individuals?"

Luke gave a half smile. "A few."

She gave a quick smile, but turned serious again. "Luke, this is really hard to explain. If only you would read it with me, we could have a better conversation."

Luke shook his head.

"I really value your insight."

Luke paced again. "I can't."

"It's another mystery for us to solve together." She smiled, pleadingly, as she said it.

Luke cradled his forehead with his hand. His breath became forced. "No."

"But, Luke . . . "

His irritation escalated exponentially—and he exploded. "I don't want to read it!"

Sarah froze.

Luke closed his eyes. He sighed. *Why did I do that?*

Her eyes watered, but it was obvious she would do her best not to let him see her cry.

Luke took a step toward her. She stepped back from the sofa, away from him.

"Sarah, I'm . . . I'm sorry. I shouldn't have yelled like that."

She shook her head. "No, it's fine. You stated how you felt. I just didn't know you felt so . . . strongly." She attempted to put up a strong front, but her bottom lip quivered.

"Sarah, please forgive me." He went to touch her again, but Sarah was walking for the door. "I let my frustration get the better of me."

"I . . . I'm going to go now." She was about to lose it.

Sarah reached for the door handle. His hand got there first. Her hand touched his. She froze again, then withdrew her hand. She stood stoic, except for her eyes watering. She was blinking to keep the tears at bay.

Luke opened the door and Sarah stepped out without saying anything.

He closed the door and leaned his head against it. Hearing Sarah cry on the other side of the door made his heart sink. He rolled his head back and forth and tightly shut his eyes. He couldn't believe he had done that. Frustrated, he wanted to pound the door repeatedly, but knew that would only frighten Sarah more. All he could think was, *Stupid, stupid, stupid. Luke, you are stupid.*

After a few minutes, he heard her walk away from his apartment. He went to his bedroom and sat on the bed with his back against the headboard. He took a pillow and squeezed it to his chest. The more he thought about what happened, the more frustrated he felt. He had to pound something. He took his pillow and pounded it over and over and over.

I am an idiot. He could have been holding Sarah, but now

he was holding a stupid pillow. So, she wanted to read this book and discuss it. If he was with her, wouldn't it be worth it? But no, he had to insist on things his way. Would he ever be able to make this up to her? Would she let him?

Luke rolled over and lay on the bed with his head on the pillow he had just pounded. He had a lot to make up to Sarah. Now he had to figure out how to do it.

NINE

The Mauchard Brothers

Philippe opened the door and looked in. "Hey, René. You're back."

René looked up. He motioned to Philippe to enter and pointed to his ear at the same time, indicating he was on the phone. Philippe entered and sat on a leather sofa to wait for René to finish his call. He looked around. This had been his dad's office. He remembered sitting on this very sofa playing games on his father's phone while he finished working. Now this was René's office. Of course, Philippe had an identical-sized office on the other side of the large conference room between their two offices. Well, almost identical. René liked to point out that his office was one meter longer in width than Philippe's.

Philippe looked over at his brother. Older brother. He chuckled to himself. How often did the two of them baffle everyone? René was only one year older than he. Well, actually two days shy of a year. Often they would have birthday parties on the day between their birthdays and tell everyone they were the same age. People would get so confused. The two of them would offer prizes for people who did not know them well, if only they could solve the riddle: they were not twins but were the same age; how could this be? Rarely did anyone figure it out.

The two of them never looked like twins, which threw their friends off even more. In spite of all the medical advancements, Philippe still developed premature graying hair. Most of the women he went out with said it made him look distinguished. Of course, they may have just wanted him to feel good about himself so he would keep buying them drinks. Yet, René had this condition worse—or used to. He turned it into a strength. René was born with hypotrichosis, a deficiency of hair caused by genetics. To the doctors' credit, they prevented any other genetic complications that might have accompanied such a condition. Philippe looked over at his brother's bald head; René had always had this look. It bothered René when they were kids, and then teens, and he compensated by becoming muscular so everyone would think twice before making comments. He considered being a model at one point; agents learned he had no body hair and thought he would be in high demand. Their father talked René out of the idea. Most of all, what their father did was bring both of them into his plan for the world. René became consumed with his father's vision and passion. So, Philippe guessed it only fair that René now become their father's chief replacement.

René stood, walked over, and sat next to Philippe in an adjacent high-back leather chair. "I expected you this morning."

A wicked grin came across Philippe's face. "I had my standing date with Granted Fantasy."

René shook his head.

Philippe reached over and tapped René's knee. "Deluxe

special, I might add."

"You and your escort services. I think you're addicted."

Philippe's eyes widened. "No, no. This is so much more. They're capable of creating whatever fantasy you can imagine." He shrugged. "Besides, it's perfectly legal. Might as well take advantage of it. Right?" He smiled. "So, tell me about your trip to America. Was it a success?"

René nodded. "Everyone there appeared ecstatic. You were definitely right in bringing this out into the open. It will keep harmful rumors down, and we can proceed unencumbered with the public actually egging us on." He laughed. "How'd you get so smart?"

Philippe smiled. "I just keep asking myself: What would dad do?"

René nodded. "That's certainly a tactic dad would have embraced."

They heard a knock at the door, and then it slowly opened.

"Mr. Mauchard, I'm sorry. But I think you may want to see this."

"What is it, Sonja?"

"It's the temperature and humidity readings for the inner vault."

Sonja came over and handed an electronic tablet to René.

He looked up at her. "What am I looking for?"

"Well, every month when the data are archived, it goes through a quality control process. It detected a total of a two-week gap, but the days are not consecutive."

Philippe looked from Sonja to René. "What? Let me see." He took the tablet from René. His hand went to his chin and then he pointed at the page the device was showing. "Is this an error, or is it deliberately erased by someone?"

Sonja shook her head. "I don't know, sir. I know the IT department is looking into that right now."

René nodded. "Thanks, Sonja. Keep us informed." He handed the tablet back.

"Yes, sir."

As Sonja left, René drummed his fingers on the chair arm.

"What are you thinking, René?"

"It seems improbable, but could someone have gotten into the vault?"

Philippe turned up an eyebrow. "How is that even possible?"

René shook his head. He stood. "Let's go find out."

"Now?"

"Yeah, come on."

Philippe stood, confused. Was René going to get The Six together? Could he do that on the spur of the moment? He took a step toward the door, but René headed toward the conference room.

"Where are you going? Don't you have to get The Six together?"

René smiled. "Let me show you the ultimate secret."

Philippe squinted, but followed him into the conference room. René went to the recessed cabinet along the inner wall and pressed something on the underside of one of the shelves. The cabinet slid to the left, revealing an elevator.

René turned and smiled. "What do you think?"

Philippe's mouth dropped open. "What is this?"

René laughed. "You know dad never left anything to chance. He trusted The Six, but didn't want to depend upon them without options for himself."

René took a step toward the elevator and the doors opened. He motioned for Philippe to come with him.

"So, this goes to the inner vault?"

The elevator doors closed and the car began to descend.

René nodded. "It descends between the fifth and sixth levels of the vault and opens directly into the inner vault."

Philippe shook his head. The whole time he was one of The Six, their father had kept him in the dark about this. Were there other things he didn't know?

The elevator came to a stop, the doors opened, and a white wall rose. They stepped out into the inner vault. There was nothing in the room except for a white fluted and pleated pedestal.

René walked to the pedestal and pressed an area under the top between two pleats. The top of the pedestal turned from white to clear. He lifted the top of the pedestal and a case rose into view. He opened the case. Philippe came up beside him.

"It's there."

René nodded. "But something's off."

"What do you mean?"

"Think about how meticulous dad was to detail. What do you see here?"

Philippe scanned the case. René was right. Something looked off. He noticed the mini drive, while in its place, lay just slightly askew. One side appeared slightly higher than the other, and the foam was slightly askew as well. It was subtle, but definitely not the way his father would have left it. "So, someone did get in."

"Looks like it."

"René, this isn't good. What do you think is their agenda?"

He shook his head. "I don't know, but this is troubling on several levels. First, few people know about this, so how did it leak out? Second, it will be disastrous if this information gets out. And third, how could this entry have gone unnoticed?"

Philippe nodded. This was troubling, puzzling. Who could have done this? He turned to his brother. "René, this had to be the work of immunes."

He nodded as he took out his phone. "My thoughts exactly." He paused a few seconds. "Sonja, contact Pierre, head of security. I want the entire vault swept and every entrance checked." Another pause. "Yeah, and make an appointment with Jean-Paul and Philippe as soon as possible." René put his phone back in his coat pocket.

"Why do you want me to meet with Jean-Paul?"

"We need a biostatistician with a knowledge of genetics to figure out how many immunes would likely be alive today."

"How many could there be? Dad pulled them all out of society years ago."

"I don't know, but we can't afford to take chances. There's too much at stake."

Philippe nodded. That was true. They couldn't afford for immunes to become a problem. Maybe this proved they already were. The lottery may have to be expanded.

TEN

BRASILIA

Luke sat at his desk but couldn't get any work done. Ever since lunch, and not seeing Sarah in the cafeteria, he couldn't stop thinking about her and how he had made her cry. He sat back and sighed.

Scott leaned over his desk toward him. "Hey, you OK?"

Luke gave a half-smile. "Yeah, I just have a mental block. I'm going to get some fresh air and think."

Scott smiled. "Good idea."

Luke went to the balcony and looked over the railing. It was a gorgeous day. The sky looked almost cloudless and a vibrant blue—just the opposite of how he felt inside. He wanted to give Sarah the space she needed, but he didn't want to give her too much space where she would think he didn't care. Pacing across the balcony for several minutes, he contemplated the right thing to do. He stopped pacing, leaned against the railing, and took a deep breath, letting it out slowly. It was obvious what he had to do: go see her. Waiting until after work would just eat at him. He needed to go now.

He had almost made it to the elevator when Larry snagged

him.

"Luke, there you are. We have a problem. You may need to go to Brasilia. Come with me."

"Now? I need to do something first."

Larry shook his head. "I have Brasilia on a video conference right now. Come with me."

Luke looked from Larry to the elevator and rolled his eyes. He reluctantly followed Larry into one of the pod rooms. Brian was talking to Dr. Cortês.

Larry put his hand on Luke's shoulder. "Find out the issue. I'll be in my office."

When Dr. Cortês saw Luke come into view, she stopped midsentence. "Dr. Loughton, thanks for agreeing to help."

Luke sat next to Brian. "So, what is the problem?"

"The gravity calculations seem to be off."

Luke looked at Brian quizzically. "Impossible. I did them myself."

Brian pointed to the screen. Luke looked at Dr. Cortês and another woman. He knew she was the one he had worked with before, but for some reason couldn't remember her name.

Cortês leaned forward. "Dr. Loughton, we're not questioning your calculations, but when we put the code into the 3-D simulator, we didn't get the results we expected."

She looked at the woman next to her. "Dr. Mendez has tried several times."

Mendez. Yes, that's it. How could he forget the name of someone so beautiful?

"Hi, Dr. Loughton." She pushed her long, slightly wavy, black hair behind her shoulder. "I would appreciate any insights you may be able to give." Her dark eyes twinkled with her sultry smile, which curved slightly upward at the edges.

Luke shook his head. "I'm not sure what the issue is. I'm going to put you on mute a few minutes. I'll pull up my calculations, and then we can compare notes."

Cortês and Mendez nodded. Brian pushed the mute button. He rolled his chair to the other side of the table so his back was to the camera. Despite the mute function, he kept his voice low.

"Wow, you never told me she was smoking hot."

Luke smiled. "Which one?"

Brian's eyes went wide. "Either one. But Dr. Mendez . . . " He shook his hand. "Wow."

Luke pulled up his gravity calculations. "Well, you'll have no competition from me. So go for it."

Brian leaned over the table. "OK, here's what you have to do."

Luke squinted. "What?"

Brian looked intently at Luke. "You have to find some reason I have to travel to Brasilia." Brian paused. "Please."

Luke gave a half-smile. "Brian, groveling doesn't become you."

"Oh, this isn't groveling. You want groveling? I'll give it to you."

Luke's smile broadened. "No, please don't."

Luke put the connection back online. "OK, I have my calculations. Let's compare notes."

Luke and Brian spent the next five hours with Dr. Mendez, but nothing looked out of the ordinary.

Mendez leaned back in her chair. "Dr. Loughton, I need a break. Give me fifteen minutes and we'll start again."

Luke nodded and put the line on mute. He leaned back and stretched. Brian did the same.

"There has to be a faster way to do this," Brian said. He paused for effect, then raised an eyebrow.

"No, I'm not sending you down there."

"Aw, come on, Luke. It would make things faster."

"But you didn't write the code."

Brian folded his arms. "We've coded together long enough for us to understand how we each code." He gave a smirk. "So, if someone has to go, you're going to pull that card?"

Luke put his hand on Brian's shoulder. "If anyone does have to go, I'll recommend you." Luke hesitated, then let it come tumbling out. "I have other things here to work out."

Brian unfolded his arms and leaned forward. "Uh-oh. Something rotten in paradise?"

Luke nodded slightly. "Something like that. I—"

The door flew open; Larry entered the room. "How's it going?"

Luke shook his head. "Too slow."

Brian stood. "Sir, I think I should go down there and work this out in person."

Larry shook his head. "Hold your horses, bronco. Let's give this a shot before we make that decision. I'll order dinner and you guys can work late."

Luke looked at Brian and briefly closed his eyes. "Yes, sir," each said simultaneously.

Luke stood. "The break's almost over. I'm going to check my messages. I'll be right back."

Both Larry and Brian nodded.

There was one message, from Oliver. "Dr. Loughton, this is Oliver Stone in HR. I need to check your passport information. Please call me at your earliest convenience."

Luke looked at his watch. Oliver had called almost an hour ago. He hit the callback button.

"Oliver Stone." His voice sounded extremely businesslike. It almost didn't sound like the Oliver that Luke knew. At all.

"Oliver, this is Luke."

"Oh, Luke. Thanks for calling back." He sounded like his old self again.

"What's up?"

"Paris. I'm leaving tonight."

Luke gave a grimace and shook his head. "Oliver, Larry has me working late tonight. I just can't get away. Can you go later?"

"No, I need to leave tonight. I have a tight window of opportunity."

"I . . . I just can't."

"OK, OK. That's fine. We'll work it out. See you when I get back."

"Be careful."

"Yeah. You too."

Luke hung up and sighed. Of all the times to have an all-nighter. He looked at his watch. *Should I call Sarah?* He decided to at least try. There was no way he would get to see her before she went to bed. He picked up his phone and dialed.

"Medical department. Kathleen speaking."

"Hi, Kathleen. This is Dr. Loughton in Astrophysics. Could I speak to Dr. Morgan?"

"I'm sorry, Dr. Loughton. She isn't here."

Luke looked at his watch again. It was very close to 18:00. Luke looked up and shook his head. "OK. Thanks, Kathleen. I'll catch her tomorrow."

He sighed. Larry would be upset if he didn't get back to the meeting. Luke stopped by the break room, grabbed a couple of sodas, and headed back to the pod room. Brian was sitting at the table. Luke placed a soda in front of him.

"Oh, thanks." He looked up. "Are you ready to start again?"

"I guess."

"Larry said he'd be back in about an hour with pizza." Brian gave a smirk. "He goes all out."

Luke held up his soda. "Here's to fun."

Brian clinked his can with Luke's. "Hear, hear."

They laughed. Brian took the video conversation off mute.

Luke took his seat. “Dr. Mendez, ready to start again?”

She nodded.

Brian smiled. “Let’s get started then.”

ELEVEN

Sarah Missing

Luke stirred. Had he heard something? He heard the sound again. It was his phone. He glanced at the clock: 08:11. After two late nights, Larry finally let Brian go to Brasilia and allowed Luke to have the morning off. The phone rang again. He put it to his ear, still groggy. "Hello."

"Lukey. I tried you at your office, but you weren't there. Are you all right?"

"Natalia?" Luke sat up and ran his hand through his hair. "Is . . . is something wrong?"

Natalia gave a giggle. "Just the opposite. He's coming, Lukey. My father. Oliver's bringing him home."

"Really?" Luke jumped from his bed and began pacing. "When are they coming?"

"They should get here sometime tonight. Can you come here around 18:00?"

"Sure. I'll be there."

"OK. Great. I'll see you tonight."

Luke set back down on his bed. This was truly incredible. After all these years, Natalia and her father would be reunited.

He thought about his own parents. He had seen them only once since he left at the age of ten for government boarding school. Yet, for some reason, they didn't recognize him. He had been taught they were a means to an end. He never had a real desire to reconnect with them. *Why did Natalia?* Maybe if he knew his parents had been put in prison for that many years, he'd have sympathy for them, too. Yet it seemed Natalia was having different thoughts since she started reading this . . . Bible.

A thought struck him. He stood. Maybe this would be the perfect reason to connect with Sarah. She would definitely want to go. Well, Natalia likely would have already told her. But maybe, just maybe, she would be willing to share a cab to Jeremy and Natalia's place. That would be just enough time to apologize for everything.

He called Sarah's office. "Kathleen, this is Dr. Loughton. May I speak with Dr. Morgan?"

"I'm sorry, Dr. Loughton, but she isn't here."

"What? Why? Where is she?"

"Well, I can't tell you that. All I can tell you is she took a few days off."

Luke sat back down. "Did she say when she would get back?"

"All her e-mail said was she was taking a few days off. She didn't specify the actual number of days. Maybe Dr. Wilson, her supervisor, knows more details."

"OK. Thanks, Kathleen."

Luke disconnected and put his hand to his chin. Where could she have gone?

Another thought sent him back to his feet. *Could she have gone with Oliver?* Surely she wouldn't—or would she? The thought made him nervous.

He dialed Natalia as he paced at the foot of his bed. He

patted his leg with his other hand while he waited for her to answer.

"Hi, Lukey. Everything OK?"

"Did Sarah go with Oliver?"

"Yeah. But I thought you knew that."

"No. No, I didn't. Did she say why?"

There was a pause. "Lukey . . . what's going on?"

"She's coming back with Oliver, right?"

"Why . . . why wouldn't she? Did . . . you do something? You two have an argument or something?"

Luke sighed. "Something like that."

"What happened?" She sounded sincere, but Luke really didn't want to start such a conversation over the phone.

"We can talk about that later. If you hear from Oliver again, just please confirm she's OK."

"OK." Natalia sounded confused. "I'll see you tonight."

"Tonight. Bye."

Luke headed to the shower. He let the water run over his body as he stood motionless in thought. *Why would Sarah go with Oliver? Did they ask her to go, or did she go willingly?* Why wouldn't she at least leave a message? Maybe things were worse than he thought. Had she already made up her mind to not forgive him? Luke shook his head. He couldn't let his mind go there until he heard from her.

He made it to work just before 13:00 after stopping for a salad at a place around the corner from work. Scott gave him a nod as he sat down, but quickly went back to his work. It looked like he was working toward a deadline, so Luke didn't interrupt.

He checked his messages. One was from Brian. He called back. "How's Brasilia?"

Brian gave a short laugh. "I wouldn't know. I've been inside the entire time."

"Complaining already?"

"No way." His voice got very low. "Luke, she's not only hot, she's the total package: smart, hot, and sweet."

A smile came across Luke's face. "So, how's work?"

"Oh, that's going well also. We just found the issue. Carmella—I mean Dr. Mendez—is running the corrected 3-D simulation now."

"Carmella, huh?"

"Oh stop."

Luke laughed. "So, what was the problem?"

"I think because we didn't know there would be other ships in Mars's orbit, that wasn't taken into account. While minute, the gravitational attraction between the ships had to be factored in."

Luke shuddered. That's exactly what he had discovered when he first ran these calculations months ago—and no one remembered the discrepancies the day after he pointed them out. That, and other things, sent him down the road he currently found himself on. At least now it confirmed his previous calculations. He half-chuckled to himself. When the calculations were right, they were corrected to be wrong. Now they were being corrected back to his original calculations. But he wouldn't even try to explain that to Brian.

"Congratulations, Brian. Good detective work. So, coming home soon?"

"I have one more day. Carmella has offered to show me around. I'm going to let her."

"Go for it, Brian. See you when you get back."

"OK. See you soon. I'll forward the corrections to you."

Luke smiled. Those he already had. "Sounds good."

He spent the rest of the day quality-checking Scott's gravitational calculations and reviewing his simulations.

He worked until 17:30 and then took a taxi from work

straight to Continental Drift. Once in the taxi, the realization of seeing Sarah hit him and made him anxious and nervous at the same time. He wanted to see her but had no idea how she would respond.

He was happy for Natalia but wanted a good outcome for himself as well.

Tonight would, hopefully, have more than just one happy reunion.

TWELVE

Natalia's Father

Natalia opened the door. "Lukey!" A smile spread across her face. "Come on in."

Jeremy stood at the bar. "Want something?"

Luke nodded. "Absolutely. Something hard, please."

Jeremy stopped and looked at him. "Everything OK?"

"Just pour, Jeremy."

Jeremy cocked his head like he wanted more information, but poured Luke's drink without comment.

Natalia came up and put her hand on the back of Luke's shoulder. "It will be a few minutes before the others arrive. Come sit down. Tell us what happened."

Luke walked over to one of the cushy white chairs and sat. He took a few sips of his vodka. He knew this might be a stressful night, and he wanted to be more relaxed. Natalia and Jeremy sat on the sofa.

Natalia leaned forward and put her hand on his knee. "Tell us what happened, Lukey."

"It was an argument, Natalia. We had an argument."

"Hey, buddy. We're here to support, not condemn," Jeremy

said. "You know that."

Luke looked at Jeremy and sighed. Yeah, he knew that. It was just a little embarrassing to admit he had hurt Sarah's feelings. He nodded. "Yeah, I know."

"So, what happened?" Natalia's voice sounded soothing, reassuring.

Luke leaned forward and twirled the glass in his hands. "Sarah came over late one night. She had been reading the Bible and wanted to talk about what she had read." He glanced up and looked back down at his glass. "I . . . I've been really struggling with reading it and I didn't want to discuss it. She kept pushing and . . . " He shook his head. "I exploded on her. She clammed up and left." He took another sip. "I've tried to get in touch with her to apologize, but it seemed like something kept preventing me from seeing her. Either work, or, now, her going with Oliver without telling me." His sighed and shook his head. "I . . . I don't know if she will ever forgive me."

Natalia patted his knee. He looked at her and she gave a supportive smile. "Couples have arguments all the time. She'll come around. She knows you love her."

"Yeah, sometimes it just takes time to get one's perspective back," Jeremy said, nodding. "You'll see."

Luke sat back and nodded. He wanted to be positive and certain about what they were saying, but doubt haunted him. He really hoped both of them were right. How long would it take for her to get her "perspective," as Jeremy put it? Although he repressed it, he could feel his eyes starting to water.

The doorbell rang. Luke sat up, cleared his throat, and blinked rapidly to try and dewater his eyes. Jeremy reached over and patted Luke's shoulder and went to the door.

Natalia stood. Luke could see she felt nervous. He sighed, mentally. Here he was blabbering about his problems when this was really her night. Her chance to reconnect with her father.

He put his hand on her shoulder. "I'm sorry, Natalia. This is really your night and I've put a damper on it."

She patted his hand and shook her head. "We're family, Lukey. We support each other."

He kissed her cheek. She smiled. He put his hand behind her back and gave an extremely gentle push. "Go ahead, Natalia. Go meet your father."

Jeremy opened the door. Oliver and Viktoria entered. Just behind them entered an elderly man who looked quite spry for someone his age. He also had fewer wrinkles than Luke expected. And . . . it was uncanny. If he focused only on Mr. Mancini's face, he looked a lot like Natalia except for the eyes. His were more round.

Mr. Mancini shook Jeremy's hand after Jeremy invited him in. When he saw Natalia, he stopped. They looked at each other for several seconds. His eyes watered. Natalia went closer, and they suddenly hugged.

"You're . . . you're so beautiful."

"Dad, I've waited so long for this moment." Natalia gave a more intense squeeze and then released the hug. She wiped away tears from her cheeks, and smiled. She then kissed his cheek. "Dad, please, come on in."

Jeremy came over and put his arm around her.

"You met my husband, Jeremy."

Mr. Mancini smiled and nodded.

"And this is a good friend of ours, Luke Loughton."

Luke smiled and shook his hand. "Very nice to meet you, sir."

He smiled back and looked at Natalia. "And with good manners."

They all laughed.

He looked around the penthouse. "Your place is very beautiful, Natalia."

"Thank you. Are you hungry?"

He nodded. He walked toward the balcony. "Can we eat outside?" He smiled. "I've been cooped up so long, it would be nice to feel space around me."

Natalia led him out to the balcony. She looked back at Jeremy.

Jeremy nodded. "I'll bring the food outside."

Viktoria followed Jeremy. "I'll help."

Oliver looked at Luke and shuffled his feet.

Luke walked over. "Oliver, where's Sarah?"

He nodded for them to return to the seating area while Natalia and her father stepped out on the balcony. "Luke, have a seat. I have something to tell you."

Luke sat. "Sarah didn't want to see me? Did she go home instead?"

Oliver shook his head. He gave a sympathetic look. "Luke, I don't know how to say this. But . . . we lost her."

Luke's mind went numb. *What is that supposed to mean?* He shook his head. "I don't understand. Just spit it out, Oliver."

Oliver sighed. "I called both you and Sarah. I knew you couldn't make it, so I assumed Sarah wouldn't be coming. But she insisted on coming. We really needed a third person. Plus, she knew the physician at the prison."

Luke turned up his brow. "Really? How?"

Oliver shrugged. "They interned together or something. Anyway, she agreed to distract him while Viktoria and I hustled Mr. Mancini out of prison."

"What happened?"

Oliver shook his head. "It was supposed to be simple: just talk and basically reminisce with him to keep his eyes off the monitors."

Luke cocked his head. "Wait. Why would a physician be

watching the prisoners? Don't they have guards there?"

Oliver cleared his throat. "This is not a standard prison. These are law-abiding citizens who just happen to be immune to the Invocation wafers and cannot be controlled. They're not criminals, so it's basically run like an assisted living place—just not very accommodating. There are a couple of guards, but they are pretty low-key."

Luke shook his head and opened his arms slightly. "So what went wrong?"

Oliver rubbed a hand behind his neck. "She was supposed to end her conversation with the guy after twenty minutes and then meet us at the rendezvous point."

"And?"

Oliver shook his head. "She never showed up."

Luke's eyes began to water. "Didn't you go back for her?"

Oliver put his hand on Luke's shoulder. "Luke, of course I did. But when I got there, both Sarah and the physician were gone. Someone else was there. I looked everywhere, but she had vanished without a trace. We had to get Mr. Mancini out before they noticed him missing. We needed to vanish without a trace as well."

Luke ran his hand across his mouth. "So, what do we do?"

"I'm going to start tonight and spend all night long if I have to, hacking and looking at any surveillance cameras I can—both at the prison and every one nearby. We should pick up at least something." He patted Luke on his shoulder. "Don't worry, Luke. We'll find her."

Luke looked Oliver in the eye to assure himself of his friend's sincerity.

"That's a commitment, Luke."

Luke nodded. He sat back. He kept blinking to keep tears from flowing. He stood. "Tell Jeremy and Natalia I'll see them later. I don't think I can be happy for them right now."

Oliver nodded.

"Oh, and don't tell them about Sarah until tomorrow, please. Let Natalia have a special night with her father."

Oliver squeezed Luke's shoulder. "You're a good man, Luke."

Luke gave a weak smile. "Just tell everyone I got called back to work."

Oliver nodded.

Luke walked all the way home. He knew it would take more than an hour, but he didn't care. He couldn't believe Sarah was missing. Now she was all alone, thinking he didn't want to be with her. This time he didn't stop them: he let the tears fall. If only he could let her know how much he really loved her.

When Luke got to his apartment, he was spent both physically and emotionally. He took a sleep aid and fell into bed. Soon, the medication took over and this very bad day slipped into oblivion.

THIRTEEN

IMMUNES

Philippe entered René's office from the conference room. René paced between his large traditional oak desk and the large picture window behind him that showcased the Eiffel Tower in the distance. "Everything OK?" Philippe asked.

René shook his head. "This report from Pierre is disturbing."

Philippe came over. René handed him the electronic report. Philippe sat in one of the chairs in front of René's desk and scrolled through the pages. "So, Pierre's men found a destroyed earwig, a removed toilet seat, and a mangled piece of aluminum pipe?" He looked up at René and blinked. "Why is that disturbing?"

René leaned on his desk with his hands. "It's not so much the items, but where they were found."

Philippe nodded. "In the Invocation Center and in the outer vault. So, you think they entered through the Invocation Center?"

René stood again and paced. "It doesn't prove that, but that is circumstantial evidence to suggest it."

"Can't a toilet seat just mean a loose toilet seat?"

"Keep reading."

"Pierre interviewed all security on each day of the deleted data?" He glanced up at René. "That's a lot of folks to interview."

"He was looking for any inconsistencies."

Philippe scanned through the rest of the pages as he scrolled. "Eight had the same story, and all sustained injuries. But it says here they were all in a rugby game." He shook his head. "What's unusual about that?"

René turned his hand in a rotating motion. "Keep reading."

Philippe looked back at the report. "They . . . never played who they said they did." He shook his head. "What does that mean?"

"Their memories were reprogrammed."

Philippe's eyes shot back to René's. "By whom?"

"That is the question."

They heard a knock on the door and Sonja poked her head in. "Sorry to intrude, but Jean-Paul is in your office, sir."

Philippe nodded. "Thank you, Sonja."

He stood and signaled with his head for René to follow. They went through the conference room into Philippe's office. In décor, it was in stark contrast to René's. The interior was extremely modern. Jean-Paul was sitting in a clear glass chair next to Philippe's cobalt-blue glass desk.

Jean-Paul stood as soon as the two men entered. Philippe motioned for him to sit down across from the yellow sofa where the two men sat.

Philippe leaned forward with elbows on his legs. "Jean-Paul, here's the scenario we need you to solve for us."

Jean-Paul gave a nod.

"If everyone who exhibited a specific trait were removed from the population, within say . . . " Philippe shrugged.

" . . . sixty years. How many people would exist in the general population who still exhibited that trait?"

Jean-Paul looked from one brother to the other. "What kind of trait?"

Philippe sat up straighter. "Does it matter?"

"Well, is it a dominant or recessive trait?"

Philippe looked at René. He shrugged.

Philippe looked back at Jean-Paul. "Can you assume it may be either?"

"Well, I could, but without knowing any specifics, this will be a very general estimation."

Philippe nodded. "Understood. We're looking for a ballpark estimate anyway."

"If you give me more specifics, I could give you more specifics," Jean-Paul said.

"I'm not sure you want to do that."

"Why?"

Philippe went to his desk and pulled out a thick document. He returned to where they were sitting and handed it to Jean-Paul.

Their visitor looked up with a scrunched eyebrow. "What's this?"

"What you will have to sign if you want more specifics."

Jean-Paul looked at the document. He then looked from one brother to the other with his eyes wide. "You . . . want me to agree to have my memory wiped after I do the calculations?"

Philippe nodded.

Jean-Paul handed the document back to Philippe. "On second thought, I think I can give a fairly good estimate with the information you've already given."

Philippe stood. "Well, if you think that's good enough . . . "

"Oh, yes sir. I think it is."

"When can you have it for us?"

Jean-Paul stood. "By the end of next week?"

Philippe nodded and shook Jean-Paul's hand. "Very good. I look forward to reading your report."

Jean-Paul bowed slightly and exited in haste.

Philippe looked at René and grinned. "A little motivation never hurts."

FOURTEEN

Sarah's Return

The alarm went off. Luke threw an arm to hit the snooze, but instead knocked the clock on the floor, the alarm still sounding. Luke groaned and sat up. He hit the snooze with his big toe. The silence was heavenly. He looked at the computer screen above his bed. "Wake up, diagnostic."

The computer said something with incomprehensive gibberish. Luke frowned. He definitely had to get the wake-up announcement repaired. He didn't think he could handle the annoying alarm clock much longer.

He fell back on the bed and folded his arms with the backs of his hands resting on his forehead. The weight of Sarah being missing hit him once again. His eyes watered again despite him willing them not to. He considered calling in sick. After all, he certainly felt sick, even if not physically sick. But he didn't want to wallow in self-pity either. Being at work could at least keep his mind occupied until he could actually do something once he heard back from Oliver.

Luke forced himself to sit up and breathe in deeply, then forced himself to exhale through his mouth. He took a shower, dressed, and headed out the door. He ordered his coffee with his phone app and headed to work. His coffee was waiting for him. He bought a protein bar as well and headed to the office.

He worked until almost 11:15, when he received a call. He let the phone ring several times as he stared at the flashing display in the lower right-hand corner of his monitor. It read: "Medical Dept." He thought that . . . odd. After the fifth ring, he pressed the flashing display and spoke into his headset.

"Hello. This is Dr. Loughton."

"Hi, Dr. Loughton. This is Kathleen in the Medical Department. I just wanted to remind you of your appointment at 11:30 to go over the findings from your last physical."

He had totally forgotten about this, and he wasn't in the mood to see anyone. "Uh, I, uh . . . would like to reschedule. I'll wait until Dr. Morgan is available."

"Dr. Loughton, it's Dr. Morgan who has the appointment with you."

Luke's head jerked back. "But . . . but you said the other day she had taken a few days off."

"That's true, but she came in this morning."

Luke was speechless. A lump developed in his throat. "Wha . . . what?" He found it hard to talk. "Are you sure?"

Kathleen chuckled. "Yes, Dr. Loughton. I'm looking at her right now."

"Oh . . . OK. I'll be right down."

Luke disconnected and stared at his monitor for several seconds. How was this possible?

Scott leaned over his desk. "Hey Luke, are you all right? You're extremely pale. Maybe you should go to medical."

Luke gave a half-laugh. "That's where I'm headed."

Luke's thoughts went wild as he took the elevator to the fourth floor. How did Sarah get back? Why didn't she call? Or, maybe she called Oliver. He shook his head. If she had,

Oliver would have called him even if she didn't want to see him. He put his thumb under his chin and tapped his index finger over his lips in thought. This didn't add up. If she didn't want to see him, why would she go over his test results? Maybe she was just doing her job. Yet she could have gotten another physician to go over them with him. He sighed. This was all very puzzling.

Once in Medical, Kathleen had him wait until Sarah was available. He looked at the large monitor in the corner that displayed some kind of documentary program, but he really didn't pay it any attention. His mind was extremely preoccupied.

The door opened, and a nurse appeared. "Dr. Loughton, if you will follow me, please."

She took him to a small room with a desk, two chairs, and an oversized monitor.

"Dr. Morgan will be with you shortly."

Luke nodded, and the nurse left him alone. The longer he waited, the more nervous he became. He couldn't believe he would be seeing her in just a few minutes.

The door opened and Sarah entered. She looked just as beautiful as he remembered. She had her blonde hair pulled back into a ponytail. Luke stood.

She looked up and smiled. "Oh, it's nice to see chivalry isn't dead. Please, Dr. Loughton, have a seat. This shouldn't take too long. I just want you to get any questions you may have answered." She sat on the other side of the desk. She typed something into her electronic tablet, and his chem labs appeared on the monitor.

"Sarah, it's so good to see you."

Her eyes shot to him. "Uh, Dr. Morgan, please. I like to keep things professional with the employees here. You understand that, right?" She turned back to the monitor. "All of your labs here are in the normal range, so . . . " She gave a professional smile. "You are very healthy." She looked at the monitor and then back at him. "Do you have any questions?"

He shook his head. "Can we talk about what happened between us, and how you got back from Paris?" He reached over and touched her arm.

Sarah recoiled and stood. Luke was taken back. "What's wrong, Sarah?"

She backed up farther. "I told you to address me as Dr. Morgan. I don't know what you are trying to do here, Dr. Loughton, but I suggest you leave."

"But . . . "

Sarah pursed her lips with a determined look on her face. "Now." Her voice firmly announced: *Your actions are highly inappropriate. Now leave.* She pointed toward the door and stood stoically.

Luke scrunched his face and stood. *What's wrong with her?* He opened his mouth to say something, but decided against it. He opened the door and left. Once in the hallway outside the medical department, he stopped and leaned against the wall. He put his hand to his temple. He was having a very hard time processing what had just occurred. This was more than just Sarah not wanting to see him. She truly didn't even know who he was. *Something is very wrong.*

Luke didn't know what to do next, but he knew he couldn't work the rest of the day. He looked at his watch. Larry and Scott were probably in the cafeteria. He headed there to find them.

He first ran into Jason as he walked down the yogurt and prepared salad aisle of the cafeteria.

"Luke, hi."

"Hi, Jason. Hey, did you see Sarah today?"

"Yeah, I did. Why?"

"Did she seem . . . different to you?"

Jason cocked his head. "Different?"

"Yeah, you know. Did she not seem herself?"

"Hmm. Not really." He bobbed his head. "Well, she did seem more formal than normal." He shrugged. "I just assumed it was because Rosencrantz was standing close by." Jason paused. "Is something wrong?"

"I'm not sure. I just saw her, and she acted like she didn't know me."

A smile spread across Jason's face.

"What? Why are you smiling?"

"Did you and Sarah have a falling out?"

"Well, sort of."

"My advice: flowers and chocolate. Admit to anything she says and just swallow your pride."

Luke gave a grimace. "I'm not sure it will be that easy."

"The good thing is, once you've groveled, the makeup session will be wonderful."

Luke gave a slight smile. "I hope it works out that way."

"I'm meeting Jared. Want to join us?"

Luke turned up an eyebrow. "Jared?"

"Oh, I forgot to e-mail you. Jared got the position in the fitness center!"

Luke smiled and patted Jason on his arm. "Congratulations. I'll check in with him sometime."

Jason smiled. "He'd like that."

"I'm looking for someone, so I'll see you later."

Jason nodded. "Sure. See you later."

If only flowers and chocolates were the answers to Luke's dilemma. He shook his head. Things were way more complicated than that. He went to the dining area to find Larry. After a few minutes, he saw Larry and Scott eating together at a table near the outside window. He approached them.

Scott saw him first. "Hey, Luke, want to join us? Sarah stand you up?"

Larry looked up. He first smiled, then turned solemn. "You OK, Luke?"

"Larry, something's come up. I need to take the afternoon off."

"Anything serious?"

"I don't think so, but not sure yet."

Larry nodded. "Sure, Luke. Let me know if there's anything I can do."

Luke nodded. "Thanks. I appreciate this."

"I'll do the QC work for you this afternoon," Scott said. "I'm almost done with my latest simulation."

Luke looked at Scott. "Thanks. I really appreciate that."

"No problem. I'll just hold it over your head forever." Scott laughed.

Luke smiled. "I would expect no less."

He turned to leave and saw Sarah approaching with a tray of food in hand. He stopped as she passed, but she didn't even look at him.

Luke stood there a few seconds. His eyes began to water. He blinked to keep the tears at bay. He swallowed hard and cleared his throat. Walking quickly, he exited the cafeteria, and then the building itself.

FIFTEEN

Memory Reprogramming

As Luke walked back to his apartment, he stopped at a café just around the corner from his building. He called Oliver.

"Luke? You never call during the day. What's up?"

"Can you meet me at the café around the corner from my apartment?"

"Sure. When?"

"Now. Can you meet me right now?"

"Uh, well, I'm still looking into what we discussed last night."

"That's why I need to see you, and see you right now. Please."

"You sound . . . odd, Luke."

"I know. I'll explain when you get here."

"OK. I'll be there in fifteen minutes."

Luke nibbled on a granola bar and drank some tea as he waited. He wasn't really hungry, but knew he needed to eat something. Sipping the tea, while somewhat soothing, helped to pass those fifteen long minutes.

Luke closed his eyes and pinched the bridge of his nose. He sighed. Would things ever become normal again? When he opened his eyes, Oliver was sitting across from him. Luke jumped and almost overturned his chair. "Geez, Oliver! I keep telling you not to do that."

Oliver grinned. "Everyone needs an adrenaline surge every now and then."

"It won't matter if my heart stops beating in the process."

Oliver laughed. "Sorry. Force of habit."

Luke took a deep breath and forced a smile.

"Luke, I'm trying to make good on my promise, but I haven't yet found Sarah."

Luke waved his hands. "That's what I wanted to tell you. You can stop your search."

"Why?"

"I just came back from seeing her."

Oliver's head jerked back slightly. "What? Where?"

"At work."

Oliver turned up his face in complete confusion. "How . . . how is that possible?" He shook his head. "Is she all right?"

Luke rubbed his hands down his face. He gave a half-chuckle. "How?" He shook his head. "I have no idea. Is she all right?" He shrugged. "Physically, yes. Otherwise, I don't know."

Oliver leaned in. "Luke, what are you trying to say? Just spit it out."

Luke was suddenly overcome with emotion; much as he didn't want them to, his eyes watered again. He held tears at bay as much as possible, but a few spilled over his bottom eyelids. "Sarah . . . " He cleared his throat. "Sarah didn't know who I was."

Oliver cocked his head and stared at him. "Come again?"

Luke sighed. "Oliver, I saw her. She didn't recognize me. When I tried to reach out to her, she threw me out of her office for being inappropriate."

Oliver rubbed his hand across his mouth. "I can't believe it."

"What?"

Oliver didn't hesitate. "Her memory has been reprogrammed."

Luke had a look of total confusion. "But . . . that's impossible. She's immune."

Oliver nodded. "To the current compound."

It was then that the realization hit Luke. He gasped. "Professor Mercure."

Oliver nodded. "I'm afraid so."

"But, Jeremy was convinced it would take much longer."

Oliver gave a short shrug. "Apparently, serendipity was on Professor Mercure's side."

Luke put his head in his hands. He closed his eyes. A tear dropped to the table. He looked back at Oliver. "So, what are we looking at here?"

Oliver sat up. "Well, the drug will wear off and most of her memories will return. The significant ones anyway—like remembering you."

Luke was thrilled to hear that. "But when will they return?"

Oliver shrugged. "Sometimes between now and a month from now."

Luke's eyes went wide. "A *month*?" He said it louder than he meant to.

Oliver held up his palms and patted the air. "Calm down." He looked around. "I'm just saying, based upon the fact we take the Invocation wafer every month, it will probably last as long as, or shorter than, the compound in the wafer."

Luke ran a hand through his hair. All of this was just too overwhelming. "So, are we already defeated?"

"Not necessarily. We need to talk to Jeremy and get his

chemical insights."

Luke nodded. "Let's go."

"Where?"

"To see Jeremy."

"I didn't mean right now."

"Well, I do. We can't wait about this." Luke stood. "Let's go see Jeremy." He pulled out his phone and ordered a taxi.

Oliver stood. "I doubt the restaurant is open yet."

Luke smiled. "Well, I guess it's good I have his personal number."

The taxi pulled up. After receiving the destination, the vehicle pulled into traffic.

Luke called Jeremy.

"Luke? Is anything wrong?"

"Yes, Jeremy. A lot is wrong. Oliver and I are on our way to see you. Can you see us as soon as we get there?"

"Of course. I need to get something in motion here, but I should be done by the time you get here."

"Thanks, Jeremy."

Luke sat back and sighed. One stupid argument put Sarah in this position. He should have been with her. Could he ever make this up to her?

* * * * *

"Destination achieved."

Luke inserted his credit disc and exited the cab. Jeremy was waiting for them at the door and led them to a secluded part of the bar.

Jeremy looked from Luke to Oliver. "OK, what's happened?"

Luke explained everything he had told Oliver and Oliver had told him. Jeremy spent most of the time with his mouth slightly open, an expression of disbelief.

Once Luke finished, Jeremy reached over and put his hand on Luke's arm. "I'm so sorry, buddy. What can I do?"

"How did Professor Mercure get a compound so fast?"

"Well, my guess is she already had one."

"What?"

"Many compounds have been made and tested, but were short-acting and not a fit for the fullerene matrix."

Oliver leaned in. "So, you're saying Sarah's condition should be short-lived."

Jeremy nodded. "I believe so."

Luke put his fist over his mouth. "But doesn't this mean they're on to us?"

Jeremy held up his index finger. "Not necessarily. I think this may be Professor Mercure thinking Sarah is after her position and sending a warning to her and whoever may be involved with her. It doesn't mean she knows anything. Yet, anyway."

Luke turned up an eyebrow. "So, you think this is only about an act of jealousy?"

"That's what I think." Jeremy gestured to Oliver. "What are your thoughts?"

He shrugged. "To be honest, I'm not sure. What you're saying, Jeremy, makes sense. If Sarah comes around soon, then the more likely you're right."

SIXTEEN

Sarah Reemerges

Luke closed the door to his apartment. He was mentally exhausted and his mind felt like mush. All he wanted was to take a shower and go straight to bed. Sleep overcame him within seconds after his head touched the pillow . . .

Luke bolted upright in bed. What had awakened him? Was it a dream? What time was it? The alarm clock indicated it was a little past three in the morning. He laid back down, trying to calm his adrenaline surge. Then he realized he was hearing the doorbell, followed by a banging on the door. He jumped out of bed and quickly headed for the door. He looked through the peephole. It was Sarah! He cocked his head and looked again. Why was she here?

Luke opened the door. Sarah, dressed in silk pajamas and a matching robe, simply stood there, staring at him. She looked like a frightened kitten. He didn't know what to do or say. *What is she thinking?* He decided to invite her in, but before he could do so, she ran to him and wrapped her arms around him, squeezing tightly. She put her head on his bare chest and stood that way for several minutes. He slowly wrapped his arms around her and hugged back—what he had wanted to do for so long. Without moving, he reached for the door and shut it.

"Sarah—"

Before he could finish, she looked up and kissed him. She prolonged it and pressed herself into him. He reciprocated. She pushed him back into the bedroom and onto the bed, still giving passionate kisses. He wrapped his arms more tightly around her and continued to reciprocate her passionate and prolonged kisses. After several minutes, he pulled away. He didn't want to take advantage of her vulnerable position. Although he wanted to go further, he wanted her to be levelheaded before they made such a commitment. He put his forehead to hers, breathing rapidly. "Let's slow down a bit."

Sarah breathed rapidly herself. She nodded.

"I'm really glad you came by. Are you OK?"

She put her head back on his chest and kissed it. "Oh, Luke. I was so scared."

He turned on his side, propping himself up with his elbow, and rubbed her arm with his free arm. "Tell me what happened."

She put her forehead on his chest for a moment and then looked into his eyes. "I'm not really sure. A lot is still jumbled. I remember us talking about Natalia's father and wanting to rescue him. The next thing I remember is waking up at my apartment and going to work." She shook her head. "The time gap didn't register. It was so weird, though. I knew what to do, but at the same time no one seemed familiar. I had to keep looking up information. I couldn't seem to remember people or where things were located. It was almost like my first day on the job—but things felt familiar and new all at the same time."

"You're OK now?"

She nodded. "I think so. When I realized the gap of time I lost, I came right over. I . . . I don't want to be alone. Can I sleep here?"

"Of course."

He turned on his back and put one hand behind his head. Sarah scooted up close to him and put her head between his chest and shoulder. Luke rubbed her back with his other hand as she rubbed his bare chest and side with her hand. Her touch was intoxicating—more than he ever hoped to have again. After a few minutes, she was breathing regularly. He stayed awake a little longer, just enjoying being next to her, something he thought might never happen again. He fell asleep not long thereafter . . .

Luke awoke to the sound of his alarm. He reached over and shut it off. He turned over, but realized he was alone in bed. He sat up and looked around. Sarah wasn't there. He walked into the living area. She was sitting on the sofa with her hands wrapped around her knees. She seemed to be staring at nothing, lost in thought.

He walked over and sat on the back of the sofa. Sarah looked up and smiled. "I couldn't sleep, but didn't want to wake you."

He rubbed her arm. "Are you OK?"

She nodded. "Yeah, I just wanted to think. I've been trying to remember what happened, but it's not coming back to me."

He walked around the edge of the sofa and sat next to her. "Sarah, in case you do remember, I want to tell you how sorry I am that I hurt you."

She cocked her head and scrunched her face. "What are you talking about?"

"Well, before you went to Paris, we had an argument."

"An argument?" Her voice was low.

He nodded and gave a weak smile. "Yeah, I was being an

idiot."

She reached out and grabbed his arm. "Don't say that."

He put his hand on hers. "I was. I made you cry. I'm so, so sorry. Please forgive me."

She smiled, reached over, and kissed him on his cheek. "I don't remember anything about it, but I forgive you anyway."

He smiled and gave her a kiss. He gave her a second one and prolonged it. Once their lips parted, she giggled. "Don't start that now. I have to get to work." She patted his chest. "And so do you."

He faked a cough. "I think I'm coming down with something. I need a personal physician to monitor my condition."

She laughed and pushed him over on his back. She fell on top of him and gave him a quick kiss. "Nice try."

She jumped up and headed for the door.

Luke sat up and put his chin on the back of the sofa, giving Sarah a pouting look.

Turning back, she opened her mouth to say something, but burst into laughter after seeing his expression. She returned his pout. "See you at lunch?"

He nodded. She blew him a kiss and left.

He put his chin on his hands and closed his eyes. Was he dreaming? He couldn't believe he was back in Sarah's good graces and that she loved him even more. He got up to get ready for work. He saw his phone on the nightstand. He picked it up and texted Jeremy and Oliver: *Sarah came by. Some memory loss, but seems back to normal.* He put the phone down, but then picked it back up. He texted Jeremy: *Sarah remembered nothing about our argument. Maybe there is a God.*

Luke was on cloud nine, so happy. With Sarah back in his life, he was determined to not let what happened between them happen again. He would learn from his mistake. He wanted to take advantage of this second chance.

SEVENTEEN

Trouble in Hohhot

Over the next couple of weeks, Luke felt he was finally reaching some sense of normalcy. Work went uneventfully. Brian returned to Mars City with a huge crush on Carmella. The two of them made plans to spend a weekend together when she came to the States for a conference in a couple of months.

Jared had Luke enter some of his classes to strengthen Luke's core, and the two of them ran another 5K together. This time, Jared won. Since being employed at the company gym, and teaching so many fitness classes during the week, Jared's strength had increased tremendously. Luke realized there was no way for him to keep that fit, so he settled on completing the race as close to Jared as possible. Finishing fifteen seconds behind Jared was a win in his book.

But there were far more serious issues at work. He had to face his fear and begin to read this *Holy Bible*. He didn't want to, but he certainly didn't want to repeat the previous altercation he had with Sarah. She still had not remembered, and he didn't want anything to jog her memory of the event. He only made Sarah promise not to discuss it until he had caught up with her reading. They both made notes to discuss as they read.

While at his desk at work reviewing some data, Luke's phone rang.

"Hey, Sarah. What's up?"

"I just got a call from Natalia. She wants us to come over tonight."

"Oh, no can do."

"Why is that?"

"Oh, I have a date with a very hot lady tonight."

Sarah snickered. "So, you need some persuasion to change your plans?"

"It would have to be substantial."

Sarah's voice got low and sultry. "Well, if you break your hot date tonight, I'll see that you're well compensated on your next one."

Luke tugged at his collar a few times. He suddenly felt warm. "You drive a hard bargain."

Sarah laughed. "Or . . . " Her voice had a singsong lilt to it.

Luke smiled. This was starting to sound interesting. "Yes?"

"I'm getting off at 15:00 today. If you can meet me at 16:00, I could provide an appetizer before we go."

"Hmm. That sounds intriguing." The way she said *appetizer* made him very curious. "I think I can arrange that."

"OK. See you then."

Luke hung up and smiled to himself. His grin lasted a long time—at least until Larry showed up in front of his desk.

"Luke, we have another problem."

Luke finished typing his sentence and looked up. "What is it now, Larry?"

"It's Hohhot."

"China?"

Larry nodded.

"What do you want me to do?"

"They're on a video conference in pod room D. They have some kind of issue and want our help." He paused. "You took Chinese in college, right?"

Luke rolled his eyes. "Yes, but that doesn't mean I can carry on a conversation. Besides, I wasn't exactly top of my class in the subject."

Larry motioned for him to follow. "Doesn't matter. You're the best I've got."

Luke followed Larry toward the pod room. "They have an interpreter, don't they?"

Larry glanced back. "That's what they call him, but he doesn't seem to grasp the English language very well."

"Great. Well, won't we be a pair?"

When they were entering the pod room, Luke grabbed Larry's shoulder. "Just so you know, if I start another World War . . . " He tapped Larry's chest. "It's your fault."

Larry grinned and gestured for him to enter. "Just do your best."

Luke entered and saw Scott sitting there, nearly beet red. He wasn't sure if Scott was laughing or crying.

"What's going on, Scott?"

Scott pressed the mute button and turned away from the camera. He could hold his laughter no longer. He took a notebook and fanned himself. "I'm sorry. But this so-called interpreter is either translating literally or just making something up."

"So, what was so funny?"

"I asked a simple question. 'What do you think is wrong?' He responded, 'No good furry dancing pictures we see.'"

Scott broke out laughing again. "I'm sorry. It just struck me as funny, and I can't stop laughing."

Luke tried to keep from laughing, but chuckled—more

at Scott than what the interpreter said. "OK, calm down. We have to appear dignified."

Scott breathed in and out slowly. "OK. Sorry. Yes, you're right." His face slowly turned back to a fleshy color. He turned back, put his hand on the mute button, and looked at Luke. "Ready?"

Luke nodded. "What's the interpreter's name?"

"Chen." Scott took them off mute.

"Mr. Chen. From what my colleague has told me, it seems your 3-D simulator is not working correctly and the images are blurry? Is that correct?"

Mr. Chen looked confused. "Repeat, please."

Luke had a sinking feeling about this. If only he could remember *any* of his Chinese. What would be the word for *simulator*? He repeated his question and added, *"Mónì qì pòsuì?"*

Chen's eyes lit up, and he nodded vigorously. "*Shì, shì. Mónì qì pòsuì.*"

Scott raised his eyebrows. "What did you just confirm?"

Luke glanced at Scott. "He just agreed that their simulator is broken."

After a few more minutes of minimal communication, Luke realized going further was hopeless. There was no way they could troubleshoot in this way.

Larry reentered. "Progress?"

Luke held up his finger. "One moment."

Chen looked confused again.

Luke put his hands to his head. How should he say "one moment"? It had been way too long since he tried to speak this language. "Uh, *Yīgè shùnjiān.*"

Chen nodded. "*Shì.*"

Luke nodded to Scott. He put them back on mute.

"Well?"

Luke shook his head. "Larry, this will be impossible. There's something wrong with their 3-D simulator. It's going to be next to impossible to understand the problem. Someone will have to go over there." He looked at Scott.

Scott held up his palms. "Don't look at me. I'd just start laughing again."

Luke shook his head and looked back at Larry. "I'll go, but give me some time to get ready and to find an interpreter who can understand some of the technical terms."

Larry nodded. "OK, but you need to do it in less than two weeks. Otherwise, they will be behind schedule."

"Understood."

Luke turned back to the screen. Scott took them off mute. "Mr. Chen, I will come see you soon. OK? Uh . . . *wŏ huì hĕn kuài jiàn dào nĭ*." Luke hoped he said that correctly.

Mr. Chen nodded. "*Xièxiè*. Thank you."

Luke bowed. "Good-bye for now. *Zàijiàn*."

Mr. Chen bowed. "*Zàijiàn*."

Luke nodded to Scott. He ended the call.

Luke sat down and let out a breath. "Well, that was fun."

Scott raised an eyebrow. "I'm impressed."

Luke shook his head. "That was about all the Chinese left in my brain."

Scott laughed and patted him on the back. Larry did the same. Luke looked at his watch. He needed to go or he would be late for his "appetizer," whatever it would turn out to be. And he sure didn't want to be late for that.

He looked at Larry. "I need to leave. OK with that?"

Larry nodded. "Sure. You've earned an hour credit."

Luke patted Larry's shoulder as he walked out. "Thanks."

Luke's pace quickened the closer he got to his apartment. He made a brief stop by his place to freshen up before he went to Sarah's.

He knocked on her door with great anticipation. She opened the door and his jaw dropped. Sarah wore a towel and nothing else. She smiled, pulled him into her apartment, and closed the door.

"I'm . . . I'm speechless."

"That's OK. Appetizers require no conversation." She kissed him and leaned into it.

He knew he was going to enjoy this.

EIGHTEEN

Principles of Community

Natalia greeted them. "Come in." She gave each of them a hug and kiss.

Viktoria and Oliver were already there. After handshakes and hugs, all found a seat. Jeremy brought drinks and small sandwiches.

After some initial chit-chat, Luke turned to Matteo, Natalia's father. "All our lives, we were never told about anything before 2030. What was it like then?"

After taking a sip of tea, Matteo held his cup with both hands. He looked at Luke, but his focus seemed to be on memories and something in the distant past. "I can't really tell you whether life was better or easier prior to the 'Enlightenment.' That's what they called it when they took all religion away. But I will say it was better when people could make their own decisions."

Sarah leaned forward. "So, tell us what it was like during the transition. Why did people accept it?"

Matteo set his cup down. "Even before 2030, there were subtle changes that occurred. I'm not sure how, but Édouard Mauchard became powerful enough to influence governments, elections, and public opinion around the world. He created the Illumi-Alliance and the rest, as they say, is history."

Sarah shook her head. "But how did he become so influential?"

"Money and greed, I'm afraid. People tend to follow the wealthiest, and he was worth billions. Once he put the Illumi-Alliance in place, he achieved the power to manipulate the world's economy and world governments. Everyone became his chess pieces."

Oliver cleared his throat. "Uh, but Mr. Mancini, surely not everyone was compliant. Didn't he receive any resistance?"

Matteo nodded. "Oh, absolutely. Yet Mauchard was poised for that. First came legislation that countered biblical principles."

Luke thought that odd. "What do you mean? What did they change?"

Matteo turned to Natalia. "Do you have a couple pieces of paper?"

She nodded, left the room, and returned with several sheets of paper and some pens.

Matteo handed a piece of paper to Luke. "Before 2030, although many were no longer truly religious, all legislation was still based on what we called the Ten Commandments. I'm going to write those—and you write down the Ten Principles of Community."

Luke nodded. "You're saying they're similar?"

Matteo smiled. "You be the judge."

Luke shrugged. "OK." He wrote down the ten principles. He found it easy to do since he had been taught these his entire life. Once finished, he sat back upright.

Matteo handed him his piece of paper. "OK, now compare the two."

Luke laid the two side by side in front of him. He was surprised at the penmanship of Matteo. His handwriting looked quite stable for someone his age. Luke saw several similarities between the two lists—but some major differences as well.

Ten Commandments	Ten Principles of Community
1. Have no other gods before the One God	Serve the Community
2. Do not worship any idol	Community is your priority
3. Do not take God's name in vain	Have respect for Community
4. Keep the Sabbath holy	Always attend Invocation
5. Honor your father and mother	Fathers and mothers support Community with the gift of their children
6. Do not murder	Do not murder
7. Do not commit adultery	Respect another's partner
8. Do not steal	Do not steal
9. Do not lie about someone	Respect others
10. Do not covet	Respect others' property

Luke scanned the list and glanced back at Matteo. "It seems the major difference is what was termed 'God' is now replaced by 'Community.'"

Matteo nodded. "Yes, and that changed everything. Sin was no longer sin."

Sarah cocked her head. "What do you mean? I've only heard that term used as an expression. You seem to imply it is something more serious."

"Indeed. It is anything that goes against God's teaching."

Luke had a hard time with that statement. He had always been taught God was an antiquated myth. Now he was supposed to believe God is a *real* entity? Why should he? "Like what?" he asked.

Matteo shrugged. "Anything not consistent with loving God with all your being or loving others as yourself."

Luke scratched his head. "Sounds like *why* you do something is more important than *what* you do."

Matteo nodded. "If your motives are correct, then your actions will be as well."

Luke rubbed the back of his neck. He held up his palm. "Mr. Mancini, no disrespect, but I'm having a hard time with all of this. Believing in God seems like a big stretch to me."

Matteo nodded. "I know it's hard, but it's foundational to understanding what the Bible says. Yet, you—yourself—are the proof of this."

Luke cocked his head. "How's that?"

Matteo gestured to Sarah. "You're a physician, right?"

Sarah nodded.

"Did they teach you how proteins are made and folded?"

Sarah bobbed her head. "Sort of, I guess. That's the purpose of the ribosomes."

Matteo nodded. "Yet what they don't really teach is that proteins are needed to make proteins."

Natalia reached over and touched her father's arm. "Dad, as a molecular biologist, did you learn something new?"

He looked at his daughter and smiled. He patted her hand. "No, it was discovered a long time ago. Yet it doesn't fit neatly in the no-need-for-God mantra."

Luke looked at Sarah for confirmation. She just shrugged and shook her head. He looked back to Matteo. "Tell us."

"While it's true ribosomes are important in the manufacture of proteins, they are formed unfolded."

"They can't fold on their own?" Luke looked from Matteo to Sarah.

Matteo looked back at Sarah. "Remember the Levinthal Paradox?"

Sarah squinted her eyes in thought. "Isn't it that there are an astronomical number of possible conformations for a protein, but the right conformation is almost always chosen?"

Matteo nodded. "Yes, the protein needs some guidance. There are carrier, or chaperone, proteins that take the protein into a double-ring protein structure called a chaperonin. It is there the proper protein conformation is made."

Luke shook his head. "That's interesting, but I don't understand the importance."

"As they say, the devil is in the details." Matteo chuckled. "But in this case, God is in the details. If you have to have a chaperonin, which is a protein itself, to create a viable protein, how could the first chaperonin be formed without a chaperonin?"

Luke cocked his head. "Well . . . " He looked at Sarah for help. She shrugged. He turned back. "I . . . I don't know."

Matteo nodded. "Just think about that as you start to read and understand the Bible."

Luke sat back. Yes, this was definitely something to mull over.

Viktoria interjected. "I don't mean to change the subject, but can you tell us what happened to your wife? Do you know where she is?"

Matteo's eyes began to water.

"Oh, I'm so sorry," Viktoria quietly said. "I didn't mean to bring up an unpleasant subject."

Natalia reached over and put her hand on her father's arm. He put his other hand on top of hers and gave a weak smile. He turned back to Viktoria.

"No, that's OK. I don't really know where she is. I would see her periodically at the prison, but I haven't seen her in quite some time."

Sarah put her hand to her mouth. "You mean they kept both of you at the prison, but didn't let you communicate or see each other? That's . . . that's despicable."

Matteo gave a weak smile. "We would look for each other when they allowed us outside for exercise. I would look for that swath of white hair and find her. We often walked the garden trail they created for us." He sighed. "That was about the only pleasant part of the place. But the last time I was outside, I couldn't find her."

Luke looked at Sarah with eyes wide. She looked back at him in the same way.

"Uh, I think we saw her." All eyes turned to Sarah.

"What?" Natalia put her hand to her mouth. "Where?"

"At the Neuroscience Center." Sarah turned to Matteo. "You said your wife had a patch of white hair?"

Matteo nodded. "When younger, she would color it to all sorts of outrageous colors." He chuckled. "She was both bold and fearless."

Natalia visibly trembled as she looked at Sarah. "Do you know where they took her?"

"Hohhot."

Natalia looked at Luke. "Really? She's in China?"

Luke nodded. "As far as we know."

Viktoria turned to Oliver. "We have another rescue mission."

Luke chimed in. "Count me in."

Sarah grabbed his hand. "Me too."

NINETEEN

Immunes Reemerge

Philippe looked up when he heard the conference door open.

René stuck his head in. "Did you get the report?"

Philippe nodded and motioned for him to come in. "Yes, but I've asked Jean-Paul to come and go over it with us." He glanced at the clock on his desk. "He should be here any minute."

René sat on the yellow sofa. "I expected it almost a week ago. What happened?"

Philippe gave a slight shrug. "He spoke at a conference, so I gave him extra time."

René smiled. "You're getting soft in your old age."

Philippe raised his eyebrows. "Old age? Remember, you're always a year older than me."

René laughed. "True." He held up his index finger. "Except for two days of each year."

Philippe smiled and gave a nod.

A light knock interrupted them, and Sonja stuck her head in. "Mr. Mauchard, Jean-Paul is here."

Philippe waved his hand toward himself. "Send him in."

Sonja opened the door wider and gestured fc to enter.

Philippe stood, came around his desk, and m Jean-Paul to have a seat. Phillippe sat on the sofa n Phillippe held up the report on his tablet. "Thanks, Jean-Paul, for the report, but can you go over the highlights? I'm definitely not a geneticist, so if you could summarize at a high level, I would appreciate it."

Jean-Paul nodded. "Yes, sir. Of course." He took out his tablet and scrolled down a couple of pages. "We first assumed simple Mendelian genetics. If the trait is dominant and you remove all those exhibiting the trait, then the trait would not return, but more than 75 percent of the population would have to be removed to wipe it out."

Philippe rubbed his chin. "And if it's a recessive trait?"

"The math usually works in a 1:3 ratio. If you take out the one-third with the recessive trait, the trait would initially return in a 1:5 ratio, but get back to a 1:3 ratio quickly."

Philippe shook his head. This didn't sound good. He knew his father didn't take out a third of the population. He looked back at Jean-Paul. "Is that it?"

Jean-Paul scrolled a few more pages. "Well, as you can possibly imagine, life is usually more complicated." He glanced up, giving a slight smile. He turned his tablet around. "Here, I have used eye color as an example of a more complicated system. If we take, say, green eye color to represent prevalence of the trait you're interested in, it would represent about 2 percent of the population." He scrolled to another page. "Now, if you take all those who exhibit this trait from the population, the trait would slowly reappear over time. There are a lot of complicating factors to take into account to know the rate of increase, as the population with this trait would likely wax and wane with an overall increase over a sixty-year period." He looked back at Philippe. "Sixty years later, you would likely be up to one-hundredth of one percent." He sat back. "Does that help?"

Philippe nodded. "Thanks Jean-Paul. That is helpful."

Jean-Paul breathed a sigh and sat back as if he felt a weight had been lifted. Philippe half-laughed to himself. Perhaps it had. He had, after all, given Jean-Paul a type of ultimatum.

Jean-Paul raised an eyebrow. "Can I answer any other questions?"

Philippe shook his head. "No, that's good enough for now." He stood. Jean-Paul followed. They shook hands. Jean-Paul turned to leave, but then turned back.

"I should mention one other thing, though."

Philippe raised his eyebrows. "Yes?"

"Those numbers are based on assuming all combinations of eye colors would be occurring simultaneously. That's rarely the case in reality. Therefore, I would say if the trait you have a concern about was in only 2 percent of the population, you're probably only back to about one tenth of this prediction. My estimate would be the maximum."

Philippe nodded. "Thanks, Jean-Paul. That is helpful to know."

Jean-Paul turned and let himself out.

Philippe sat back down and looked at René, raising his eyebrows. "What do you think?"

René nodded. "That would be more in line with the number of individuals Dad had taken out of the general population." René sat back and put his hand to his chin. "Even if we're talking about one one-thousandth percent of the population, that's at least one hundred thousand people." He sighed. "That's certainly more than I thought we'd have to contend with."

Philippe nodded. "And the immune trait isn't as easy to identify as green eyes." He paused. "How do you want to deal with this potential issue?"

René sat for several minutes, thinking and drumming his fingers on the arm of the sofa. He turned to Philippe. "How much progress has Professor Mercure made?"

Philippe cocked his head and gave a slight shrug. "She's only just begun. But she at least knows what to target now, so that should help."

René twisted the corner of his mouth. "Yes, but will that produce results in time?"

"She seems confident."

"I sure hope she comes through. If not, and if Dr. LaMarre's reintegration techniques don't work, we may have to repeat what Dad did all those years ago."

Philippe stiffened. "René, that created such chaos at the time."

René nodded. "Yes, but that was a huge paradigm shift at the time. Not so today. Besides, we can implement it under the guise of the Mars lottery."

Philippe gave an approving smile, eyebrows raised. "That may actually work."

"Get Dr. LaMarre poised for a large increase in Mercy Farewells. Most of these, though, will be in secret. The more the general populace doesn't know, the better."

"Agreed." Philippe stood. "I'll at least brief Dr. LaMarre on the potential need and have him ready."

René tapped his knees with his palms and stood. "Good. I'll check on those getting the lottery ready and see how this can get incorporated." He rubbed his chin. "I'll also get our Illumi-Alliance forces to be more vigilant in their lookout for immunes." He looked back at Philippe. "Let me know how things go with Dr. LaMarre."

Philippe nodded.

René exited through the conference room back to his office.

TWENTY

WORKOUT

Luke grunted as he did another crunch. He breathed hard. "Thanks, Jared, for helping me with my core exercises after work these last few weeks." He sat with his arms over his knees, breathing hard, resting.

"No problem." Jared bumped Luke with his foot. "Hey, what are you doing?"

Luke looked up at him. "Resting."

Jared shook his head. "No, no, no. Get up. You agreed to an even fifty sets."

Luke rolled his eyes. "That's what you said. Not what I agreed to."

Jared reached down and pulled Luke to his feet. "Come on. Two more sets. Now, sprint."

They both ran hard and fast staying in place. Sweat already was pouring out every pore of Luke's body, but he felt even more was about to drain. Still, he kept going.

Jared dropped. "Burpee."

Luke squatted, kicked his feet out straight, did a push-up, jumped his feet up to his elbows and then back into a squat, and jumped back up holding his hands in the air. He did this five times.

Jared dropped again. “High planks.”

Luke went to all fours and alternated bringing each knee to his elbow, doing that five times.

Jared dropped lower. “Low planks.”

Luke went down like a push-up and stayed down, repeating bringing each knee to his elbow.

Jared flipped onto his back. “Crunches.”

Luke flipped over, bent his knees, and crunched his torso toward his knees and back again.

After doing five, Jared barked: “Repeat the set. Last one.”

Luke rolled his eyes but did it all over again. He couldn’t really complain since Jared did everything with him. The only difference was Jared’s exercises were in perfect form. By this point, Luke was just trying to get through the set to say he had done it. Every so often, Jared would yell, “Improve the form!” Luke would grunt and try his best to improve.

Once the set was over, Luke crashed onto the floor and tried to catch his breath. “You’re . . . quite . . . the taskmaster.” He looked over at Jared, who sat breathing hard, but not sucking in air like he was.

Jared stood. “OK, time to cool down.”

Luke looked up at him. “What do you think I’m doing?”

“Whining.” Jared did a rotating motion with his hand. “Come on, Luke. Get up. Let’s cool down so your muscles don’t lock up on you.”

Jared helped Luke to his feet. “Now reach up and stretch.”

Luke did so—and had to admit that felt pretty awesome.

“Now spread your legs wide. Slowly bend over and put your palms to the floor.”

Luke could feel the pull in his hamstrings. He grunted. It hurt and felt good at the same time.

"Good form, now."

"Come on, Jared, I'm doing the best I can."

"Here, let me help you." Jared tapped the back of Luke's leg. "Straighten the leg more."

Luke let out another grunt. It hurt, but after a few seconds, it started to feel good.

"OK, now straighten the back, tuck in the stomach." Jared readjusted Luke's stance to be more correct.

"Get a room."

Luke looked over and saw Sarah. He laughed. He saw Jason entering with her.

Sarah laughed. "This is a déjà vu moment. You're both as soaked now as when the two of you tried to out-compete each other at the 5K."

"Plus, you're standing too close to each other," Jason said, acting upset.

Luke knew Jason was just acting. Laughing, he quickly grabbed Jared around the neck and pulled him tightly to him. "You can't have him, Jason. He's mine."

Before he knew what happened, Jared had Luke flipped, on his back, and was sitting on top of him with his knee close to Luke's throat.

Somewhat dazed, Luke tapped the floor. "Uncle."

Jared laughed and helped Luke to his feet. "An advertisement for my defense class."

"Geez, Jared. I can't believe how much stronger you've gotten."

Jared patted him on his back. "All thanks to you, buddy."

Luke gave him a slight push. "On second thought, he's all yours, Jason." Everyone laughed.

Luke let out a long breath. "I'm giving you the next couple of weeks off, Jared. Sarah and I have to head to China for a simulator crisis they seem to be having."

Jared nodded. "OK, sounds good." He looked at Jason. "Maybe you could take his place?"

Jason gave a wide-eyed, raised-eyebrow look. "I don't know about that."

Jared laughed. He shook Luke's hand and pointed at him with his index finger. "OK, look me up when you get back. I'm going to get cleaned up and head out."

Jared and Jason headed out together with Jared still trying to talk Jason into doing core exercises.

Sarah looked at Luke. "Why don't you get cleaned up? We have just enough time to grab a bite before we go over to Jeremy and Natalia's. We need to coordinate with Oliver and Viktoria as to how to rescue Mrs. Mancini."

Luke nodded. "OK. I'll be right out." He reached over and gave her a quick kiss while careful not to touch her with his sweaty body. "I'll be out in ten."

Sarah nodded. "I'll let you know what I found out from Jason on our way there."

Luke turned. "Good. After all, this was all your idea to give you an excuse to talk to Jason while you were . . . "—Luke made air quotes—"waiting for me."

Sarah laughed. "Well, you can't complain. Your core is quite toned now."

He grinned. "A true win-win."

Sarah smiled. "Two wins for me."

TWENTY-ONE

JOHN ONE

As Luke and Sarah left the building, he ordered a taxi with his phone app. They were outside for only a few minutes when the taxi arrived.

"Have you started reading your Bible?"

Luke nodded. "Well, I've started. I found the first chapter of John hard to understand. It sounds a little cryptic."

Sarah leaned into his arm and smiled. "Think metaphorically."

Luke cocked his head. "How's that?"

The taxi pulled up. Luke opened the door for her and jumped in the other side. He announced their destination and inserted his credit disc. A low, sultry, mechanical female voice responded. "Continental Drift. Arrival time, sixteen minutes." The car pulled out into traffic.

Sarah scooted closer to Luke as he put his arm around her. "John uses the term 'Word' to mean the one who came and was the embodiment of God's voice."

"Oh, so if you listen to what he said," Luke interjected, "it would be the same as listening to what God would say?"

Sarah nodded. "That's because John is claiming they are one and the same, yet different."

Luke turned up an eyebrow. "Yeah, that last part is what's hard to grasp. They are the same, but different. Do you understand that?"

Sarah gave a half-shrug. "Sort of. I'm not sure I completely understand it, but I think that's the point. God is different from us, yet was willing to identify with us to bridge the gap that somehow divided us."

"Maybe Mr. Mancini can give us his perspective on this."

Sarah nodded and laid her head between his shoulder and chest. They traveled in silence until the car announced, "Destination achieved."

* * * * *

It surprised Luke when Sarah chose the North American floor and asked for a hamburger.

"You really want a hamburger?"

Sarah nodded. "I thought that would be the fastest thing to eat." She smiled. "Plus, I'm dying to see what they do with something so American." Luke chose the same.

They were both amazed at what was served. At first glance, everything looked fairly plain, but the taste was awe-inspiring. The hamburger was served with mango salsa and had a red cabbage slaw on the side that tasted tangy but had a light freshness to it as well. They both agreed the pièce de résistance was the dipping sauce for the French fries.

Sarah dipped a fry into the sauce and took a bite. Her eyes lit up. "What is this?"

Luke took a bite. It had a peanut taste with an added sweetness. He took a closer look at the sauce, dipped his finger into it, and tasted it without the fry. "I think it's some concoction of peanut butter and honey." He looked back at Sarah. "I can't believe how good this is with the fries." He shrugged. "Who would have thought?"

They both looked at each other, smiled, and said simultaneously, "Jeremy." Both laughed.

Rather than ordering dessert, they headed up to Jeremy and Natalia's penthouse. After greeting everyone, Jeremy offered them a frothy hot drink.

Sarah breathed in the aroma and her eyes lit up. "I was hoping you'd serve this." She took a sip and licked the froth from her lips. "I just love the mocha flavor with a hint of mint."

Jeremy smiled. "Made just for you, my dear."

Sarah chuckled. "I can see I'm becoming way too predictable."

Luke turned to Matteo. "Sarah and I were discussing the first chapter of John on the way over. Can you give us your perspective?"

Matteo smiled. "It's fairly simple, really. That is, after you take the first step."

Luke cocked his head. "First step?"

Matteo nodded. "You first have to accept that God exists."

Luke sighed and put his hands in his coat pockets. He hadn't come to grips with that yet. He, and everyone, had been taught each person was the master of their own fate, with the help of Community. His fingers touched the piece of confetti, which he continued to carry with him. He took it out and passed it to Matteo. "Does this mean anything to you?"

Matteo smiled. "Of course."

Luke's eyes widened. "Really? What does it mean?"

Matteo handed the piece of paper back. "This is your journey, Luke. It will mean more if you discover it for yourself."

Luke's heart sank. He thought back to how this journey had led him to discovering *T-H-B*. This didn't really instill a sense of eagerness on his part. "Not even a hint?"

Matteo chuckled. "It's tied to the first step we just talked about."

Luke sat back. *What did he mean by that?* If he didn't believe in God, he would never understand the cryptic letters?

As he sat there pondering, another thought came to him.

"Mr. Mancini, Oracle Tatum stated there were other books taken away. Why was the Bible the only one the Illumi-Alliance sequestered?"

Matteo nodded. "The Bible is the only book that states one cannot do anything about their sin. Others say one has to do something or be good enough to enter Heaven or paradise. The Bible states God himself took care of the problem. We only have to accept what he did."

Luke had not expected such a statement. He would have to think about that. It stood very much against what he had been taught all of his life. He was supposed to be the master of his own fate and not dependent on anyone else.

Sarah changed the topic. "Mr. Mancini, how did you and your wife get separated?"

Matteo's expression went from one of contentment to one of painful memories. It was almost as if the spark in his eyes cooled. Although he didn't actually cry, his eyes noticeably glistened.

He sat back and looked at Sarah. "I don't know if you can imagine how heart-wrenching it is to have your child taken from you knowing the likelihood of seeing them again is remote." He looked over at Natalia and gave a weak smile. "I'm truly one of the lucky ones."

Natalia reached over, took his hand, and gave a squeeze.

Matteo gave a slight shrug. "We all agreed, in principle, that Community would be better with this plan. Yet once your child is born and you've made such an attachment with him or her, the thought of giving them up is unthinkable."

Sarah leaned forward. "So, what did everyone do?"

"In the beginning, altercations occurred. That's when Mauchard and the Illumi-Alliance started wiping parents' memories of their children."

Sarah gasped. "That's . . . that's horrible."

Matteo nodded. "Yet, from the side of Community, it became a necessary step. There's no other way for such a plan to be successful. Over time, with teaching this practice, people began to accept it, and the number of those who resisted decreased. Yet they still wiped the parents' memories."

It dawned on Luke that this was probably why his parents didn't recognize him. He had been resentful of them for all of these years, but he was now realizing they had never really been given a choice. If not immune, they never would have remembered him.

Natalia reached over and rubbed her father's arm. "Dad, tell them about Mom."

Matteo nodded. "Neither Xiaofeng nor I wanted to give up Natalia. Yet the day after her tenth birthday, our Oracle came for her. There was a . . . "—he did air quotes—" . . . celebration." He choked up and cleared his throat. "Held with cookies and tea. Apparently, it knocked us out and we were reprogrammed. When we awoke, Natalia was gone and we didn't even realize she had ever been with us."

Luke thought back to what he had been taught. This was a happy time for everyone. Parents were proud to give their children to the betterment of Community and children were anxious to become part of Community. He had never missed his parents until he saw them that day. Then, he had not wanted to see them again out of bitterness and disappointment. Matteo was painting a very different picture.

Sarah shook her head. "So, what happened after that?"

"Xiaofeng had some type of resilience to the reprogramming. About a month later, she started talking about Natalia and wanting to find her." He shook his head. "I thought she was delusional, and I had her see a physician. He recommended that she be institutionalized. I consented." His eyes watered once more. "I thought it would be a short-term thing, but . . ." Matteo choked up again. "She just vanished."

Natalia rubbed his arm and wiped a tear.

"I was told there was no record of her being at the institution. I spent the next year looking for her everywhere." He gave a slight shrug. "I guess I caused too much disturbance, as I was taken and put in the prison outside Paris." He gave a slight smile. "One day, when in the prison courtyard, I saw her. She had been there the whole time I had been looking for her. She again told me what she remembered. Of course, I believed her this time."

"But your wife got out, right?" Luke asked.

Matteo looked at Luke and nodded, giving a slight smile. "Several times, actually." His smile faded. "But unfortunately, she always returned."

Luke turned up an eyebrow. "Why? What happened?"

"For some reason, the Illumi-Alliance started a reintegration program. Maybe they had a change of heart, or maybe the prison got too crowded." He shrugged. "At any rate, they chose several individuals to put back into society. Xiaofeng was one of them." He looked over at Natalia and took her hand. "She was determined to find you."

Natalia smiled, her eyes now watering.

"Each time, the effects of the drug wore off and she would attempt to find Natalia. Yet, she always got caught before she would find you."

Sarah sat up suddenly and let out a slight gasp. Everyone turned her way.

Luke reached over and held her arm. "Are you OK? What's wrong?"

"Immunes. They've been targeting immunes." She looked at Luke. "Remember what the guy told Xiaofeng . . . Mrs. Mancini?"

Luke shook his head.

"He said this would be her last time. He likely used a different drug. They've been trying to find the right compound which would work on immunes. It wasn't a reintegration program at all." She bobbed her head. "Well, sort of. But their main goal was to find the right compound, one that would work on immunes."

Natalia stiffened. "What did you mean by 'her last time'?"

Sarah put her hand to her mouth. She looked at Matteo. "How long did it usually take for her to be returned to the prison?"

"It varied. The longest, I think, was about three months."

Sarah turned to Oliver. "We need a plan to extract her as quickly as possible. Do you have one?"

Oliver smiled. "I thought you'd never ask."

TWENTY-TWO

Hohhot Revisited

"Thanks for coming with me. There are very few people at work who can speak and understand Chinese."

Sarah looked at Luke and smiled. "I'm glad both your boss and mine agreed to it, even if it took them two weeks to decide. Ken, my supervisor, was not very keen on me coming, but apparently your supervisor acted desperate. I'm sure me not being Chinese was the hardest sell."

Luke laughed. "Well, I had to sell myself at first. I had no idea you could speak Chinese."

Sarah smiled. "My roommate, when I interned at the American Hospital of Paris, was Chinese. We had a pact. I would speak only Chinese, and she only English, when we interacted. Then we both spoke French when at work. It turned into a good learning exercise."

"And you still remember everything?"

She nodded. "Pretty much. Before I came, I had a long talk with my previous roommate, who's now in Shanghai, and it rekindled those neurons." Sarah laughed. "I must have been on the phone for two hours with her. She'll likely think twice about accepting a phone call from me again."

Luke put his arm around her. "I'm sure she loved catching up with you."

Sarah nodded. "Yeah, I think she did."

Luke looked out the window from their train and watched the landscape go by. They passed by several tiered farms going up the mountainside. The farms were impressive and picturesque. Luke glanced at his watch. They still had almost four hours to go before reaching Hohhot.

Sarah leaned against him, her feet in the seat, reading something on her tablet. She glanced up at him. "Luke, have you read the third chapter of John?"

Luke nodded. "Several times, actually." He shook his head. "I don't get it. I mean, I consider myself fairly intelligent, but the words in this book just throw me completely."

"Yeah. One has to have a different mind-set, for sure." Sarah pointed to her tablet. "What do you think about this verse, which says, 'Because God loved the world, he gave his only son, and whoever believes in him will not perish, but will have eternal life'?"

Luke shrugged. "You tell me. I mean, I'm starting to buy Mr. Mancini's argument for the need for a divine Creator in order for life as we know it to exist. Then, it would make sense that he would love us. But how does he have a son, and why would he send him to earth to die? If he's a god, why would he do that? I mean, doesn't he set the rules? Wouldn't they be in his favor?"

Sarah rubbed the arm he had around her. "Yeah, I had the same thoughts. I asked Mr. Mancini about that."

Luke jerked his head back. "Really? When?"

"Luke, I've been seeing him almost every other night. I've really been trying to wrap my head around all of this."

"So what did he say?"

"He said we have to believe in God as well as Satan."

Luke held up his palms. "Whoa, whoa. You mean, like, the devil?"

Sarah nodded.

"Like what we see in horror films?" Luke shook his head. "*Pfft*. That's just fantasy."

Sarah took his hand in hers. "The film version is the fantasy part. But apparently, he is real. I'm starting to come around. I mean, just look at all we have learned about our world. I'm beginning to believe evil is real and not just a part of human nature."

"Yeah, but still . . . "

"But still, what? Think about it, Luke. We have been taught we are good and that we are to look out for the needs of Community. Yet, what have we found out? We're actually being manipulated for someone else's agenda. How is that good—or even for our good?"

Luke thought about this for a few minutes. *She makes sense. But . . . a devil?*

Sarah gently shook his hand. "You OK?"

Luke smiled. "Yeah, I was just thinking. OK, let's say you're right. What is this verse trying to teach us?"

"Remember Oliver telling us about what he read in the first book, called Genesis? Because Adam and Eve succumbed to his lie, everyone became separated from God because of that sin."

"OK, wait."

Sarah looked up at him. "What's wrong?"

"I have a hard time with that term."

"Sin?"

"Yeah. What does that really mean, anyway?"

"Mr. Mancini said the simple definition is anything against what God says or against his standards."

"Like the Ten Commandments?"

Sarah nodded. "Yeah, I think that's part of it. Those are the fundamentals, but their concepts go wider."

"What do you mean?"

"Our time together the other night was probably wrong."

Luke scrunched his brow. "What?" He had never heard such a thing. *How could it be wrong for a sexual being to have sex?* "Is that what you really believe? You didn't think our time together was special?" He kissed her on her forehead. "I sure did."

She kissed his hand. "Of course I did. But . . . I'm not sure it was the right thing. I talked to Mr. Mancini about it."

Luke sat up even more straight than he had been. "What? You talked about us . . . being together?"

Sarah patted his hand. "No. No, of course not. I just asked him about the concept in general."

"So what did he say?"

Sarah shook her head. "He wasn't very direct. He stated that once I receive the Holy Spirit, He would guide me in such decisions."

"Receive the *what*?"

"The Holy Spirit. He said once I accept the death of God's son as payment for my sin and as the hope of my future, the Holy Spirit would be given as a means to guide me in my choices and decisions based upon Scripture."

Luke shook his head. "All of this is so . . . different from anything I've ever heard."

Sarah nodded.

Luke cocked his head. "What about our stay in Hohhot? We had decided to make only one reservation." He had looked forward to more intimate time with Sarah.

Sarah glanced up at him with a small grimace. "Sorry. I had another reservation made for me." She grabbed his arm and rubbed it. "I still want to spend time with you, but set a limit on how far we go."

Luke nodded, but he was sighing on the inside. So much for his plans. It seemed his *T-H-B* discovery now had put a crimp in his plans. Yet, he had to admit, he was also intrigued at the same time.

Sarah spent the remainder of the time reading to Luke. He listened as he watched the scenery outside their window transition from plains to more mountainous terrain. He found this country beautiful.

The intercom sounded. "Hohhot station."

Sarah sat up, donned her shoes, and made preparation to disembark. Luke pulled their luggage down from the rack above them, and they walked to the end of the car with the other passengers.

* * * * *

Once they checked into their hotel, Luke and Sarah walked through the city since they didn't have to start work until the next day. Not far from their hotel was Qingcheng Park. It looked beautiful with several ponds scattered throughout; there were manicured landscapes and ornate and colorful shrubbery. It seemed peaceful and inviting.

Once they left the park, they came to the Invocation Center.

Sarah pointed. "Isn't it beautiful? I'm always amazed at the diversity of these Centers."

Luke nodded. "I guess it's apropos that this one has five pagodas on its roof."

Sarah nodded. "The symmetry is breathtaking. The pagodas on the corners are the same, with a different style above the building's entrance. I wonder what this was before it became an Invocation Center."

Luke shook his head. "It's obvious this building was around way before 2030." He shrugged. "Maybe it was some type of religious building."

Sarah nodded. "There's nothing left here to let us know."

As they headed back to the hotel, they stopped for dinner. Luke then escorted Sarah back to her room. He had envisioned romantic plans for this night, plans that, undoubtedly, he would now not realize. Sarah opened her door and turned. He gave her a passionate kiss and prolonged it. At first, she reciprocated. For a moment, Luke felt she had changed her mind. He pushed them toward the door, but Sarah broke from the kiss.

She put her forehead on his. She was breathing hard. "Luke, please don't make this harder than it already is."

Luke sighed. "I'm sorry, Sarah. I think your willpower is stronger than mine."

She slowly shook her head. "No. No, it really isn't. I need you to be with me on this."

He couldn't say he was, but he respected her too much to push his will on her. "I will support you as best I can. That's all I can do."

She looked into his eyes. "That's all I ask. Thank you."

She stepped into her room. Luke remained where he stood.

"I love you." She closed the door.

Luke leaned against the wall and sighed. This was going to be much harder than he wanted. He turned and headed toward his room. He knew a cold shower was on his agenda before bed.

TWENTY-THREE

DR. LIWEI

The next day, Luke tried but couldn't order a taxi with his app. He went to the hotel's concierge. He gave Luke a special credit disc with a button in its center which, when pushed, would send a hotel taxi his way. The disc would then charge the taxi use to his room.

Once Luke and Sarah exited the hotel, he used the disc and a taxi soon pulled up. Luke opened the door for Sarah and climbed in the other side. The taxi's mechanical voice sounded male and, in Luke's opinion, rather gruff. It also spoke in Chinese. Rather than asking it to change to English, Sarah gave the destination in Chinese. The mechanical voice responded and pulled away from the hotel and into traffic. It headed north out of the city.

Sarah sat back. "We should be there in about half an hour."

After a few minutes, Sarah looked over at Luke. "Who is it we are supposed to be meeting?"

"A Dr. Chen."

Sarah stared at Luke.

"What?" he asked.

"You want me to go into a Chinese facility and ask for a Dr. Chen?"

Luke nodded.

Sarah laughed. "Are you going to pick him out of a lineup or something?"

Luke gave her a puzzled look.

She put her hand on his chest. "Luke, any idea how many people with the last name Chen likely work at such a facility?"

Luke suddenly felt foolish. "Oh, yeah. That could be a problem." He pulled out his phone and checked his messages to find the invitation. "Qiang Chen." He looked back at Sarah. "He's the one I spoke with about their simulator issue."

Sarah nodded. "That helps."

Luke debriefed her on all he knew and what he hoped to accomplish.

The taxi pulled up to a large building and made an announcement. Luke inserted his disc and exited the cab. He helped Sarah out, and the taxi pulled away.

Luke whistled. "Wow. Have you seen anything like this? I would never have expected this." The building stood several stories tall and looked quite wide. The entire building seemed to be of glass, but random panes were of different colors.

Sarah shook her head. "It's awe-inspiring."

They entered through a cobalt-colored archway and large glass doors into a beautiful atrium. Next to the receptionist desk was a large waterfall that meandered over attractive rocks, entering into a small pond at the base; there, iridescent lavender-colored lotus flowers floated about. Their small movement from where the water entered the pond was nearly mesmerizing.

The receptionist also wore a lotus flower in her jet-black hair, which made the flower stand out all the more. Her hair was long and draped over both shoulders. She offered a bright smile as they approached.

The woman and Sarah conversed in Chinese for a few minutes. Luke made out a few words. The receptionist picked up her phone. She let Dr. Chen know his visitors had arrived. The woman gestured to the overstuffed chairs opposite the waterfall. They sat and waited.

Sarah kept looking around. "This is way more opulent than I would have expected."

Luke nodded. "It some ways, it puts our building to shame."

Sarah laughed. "I wouldn't go telling Mr. Rosencrantz that, though."

Luke smiled. "Don't worry. I value my job."

A man with short black hair wearing a lab coat approached. The man's name appeared over his left shoulder but was written in Chinese characters. He bowed and Luke and Sarah bowed in return.

Sarah made introductions in Chinese.

Luke bowed and gave a greeting. "*Nǐ hǎo.*"

The man bowed again.

Dr. Chen took them up to a tenth-floor conference room. Other introductions were made. Dr. Chen had brought two other engineers and the man in charge of the 3-D simulator, a Dr. Liwei.

Through the help of Sarah, Dr. Liwei explained the problems they were having. He even gave a demonstration of the fuzzy images the 3-D simulator was showing. Luke thought it may be a coding problem and asked to review the computer coding. Sarah asked Dr. Liwei if they could view the 3-D simulator.

After an hour of reviewing code, Luke was still unsure of the issue. He sat back and sighed. *What else can I do?* He got up to see if Sarah had found anything in her side discussions with Dr. Liwei. At that moment, she and Liwei entered the room, laughing.

"What's going on?"

Sarah smiled. "Problem solved."

Luke turned up his brow, feeling completely confused. "Really? How?"

"Everyone was thinking too technical. When I think of fuzzy pictures, I think to adjust the lens."

Luke's jaw dropped. "No. You're kidding. That was it?"

Sarah shrugged. "Well, it was slightly more complicated, but that was basically it. Being loose, it responded to the computer settings sporadically. That's why the picture seemed fine at times and fuzzy at others."

Luke laughed. "No one will disagree with your coming now."

Dr. Liwei responded.

Luke looked at Sarah. He knew he had said something about perspective.

Sarah laughed. "He said that it sometimes helps to have someone with a fresh perspective."

Luke chuckled. "Can't argue with that."

Just then, the door swung open and slammed against the doorstop. Sarah did a light shriek simply from being startled. Luke jumped and turned to see what had happened. Dr. Liwei's eyes grew wide.

Two Illumi-Alliance soldiers entered. They said something in Chinese, grabbed Dr. Liwei, handcuffed him, and dragged him out of the conference room. Dr. Liwei kept saying something in Chinese over and over again.

The soldiers essentially ignored Luke and Sarah. It happened so fast that Luke simply stood there, stunned. After they left, he looked at Sarah, mouth open. "What . . . what just happened?"

Sarah turned and looked at him. Her eyes glistened. She

seemed dazed. "They . . . they accused him of being an immune and sabotaging the 3-D simulator."

"But why would he do that and then help to correct it?" Luke shook his head. "That doesn't make any sense."

"Dr. Liwei kept saying they had the wrong guy, but they just ignored him."

Luke nodded. "Once they have orders, nothing deters them from carrying them out."

"What can we do?"

Luke's eyes widened. "*Do?* What *can* we do?"

Sarah closed the door. "Luke, Dr. Liwei is innocent here."

"You can prove he isn't an immune?"

Sarah opened her mouth to say something, stopped, paced, and then turned back. "Whether he's an immune or not is not the question. He's innocent of this particular charge."

Luke grabbed Sarah's arms and looked into her eyes. "His *crime* is being immune. The charge is obviously made up. It's just a smoke screen." He threw up his arms. "Who knows? It may be a warning for us. Or . . . or a message for all immunes."

"What? What do you mean?"

He took a step closer and lowered to a whisper. "Sarah, in Paris: we didn't exactly leave a pristine crime scene."

Now Sarah turned up her brow. "But, you put the mini drive back."

"Yes, but the crushed earwig, the toilet seat, and the aluminum bar were left behind."

Sarah's eyes widened. "Why would they even look? What would make them suspicious?"

Luke shrugged. "I don't know. Maybe it's just my paranoia."

"Are you backing down from our true assignment?"

Luke shook his head. "No. Of course not."

"OK, then. Let's go find Oliver."

"Shouldn't we first talk to Dr. Chen?"

Sarah shrugged. “He already knows the simulator problem is now solved. Dr. Liwei told him on our way back here.”

Luke cocked his head. “Ok, then. Let’s go.”

TWENTY-FOUR

Oliver's Appearance

Luke and Sarah hurried to the elevator, descended to the lobby level, and exited the building as quickly as possible. Luke pressed the button on his credit disc. He wasn't sure how long it would take for a taxi to arrive.

Luke heard someone running up to them.

"Hěn bàoqiàn, Hěn bàoqiàn. So'y. So'y!"

They both turned. Dr. Chen was hurrying toward them. When he arrived, he bowed and spoke very fast in Chinese, catching his breath between words.

He looked at Sarah.

She looked from Dr. Chen to Luke. "He says he's very sorry. He's thanking us for our help and asking if he can help us in any way." She put her hand on Luke's chest. "I think he's frightened we may give a bad report about what happened here."

"Tell him we were happy to help, and that's all we will report."

Sarah nodded and relayed the information to Dr. Chen.

He bowed. *"Xièxiè. Xièxiè."*

Luke and Sarah bowed in return as the hotel taxi arrived.

Luke put his hand on Dr. Chen's shoulder and gave a pat. "You're welcome, Dr. Chen."

On the way back to the hotel, Luke pulled out his phone and typed a message to Larry.

"What are you sending?"

Luke glanced up at Sarah and continued to type. "I'm sending Larry a message that we were successful." He paused and sighed. "I thought we would have more time to look for Mrs. Mancini. Being successful so fast limits our time here."

Sarah looked at Luke with a sly smile. "Are we sure we've solved the entire problem?"

Luke cocked his head. "What do you mean?"

"Well, we've come all this way. I would want to be sure all is working properly before I headed back—to ensure we're not turning around and coming right back."

Luke smiled. He pointed his finger at Sarah. "You're the sly one. I need to keep my eyes on you."

Sarah smirked. "Just trying to be thorough and save the company money. I call that thrifty in my book."

Luke turned back to his e-mail. "I'll request of Larry that we stay three more days to be sure all is in working order before we leave." He leaned over and gave Sarah a kiss. "You've earned this trip in more ways than one."

"I just want it to be successful in more ways than one."

Luke nodded, finished his e-mail, and put his phone away. "Now we have to find Oliver."

Sarah scooted closer to him. He raised his arm and wrapped it around her; she nestled in. Sarah looked up at him. "I don't think we have to worry. He'll most likely find us."

Luke nodded. She had a point. Both he and Viktoria always seemed to operate in that way.

* * * * *

Once back at the hotel, Luke escorted Sarah to her room. "Let's meet downstairs in an hour and we'll get dinner and decide what to do from here," he said.

Sarah nodded. She turned to insert her door key. The door opened as soon as she touched it. She turned to Luke, wide-eyed. He put his arm in front of her.

"Let's proceed cautiously."

She nodded.

Luke slowly opened the door and peeked in. He couldn't see anyone. He entered a bit farther. His heartrate was sky-rocketing. He could feel the vein in his neck pulse. He turned the corner, where the sofa was located. He froze. He saw a boot at the corner of the sofa. He looked around for anything to use as a weapon. He reached for a metal mask hanging on the wall next to him while trying to be as quiet as possible. He wrapped his fingers around its base. He took a deep breath and rushed into the room—ready to swing the mask in the same way he had the toilet seat back at the Paris Invocation Center . . .

"It's about time."

Luke froze, the mask poised over his head. "Oliver?" He slowly lowered the mask and let out a long breath. He fell onto the sofa. "As soon as I recover, I'm going to smash you with this mask."

Oliver laughed. "I told you I'd meet up with you here."

Luke looked at him and responded with exasperation in his voice. "Yeah, but you neglected to state exactly where and when! A little advance notice would have been welcomed."

Oliver shrugged. "Well, we're here, aren't we?"

Sarah came around the corner. "Just where is the rest of 'we'?"

"I'm here." Viktoria stepped out of the bathroom. "What did I miss?"

Oliver laughed. "Luke here tried to mask me."

Viktoria had a funny expression on her face. "What?"

Oliver laughed all the more.

Luke got up and hung the mask back where he found it. "Your husband here just scared the living daylights out of us."

Viktoria turned to Oliver and pointed at him. "See, I told you: you should have shaved this morning."

Luke rolled his eyes. "Oh, so now you have a sense of humor?"

Oliver laughed again. "Come on, Luke. I'm sorry. I didn't want to send an e-mail."

Luke plopped back onto the sofa waving his hands. "OK. OK. Let's just focus on our real mission. We only have three days to get it done."

Sarah spoke up. "Can you talk over dinner? I'm really hungry."

Viktoria put her arm around Sarah's shoulders. "I'm on her side."

Oliver held up his palms. "OK, OK. I get the message. It's has to be room service, though. We probably shouldn't be seen."

Sarah nodded. "Yes, that's probably best." She looked from Oliver to Viktoria. "What would you two like?"

Oliver shrugged. "You decide. We're easy."

Sarah laughed. "OK. I'll go order the surprise."

While waiting, Luke told about his and Sarah's day. Room service arrived before he got to the interesting part. While eating dinner, Luke and Sarah finished telling their experience at the Hohhot Aerospace Center. Oliver suddenly looked pensive.

Luke sat his wine glass down. "What's wrong, Oliver?"

"Hmm?" He came out of his trancelike state. "Oh, sorry. That just made me wonder."

Sarah stopped chewing. “About what?”

“It may be they are already targeting immunes.”

Luke clunked his silverware on his plate. “*Already?* You mean they’re on to us?”

Oliver nodded. “It would seem.” He cocked his head. “Although, they may be more suspicious than anything else at this point.”

Sarah whispered, “So what do we do?”

Viktoria put her hand on Sarah’s arm. “Just do your job and don’t be too efficient about it.”

Sarah nodded, sat back, and sighed. After a few seconds, she leaned in. “OK, so how do we finish our mission here?”

Viktoria shook her head. “We haven’t found her yet.”

Sarah’s eyes widened. “What? Has she left or been taken back to Paris for Mercy Farewell?”

Oliver tapped his index finger on the table. “That is the question.”

Luke slowly shook his head. “So, what’s the plan? Do . . . you have a plan?”

“We do.”

Luke looked at Viktoria.

“As an Illumi-Alliance officer, I’ll check out our detention center here in Hohhot tomorrow and see if she’s there.

Oliver nodded. “If she’s there, we’ll rescue her tomorrow night.”

Luke’s eyebrows rose. “And if she’s not?”

“One bridge at a time, Luke. One at a time.”

TWENTY-FIVE

Mrs. Mancini's Rescue

"Ready?"

Luke awoke, sat up, and stretched. "Sorry. I must have fallen asleep."

Sarah smirked. "Are you implying I get dressed too slowly?"

Luke chuckled. "Just tired, I guess."

Luke looked at his watch. It had only been fifteen minutes since he sat on the sofa waiting for Sarah to finish getting ready. A day of sightseeing and waiting for the call from Oliver had been more draining than he thought.

As they exited Sarah's hotel room, Luke made sure the door was secure. He laughed to himself, remembering what Viktoria had said before: a lock is not a deterrent, it just slows her down a bit. He was glad she was on their side. She would be a formidable opponent.

"You know where to go?"

Luke nodded. "We're to meet them behind some type of warehouse just south of the city." He pressed the button for the elevator.

Sarah gave a sigh.

"Are you all right?" Luke asked.

She gave a weak smile and nodded. "Yeah, I just never thought espionage would be part of my life."

Luke wrapped his arm around her as they entered the elevator. "I thought you wanted an exciting life."

She gave him a chuckled sigh and shook her head. "I wanted an exciting career. This is . . . beyond my requirements."

Luke gave a short laugh. "When I look back at all that's happened with us over a short period of time, I sometimes think I'm in *The Twilight Zone.*"

Sarah nodded as they left the elevator at the front of the hotel. "I remember seeing some of those old television episodes. They always creeped me out. That's what my life is doing to me now."

Luke pressed the button on his hotel credit disc and a taxi pulled up. After they entered, Sarah gave some instructions and the vehicle pulled into traffic.

They didn't talk much; Sarah nestled next to him, and he put his arm around her. He had to admit, while he didn't really want this covert life, it had pushed Sarah closer to him faster than life would have done otherwise. Could he complain if they were closer to each other than ever? Yet, he would like more intimacy—and that was now on the back burner. Once this rescue was over, he wanted to discuss this more with her. This "sin" thing was really puzzling.

The vehicle's mechanical voice said something in Chinese. Sarah stirred, so it meant they had reached their destination. They stepped out of the taxi and looked around to get their bearings.

He pointed to a large building several blocks away. "I think that is where we're supposed to meet Oliver and Viktoria."

They headed in that direction and meandered toward the

back of the building. Sarah grabbed his arm. "This is creepy back here. I can barely see anything."

Luke nodded and kept his eyes peeled for any glimpse of Oliver or Viktoria. He felt a tap on his shoulder. He turned with a start: Oliver. Instinctively, he made a swing at him. Oliver easily sidestepped the swing and laughed.

"One of these days, Oliver, you're going to give me a heart attack."

"Relax, Luke. You know you wouldn't want me any other way."

"Oh, stop being right all the time." Luke pushed him on the shoulder. Oliver laughed.

Viktoria came out of the shadows. She wore a black bodysuit that allowed her to blend into the darkness. When close, it highlighted every curve of her figure. Luke had to force himself to not stare.

Viktoria chimed in. "If you boys are through playing, it's time to get to work."

Oliver smiled and reached over to give her a kiss. She gave a quick smile back and turned quite serious. Evidently, this was Viktoria getting herself in the zone. Luke thought back to their time at the Invocation Center. He was glad she was with them; he would definitely follow her lead.

Viktoria led them behind several large bushes, around a couple of large Dumpsters, and up a fire escape to a second-floor window. She looked back. "There should only be a couple of guards, so this shouldn't be too time-consuming."

She jimmied the window and they were able to enter a large, cavernous room.

She led them onto a type of catwalk overlooking the floor below. There were two guards at a table. Beyond them were several rooms with doors. Luke assumed they were holding Mrs. Mancini in one of them. Viktoria went further in, stopped, and shook her head.

Oliver put his hand on her shoulder. "What's wrong?" he whispered.

"It's Caine and Abel. I can't let my partners see me here. I can't risk my cover as an Illumi-Alliance officer. There is no way I can enter."

Oliver kissed her cheek. "No worries. I'll take care of them."

Viktoria squinted. "Are you sure?"

Oliver smiled. "That's why you've been training me, isn't it?" His smile turned into a broad grin. "Or was that just foreplay?"

Luke waved his hands. "TMI. I don't need to see that in my mind."

Oliver laughed. "Don't worry. I've got this."

Oliver slid down one of the poles supporting the catwalk. He was still in the shadows; the only light was where the two agents were sitting. They appeared to be playing some type of holographic game. Luke could see some type of creatures fighting each other on the tabletop, but couldn't see them clearly enough to know the specific game.

Oliver crept up on the two on all fours, looking something like a panther; he too was dressed in all black. The two men were so engrossed in their game they didn't notice Oliver approaching closer and closer. Oliver reached up and knocked out Abel with his fist. Caine looked up and reached for his gun. In a flash, Oliver grabbed Caine's chair leg with his foot and flipped him over. He twisted around, grabbed his stun weapon, and shot Caine before he even hit the ground. Oliver turned and looked up at them, a big grin on his face.

Viktoria motioned for Luke and Sarah to follow. All three slid down the same pole Oliver had. As soon as Luke touched the warehouse floor, a door at the end of the large room opened and about a dozen Illumi-Alliance guards poured into the room, weapons raised. Oliver immediately flipped the table so it could be used as cover. The guards approached with weapons raised, but didn't fire. They evidently thought Oliver was alone. Though a few swung their weapons in various directions as they approached, all of them were basically focused on him.

Luke felt Viktoria grab his shoulder. She motioned for he and Sarah to head toward the door the guards had entered, but to stay in the shadows.

Viktoria whispered to Luke. "Stay behind me and shoot whoever I knock down." She motioned for Sarah to stay where she was for the moment.

Both Luke and Sarah nodded. Sarah grabbed Luke's arm. "Be careful."

He nodded and looked back at Viktoria.

"Ready?"

Luke swallowed hard and nodded. No, he wasn't ready, but he had to help. He could feel the vein in his neck beginning to pulsate again.

Luke was amazed at how Viktoria could run so fast in near absolute silence. He tried to stay up with her, but lagged behind. He didn't have her speed or stealth.

Viktoria slid and took out the three guards in the rear of the group. Without missing a stride, she jumped, grabbed one of the guards around his neck, twisting him around as she grabbed the next guard around his neck with her legs, throwing the first guard into another who toppled. One of the guards turned and pointed his weapon at her. Still, she was quicker. She grabbed the barrel, lifting it up as she kicked the guard's hand off the trigger. In one smooth motion, she took the rifle away from the guard and used it as a club, taking out four more guards before they were able to turn and aim at her. The last guard she hit twirled, and she grabbed him and used him as a human shield as the two remaining guards turned on her.

Oliver bolted from behind the table and ran toward them. One turned his way, but Oliver shot him before he could discharge. Oliver then felled the last one, who shot at Viktoria. Luke came up behind Viktoria, shooting each guard she had felled before they could recover.

Viktoria dropped her human shield guard. This one had received so many stun shots he was barely breathing. Luke decided it was little use shooting him again.

Sarah came running up to Luke. "Are you OK?" Her eyes were wide. She rubbed her hands over his chest and shoulders, looking for injuries.

He smiled. "I'm fine. They also used stun guns."

She wrapped her arms around his neck and pulled him close. "Oh, Luke. This . . . this is crazy."

He kissed her cheek. "I'm fine. Really. I'm fine."

He turned and saw Oliver and Viktoria in a passionate kiss. He walked over and patted Oliver's shoulder. "Uh, remember our mission."

Oliver broke the kiss. He turned to Luke and smiled. "Sorry. Got carried away."

Luke shook his head. "You two. You're just . . . "

Oliver raised his eyebrows.

"Scary."

Oliver laughed and patted Luke on his shoulder. "Come on. Let's go find Mrs. Mancini."

Sarah was already looking in the windows of the doors to each room. When she reached the third one, she turned. "She's in here."

Luke went back to where Caine and Abel lay on the floor unconscious. He looked in Caine's coat pocket and found a key. It was strange to have a physical key for a door, but the warehouse did indeed look very old. Luke walked back over and opened the cell door.

For a cell, it wasn't what Luke expected. It looked like a small living room. He could see a sofa, a desk, a reading lamp, and a monitor with several movie discs next to it. While a prisoner, it was obvious Mrs. Mancini wasn't considered a criminal—at least not in the normal sense.

She sat on the sofa along the back wall, eyes wide, shaking slightly. Obviously, she was terrified. Luke couldn't blame her. She had heard the fighting, or maybe even seen part of it, and now strangers were opening her cell door. *What must she be thinking?*

Luke mustered a soft smile and tried to project a pleasant tone. "Mrs. Mancini, we've come to take you to your husband and daughter."

Her eyes darted from one to another. "How . . . how do you know my name?"

"It's a long story." He walked over and held out his hand. At first she stared into his eyes, likely trying to see if she could really trust him. Eventually, she reached out her hand and Luke helped her to her feet. "You know my husband? And . . . " Again, she looked from one of them to another. " . . . my daughter? You also know my daughter?"

Luke smiled. "She's one of my best friends."

Mrs. Mancini put her hand to her mouth. Her eyes filled with tears and a few ran down her cheeks. "I have tried to look for her for so long." She looked back at Luke with a stern face. "Please don't deceive me. I could not bear it."

Sarah came forward and took her hand. "Mrs. Mancini, both your husband and daughter are waiting for you. It's real. You'll see them soon."

She shook her head. "This . . . this is like a dream. I . . . I can't believe it."

Sarah wrapped her arm around Mrs. Mancini's shoulders and led her out of the room. Mrs. Mancini looked around at all the guards on the warehouse floor. Her jaw fell slightly open. "These are Illumi-Alliance soldiers. How . . . ?"

Sarah smiled and patted her new friend's shoulder. "We had a secret weapon." Sarah looked at Viktoria and smiled.

Mrs. Mancini stopped and turned. "Oh, there is another man here. They brought him in just yesterday."

Sarah looked at Luke. "It must be Dr. Liwei."

Luke nodded and looked in the other cells. All were empty except for the fifth. He looked in. Dr. Liwei also was sitting on his sofa. He stood as soon as he saw Luke's face. He walked to the door, a puzzled look on his face.

Luke opened the door and stuck out his hand. "Good to see you, Dr. Liwei."

Dr. Liwei bowed. His eyes widened further when he saw Sarah.

Sarah said something to him in Chinese. Mrs. Mancini actually laughed. Dr. Liwei smiled and bowed.

Luke looked at Sarah for a translation. Sarah smiled. "I said, 'We're here to rescue you. How would you like to meet more immunes?'"

Viktoria herded all of them toward the door. "Let's get out of here."

TWENTY-SIX

Danger Escalates

Luke helped Jeremy prepare drinks. Sarah talked to Mr. Mancini. Natalia paced. Luke and Sarah had taken their scheduled flight and arrived back in Houston the previous day. Luke had reported to Larry before their flight that all seemed well at the Hohhot Aerospace Center. Larry had not heard about Dr. Liwei, and Luke wasn't going to mention what he and Sarah had witnessed unless directly asked.

He had no idea how Oliver and Viktoria were bringing Mrs. Mancini and Dr. Liwei back. Actually, he had no idea how those two did half of what they did. He was sure he didn't want to know.

Luke looked over at Jeremy. "How's Natalia holding up?"

Jeremy looked at Natalia and then back to Luke. "She's fine." He smiled. "She never thought she'd have her parents back in her life. Now she'll have both parents back." He sat the last drink on the tray. "You know, I've never really thought about my parents or had a desire to connect with them. Yet, Natalia always had that desire. I'm not sure why. I'm just glad her wish is coming true."

Luke nodded. "I was surprised she remembered things her father told her." He shook his head. "I can't remember hardly anything before I turned ten."

Jeremy nodded and picked up the tray. "Same here." He walked over to the group and handed out drinks.

Luke walked over and sat next to Sarah. The doorbell rang. They all stood.

Natalia reached for her father. "Dad, you should meet her first."

He patted her hand. "Thank you."

All headed to the door. Luke and Sarah stayed farther back. This was a moment for Natalia and her dad.

Jeremy opened the door. Oliver and Viktoria entered first with Dr. Liwei; they greeted everyone as they entered. They walked over and stood with Luke and Sarah.

Mrs. Mancini entered just behind them. As she saw Mr. Mancini, she stopped and they looked into each other's eyes, both wet with tears. Mr. Mancini held out his arms and she entered them, wrapping hers around him. He enveloped her in his arms and hugged tightly. He pulled her away slightly and gave her a kiss. She smiled and kissed him back. They hugged again.

Mrs. Mancini put her hands to his cheeks and looked deeply into his eyes. "Matteo, I can't believe I am this close to you again. I love you."

He smiled. "Xiaofeng, you being here is like life-giving breath given to a corpse. You have always been my life, and you have been given back to me." He took her hand and slowly turned her position. "Xiaofeng, this is your daughter."

Xiaofeng looked at Natalia, who smiled back and tried to hold her tears at bay. Xiaofeng glanced back at Matteo and then at Natalia. "Matteo, she's so beautiful." She held out her arms and Natalia walked into them. They embraced and both began to weep softly. Tears ran down their cheeks.

Xiaofeng smiled with eyes closed, but her tears still poured through. "Oh, Natalia, my darling. I have waited so long for this day." She pulled away and looked into her daughter's eyes and placed a hand on Natalia's cheek. "You are indeed so beautiful. God gave us an angel."

Natalia smiled as her tears continued to flow. "Oh, Mom, I waited so long for this day as well. I had wanted us to be a family again for so long." They hugged again. Once she released the embrace, she gestured to Jeremy. "Mom, this is my husband, Jeremy."

Xiaofeng smiled. Jeremy held out his hand, but she ignored it and wrapped her arms around his neck. He hugged her back and smiled. Once the embrace was released, he gestured for everyone to enter and have a seat.

As Jeremy entered the sitting area, Luke touched his arm. "Jeremy, we're going to go and give you and Natalia time to get acquainted with her folks."

Jeremy nodded. "OK, but you know you're welcome to stay. Both Natalia and I feel all of you are like family to us."

Sarah smiled. "Thanks, Jeremy. We feel the same, but this is different. Natalia needs the time to focus on her parents."

He nodded. "I understand. Come by tomorrow night, OK? I'll prepare something for all of us."

All nodded. Oliver put his hand on Jeremy's shoulder. "What should I do with Dr. Liwei? I could find a hotel to put him."

Jeremy shook his head. "No, he can stay here. We have room. Plus, he probably needs to be out of sight. Am I right?"

Oliver nodded. "The less he can be seen, the better right now." He nodded toward the party in the living area. "Mrs. Mancini has developed a rapport with Dr. Liwei, so he should be fairly comfortable here, although it may be a little awkward for him tonight."

"Don't worry. We'll make him feel welcome." Jeremy shook each of their hands. "We'll talk more tomorrow night. Thanks for everything."

Luke looked over at Natalia. She looked so happy. *Good for her,* he thought. "Jeremy, tell everyone we'll see them tomorrow evening. We don't want to interrupt their time together."

Jeremy nodded and walked them to the door.

Once in the elevator, Luke turned to Oliver and Viktoria. "Want to stop in the bar and talk?"

Oliver nodded. "Sure. I can use a drink and a bite to eat."

They found a secluded table in the corner of the bar. Luke ordered some wine and a few appetizers. He looked at Oliver. "So, what will be the repercussions of all this?"

Oliver shrugged. "I'm not sure. I did my best to reprogram those we encountered. Yet, I'm sure more than just those we encountered knew why they were there."

The waiter came with their wine and poured a glass for each of them. Luke raised his glass. "To Natalia." Each raised their glass and took a sip.

Sarah sat her glass down and leaned in. "So, Viktoria, why were the other guards there?"

Viktoria shook her head. "I don't know. I was just as surprised to find them there as the rest of you. I had heard nothing about it."

Sarah shook her head. "So, what's going on?" She glanced at Luke and then Oliver and Viktoria. "Are we in danger?"

Oliver shrugged. "To tell you the truth, I don't know."

Luke looked at Sarah and they both looked back at Oliver, eyebrows raised.

Oliver raised an index finger. "The powers that be may be suspicious, but I don't think they know anything specifically. We probably need to lay low for now and go about our regular jobs for a while."

Luke nodded. "That sounds good to me. I could use a little normalcy for a change."

Sarah shook her head. "I don't think normalcy can exist in our lives anymore. Even our routines need to be tempered with caution and wariness, I'm afraid."

Oliver nodded. "I think I agree with Sarah on this one." He gave a slight smile. "Actually, Sarah, I think it may be time to reach back out to Dr. LaMarre to see what he knows."

Her eyes widened. "What?" She looked around, realizing her response had been too loud. She lowered her voice. "I mean, what if he's the one on to me—*us?*" She looked from Oliver and Viktoria to Luke. "I think he may be the one who led me to losing my memory when we went to the prison for Mr. Mancini."

Luke put his hand on her arm. "Have you remembered something?"

She shook her head. "No. But he was the physician on duty that night. That's about all I remember."

Luke looked at Oliver. "Is it wise she contact him?"

Oliver looked from one of them to the other. "Wise?" He shrugged. "Necessary, though."

Sarah cocked her head. "Why?"

"If he is behind this, or part of this, we need to know what he knows."

Sarah gave a swallow. She nodded.

Luke rubbed her arm and addressed Oliver. "This could be very dangerous."

Oliver nodded. "When isn't it?"

TWENTY-SEVEN

Additional Resources for Mercure

Philippe could feel heat rising in his face. "What do you mean no one knows anything? You're the one who told me an immune was taken in Hohhot. So, where is he?"

He didn't have to see Pierre's face to know he was caught between a rock and a hard place. Philippe could hear it in his voice through the phone. "Sir, he was taken from the Hohhot Aerospace Center to a holding area," Pierre said. "He and another woman held there are now gone. The guards can remember nothing."

Philippe clenched his fist. He wanted to smash something, but he loved everything in his office too much. He kept clenching his fist tighter and tighter. "How . . . *how* is that even possible? You're telling me fourteen Illumi-Alliance guards were sent to secure two prisoners and they slipped through their fingers?" He unclenched his fist and forcefully tapped his index finger on his desk. "You find out what happened and report back. Your story better have a satisfactory ending within forty-eight hours from now."

"Yes, sir."

Philippe hung up. He leaned back and breathed out heavily through his nose. Something was definitely going on. If he and René didn't nip this quickly, who knows where it might lead? Somehow, immunes were getting the upper hand. He just could not let that happen.

His office door opened and René peeked in. "OK to come in without decapitation?"

Philippe gave a weak laugh and waved him in.

"What's wrong? I could hear you all the way in the hallway."

Philippe got up from his desk and went over to the yellow sofa to sit with René. He shook his head. "I'm afraid some immunes are already starting to cause trouble. I'm forcing Pierre to get to the bottom of it."

René put his hand to his chin. "Hmm. It seems we really need Dr. Mercure's solution sooner than later."

Philippe nodded. "Yes, but we really haven't given Simone . . . I mean, Dr. Mercure, much time. She's only just started."

René cocked his head and offered a raised eyebrow. "Does she deserve less motivation than Pierre?"

Philippe looked at him, realizing René knew of his slight crush on her. Not that she realized it; Simone was always so focused on her work. He gave a slight nod. "You're right. I'll go see her now and evaluate her progress."

He walked to his desk and pressed a button. "Sonja, get the car ready." He let the button go, not bothering to wait for Sonja's reply.

René stood, walked over, and patted Philippe on his shoulder. "Dr. Mercure is a beautiful woman, Philippe. But don't let that stand in the way."

Philippe shook his head. "No. No, of course not. It is true we haven't given her much time, but I'll certainly pressure her to work more quickly."

René nodded and left Philippe's office.

Philippe sat and ran his hand down his face. Things were certainly getting complicated quickly. Their best hope for getting the immunes under control lay in Simone's hands.

* * * * *

By the time Philippe made it to the front of the building, the car was waiting for him. The driver who opened the door to the limo stood just shy of two meters in height and had broad shoulders and oversized biceps. He looked more like a bodyguard, which he really was, as "driver" was a misnomer since the limo could drive itself. The large man sat in the front as a driver would.

"Take me to Dr. Mercure's lab, Henri."

"Very good, sir." He closed the door and went to the driver's side.

As the car pulled into traffic, Philippe pulled out his phone and punched up Simone's number.

"Dr. Mercure's lab. Valerie speaking."

"Hello, Valerie. This is Mr. Mauchard. May I speak to Dr. Mercure please?"

"Oh, yes sir. She's actually in her office right now. I'll put you through."

"Thank you." He waited a few seconds as the transfer was made.

"Philippe? To what do I owe the pleasure?" Philippe always found Simone's voice soothing.

"Hi, Simone. I just wanted you to know I'm on my way over to speak to you and wanted you to be available."

"Of course. Any problems?"

"Well, I can't say there isn't any, but I'd rather talk about them in person."

Simone's voice changed; her tone became more wary. "OK. Just come to my office when you arrive."

"Very well. I'll see you shortly."

Philippe put his phone back in his coat pocket. He looked out the car window thinking through how he would break the news to Simone. He certainly wanted her to work faster, but he didn't want her angry at him either. He would really like to get to know her better. He wasn't sure if the two could be done simultaneously or if the two things would turn out to be mutually exclusive.

The car pulled to the front of the building that housed Simone's lab and office. Henri came around and opened the door for him. "Shall I come with you, sir?"

Philippe shook his head. "No need this time, Henri. I shouldn't be too long."

The driver nodded. "Very good, sir. I'll have the car waiting."

Philippe nodded and headed inside. He walked past the labs and into the office area. Simone was in the corner that had both walls consisting entirely of tinted glass and looked into a garden-like area. She stood as soon as Philippe entered. She came around her desk and kissed him on both cheeks. She gestured to two chairs next to the window. "So, what's the concern?"

Philippe smiled. "Well, first of all, it is always a pleasure to come see you in person."

Simone smiled back. He hoped he wasn't coming across in a cheesy manner, but it really was the truth. Simone seemed to blush a little, so he took that as a good sign.

"Second, I wanted to follow up and see how things are going with your research."

Simone curled the side of her mouth. "Oh, you want to

know why we haven't made faster progress."

Philippe gave a weak smile. "Well, that is part of it. It's just . . . there have been some issues with a few immunes. It would be nice to be able to quell whatever it is they are planning."

Simone's eyes widened. "What's happened?"

Philippe waved his hands. "That's not really important. The important thing is to know if we have a compound which can work on them."

"Well, it's only been a few weeks. I'm still confident in our success, but it does take time to make it happen."

Philippe nodded. "Yes, I'm sure. But is there any way to put more resources on it?"

Simone shook her head. "Not without more funding. My department head thinks I'm spending too many resources on this already."

"OK, leave that to me. I'm sure a little donation may help in that regard."

Simone chuckled. "I'm sure it would." She paused. "What else is bothering you, Philippe?"

"There are some who believe Dr. LaMarre should have received this position. I gave it to you because of our friendship."

Simone sat back and crossed her arms. "Dr. LaMarre. *Pfft*. What can he contribute?"

"Well, he has instituted the reintegration initiative."

Simone sat up. "Yes—using the results of my study." She tapped her fingers on the arm of her chair. "He always was a brownnoser."

Philippe laughed. "I thought you two were colleagues."

"Oh, we are. I like him a lot, but I've worked with him ever since our internship. I know his techniques for getting what he wants."

He reached over and patted her arm. "Relax, Simone. I know I made the right choice. I can handle the comments that come in. Yet, if we don't have results, it will all be for naught and we will lose no matter how right we were."

Simone nodded. "You get me the resources and I'll definitely put them to work. Currently, the synthesis of the compounds is the slowest step. Get me at least two more chemists and another person to help out Valerie. I can definitely make their PhD thesis unique and worthwhile for them, and achieve our goal as well."

He nodded and stood. "OK, consider it done." He wanted to ask her to dinner, but was unsure if this was the right time. But would there ever be a right time? He held out his hand to help her to her feet.

She gave an inquisitive look. "Everything OK?"

He cleared his throat. "Uh, Simone. Would you care to go to dinner tonight and discuss what you need? That will help me pitch this more appropriately to your department head. What do you say?"

Simone gave a bright smile. "I would enjoy that."

Philippe smiled back. It had turned out to be a good play after all. "Wonderful. I'll have my driver pick you up around 19:00."

"I'll be ready."

Philippe kissed the back of her hand, turned, and left her office.

As he walked down the hall to exit the building, he found himself still wondering if this had been the right move. Philippe shook his head. There was nothing wrong with mixing business with pleasure. People did it all the time. His smile returned, and he began to whistle as he exited the building.

TWENTY-EIGHT

GOD'S FINGERPRINT

Luke sat back and looked around. If someone had told him a few months ago who would be in this room and what they had so far discovered would be true, he would not have believed them. He was so happy for Natalia. She now had both her parents back with her. Yet Luke had to wonder how she and Jeremy would be able to keep them hidden indefinitely.

Jeremy came by and patted him on his shoulder. "You look pensive over here."

Luke smiled. "Oh, just thinking about all that has changed for us in a short period of time."

Jeremy sat on the chair's arm next to him. "It's been a ride, hasn't it?"

Luke nodded. "Yes, but are we sure of our destination?"

Jeremy turned up an eyebrow. "What do you mean?"

Luke shrugged. "Well, there's a lot we still don't know, and it seems immunes are becoming a bigger target."

Jeremy did a quick raise of his eyebrows. "You have a point."

"Jeremy, you have to start manufacturing an antidote you can put in the Invocation wafer."

Jeremy's head jerked back slightly. "An antidote?" Now he cocked his head. "That's actually harder than it sounds."

Luke shook his head. "I'm not saying it's easy. But if Dr. Mercure is trying to manufacture something against the current immunes, we have to do something to counter that."

Jeremy put his hand to his chin. "Hmm. That's a good point. Let me think about that and see what I can come up with."

Luke nodded. He smiled when he saw Sarah approaching.

She pulled Luke up from his seat. "Come. Let's go talk to Natalia's parents."

He pointed to Jeremy. "I want you to follow through with that. OK?"

Jeremy saluted as he slipped into the seat Luke just vacated. "Aye, aye, Captain," stated Jeremy, and gave a playful wink to Luke.

Luke paused and looked back at Jeremy. "I meant it as a request, not a command."

Jeremy smiled and gave a thumbs-up gesture.

Luke followed Sarah to where Xiaofeng sat.

Sarah touched her arm. "Mrs. Mancini . . . "

She turned and smiled. "Xiaofeng, please. I thought you two looked familiar when you rescued me, but I was not in a good frame of mind then. I later remembered you from my last time in Paris."

Sarah smiled. "Xiaofeng, speaking of Paris, I was struck by the peaceful countenance you had. After all you've been through, how did you accomplish that?"

Xiaofeng's smile broadened. "I guess when you have hope, the circumstance doesn't define your outlook."

Luke squinted. "What do you mean? The hope of finding Natalia kept you going?"

Xiaofeng glanced over at Natalia and back to them. "Oh, I dreamt of this day for so long. Yet, I didn't know if it would happen." She shook her head. "No, this happy reunion was not my ultimate hope."

Luke cocked his head. "I . . . I don't understand."

She placed her hand on his arm. "Luke, I know Matteo told you about the God of the Bible . . . "

Luke nodded.

"But you can't just know *about* God, you have to accept all that he is."

Sarah glanced at Luke and turned to Xiaofeng. "We know he's different somehow from us."

Xiaofeng looked at Sarah and gave a warm smile. "Oh, so different. And yet so alike."

Luke shook his head slightly. "It sounds like . . . a riddle."

Xiaofeng patted his arm. "No, a riddle is solvable. God is not."

Luke felt as though he had entered another twilight zone. *None* of this made sense. He must have had a puzzled look on his face since Xiaofeng laughed as she looked at him. "Have you read Exodus yet?"

Both of them shook their heads. Sarah added, "But I think Oliver has."

She nodded. "So he's reading the Old Testament and you the New. Divide and conquer." She smiled. "Very scientific of you. Yet, don't forget they are all connected. Each book reveals some character of God."

Luke had always thought of God as a myth, or, at most, an indifferent being far removed from what occurred on Earth. Was there that much to really understand about such a being? "And what does Exodus reveal about God?" he asked Xiaofeng.

She leaned in. "The name of his basic nature. How he is able to do all he does and can do. *Hashilush Hakadosh,* or his being Trinity. The name is never used, but the concept is revealed."

Sarah shook her head. "But why would God not reveal his name?"

"God is so multidimensional, one name cannot describe him. He does state some of his names, and thus his character, but not this one. It has to be sought."

Sarah cocked her head. "But why?"

Xiaofeng smiled. "God reveals many things in secret because they are special and should be understood with awe."

Luke wondered if this was why this book had been locked away but not destroyed. "So, what does 'being Trinity' mean?"

Xiaofeng sat back. "In Exodus, God told a man by the name of Moses he would meet him and all the people with him at a specific mountain. God came in power: thunder, lightning, and thick smoke. He stated all should not touch the mountain because it was holy, and whoever touched it would be killed instantly."

Luke jerked his head up straighter. "That doesn't sound like he loved them very much. I thought God was supposed to be loving."

Xiaofeng nodded. "God is many things, but first and foremost, he is holy, meaning he is unique. No one and no being is like him. He stands for justice with a standard only one like him can meet. We first must stand before him in awe. These people were in so much awe they were terrified. They wanted Moses to talk to God and then relay the information to them. Today, we call him God the Father."

Luke scrunched his face. "So how is anyone supposed to relate to such a being?"

Xiaofeng's smile returned. "There are a few instances recorded where people met this part of the Trinity. Most usually fell to their face feeling unworthy to be in his presence."

Luke leaned forward, propping his chin in hand with his elbow on his knee. "So, how does the love come in?"

Xiaofeng's eyes sparkled. "Ah, that's what we come to next. After all of the commands from God, Moses and some other men met with God and had a meal with him."

Luke's eyes widened. "What? After all the smoke and fire, he now wants to play friendly?"

Xiaofeng chuckled. "He didn't change. He just revealed another side of himself. This is what we call the second person of the Trinity. He is the one who has always revealed himself to mankind in a physical form. He reveals the love of God. He's the one who appeared to Adam and Eve and countless others. He's the one you've been reading about in the New Testament."

Sarah interjected. "The one who talked to Nicodemus."

Xiaofeng nodded. "Yes, the very same. He came in human form to identify with us. By being born to a human mother, he has been designated as God the Son because God was his father in this supernatural birth. He did that to offer himself as the payment God required for mankind's rebellion and sin, which no one person would ever be worthy to pay on behalf of everyone." She smiled. "So, you see, he is a God of love as well."

Luke waved his hands. "Wait. Wait a minute. You're saying God—God the Father—required a payment no one could pay? So he—God the Son—came and made that payment on our behalf?"

Xiaofeng nodded again. "That's right. This is how he can have both justice and love be a part of him and have both exist in their purest form. How else could opposites exist in one being? How else could we be reunited with him—have a relationship with him? It was something only he could do."

Luke thought about that. Was that the key? His attention turned back to Xiaofeng. "Is that why this was the only religious book preserved from 2030?"

Xiaofeng's hand went to her chin. "I had not thought of that. But, yes, I would think so. All other religions have us responsible for deeds which will give us future rewards. That was easily incorporated into the oracles' teachings, just a different focus. Community rather than Heaven. This is the only religious book that states mankind cannot save themselves."

Luke knew this was something he would have to ponder more. He felt so overwhelmed. "And what about the third piece?"

Xioafeng leaned forward with an even brighter smile. "Ah, the cosmic gluon which makes all of this possible."

Luke scrunched his brow. "I'm not sure I'm following. You're comparing God to an atom?"

Xiaofeng laughed. "Sort of, I guess. As a molecular biochemist, it's how I think about it. After all, if God created everything, wouldn't his fingerprint be in it?" She looked at Luke. "What does a gluon do?"

Luke shrugged. "Well, in simplest terms, it keeps particles in protons and neutrons, called quarks, together. How the quarks are arranged, designated up or down, and grouped together with their partial charges, determine if they make a proton or neutron."

Xiaofeng nodded. "Exactly. This third part of the Trinity is called the Holy Spirit. Just as the quarks are never observed independently, but held together by gluons to form a proton or neutron, the Holy Spirit allows the opposites of justice and the love of God to both exist simultaneously—sort of like the work of gluons—and we observe God as all of his traits together. While each of these parts of God, if you will, are separate and distinct, they are never experienced as independent parts." She paused and smiled. "Now, next question. The association of quarks via gluons across protons and neutrons creates what in the nucleus?"

Luke thought for a moment. "The strong force, I think."

Xiaofeng grinned. "That's right. As in the nucleus, the close association of the three components of God creates a strong force which the Holy Spirit uses to draw us toward him. Like the strong force holds the protons and neutrons tightly to each other even though there is nothing physically attracting them to each other, once we come to him, we are also never separated from him."

Luke cocked his head. "That's a lot to take in."

Xiaofeng nodded. "Indeed. And to complete the metaphor, just as the electrons are everywhere and anywhere, yet are in a position when observed, God is everywhere and anywhere, yet is with us personally when we call on him."

Luke thought about that. It was hard to argue with the possibility since the elements of nature had these properties. Could they have come from God himself? It was almost too much to take in. "OK, so how does that tie into what we read in Exodus?"

"In Exodus, the Holy Spirit entered many of their leaders, drawing their spirits unto himself and helping them govern appropriately based upon God's standards. For us today, it helps our spirits connect with God and understand his will for us, creating in us a desire to emulate God's character and giving us the ability to extend God's love to others. Because he is everywhere and anywhere, he can do this for each of us simultaneously."

Sarah cocked her head. "And who gets this Holy Spirit?"

Xiaofeng placed her hand on Sarah's knee. "Anyone. Anyone who accepts these things about God through faith."

Now it was Sarah's turn to have a quizzical look. "What does that really mean?"

Xiaofeng smiled. "It means you believe in God, you believe God the Son has paid your sin penalty and is the hope for your future, and the Holy Spirit then indwells you to help you become more like his character."

Luke thought about this. "And what's the main purpose for that?"

Xiaofeng's countenance turned somber. "In spite of the oracles' teaching that Community is the ultimate goal, we are eternal beings and, after this life, will exist somewhere. Only through faith can we dwell in God's presence for eternity." She put her hand back on his arm. "Luke, it's the only way."

He looked into her eyes and saw her sincerity. He knew she really believed it. Could he?

"That goes against everything I've been taught my entire life. I think I need . . . to think about it."

Xiaofeng smiled and patted his arm. "Of course you do. I know God will help you make the right decision." She stood and pulled the two of them to their feet. "That's enough lecturing for now. Let's go join the others. We should enjoy our time together."

Luke didn't let go of Xiaofeng's hand. She turned back to him with eyebrows slightly raised.

"Xiaofeng, why did you tell me about *T-H-B* in Paris? How did you know I was looking for it?"

She smiled and patted his hand. "Anyone sneaking around that place had to be looking for something beyond what they already knew. I felt I should say that to you."

Luke looked into her eyes. "The Holy Spirit?"

She smiled and her eyes twinkled. "Yes, I think so." She tugged on his hand. "Come. Let's join the others."

Luke took Sarah's hand. She gave a weak smile. He could tell she, too, was having a hard time grasping all that Xiaofeng had said. They went over and sat on the sofa. Oliver was telling a tale about one of his dangerous exploits—and making it funny.

TWENTY-NINE

Making Plans

Luke sat on the sofa next to Sarah as Oliver told of their earlier escapade to Hong Kong. Luke soon realized he was becoming the brunt of Oliver's jokes. Oliver told of how he startled Luke when he knocked on the door to Dr. Li's lab, and how Luke had knocked a graduated cylinder off the counter and tried to keep it from falling to the floor. He gave an exaggerated version of bad juggling. Luke rolled his eyes. He remembered the incident well, and it wasn't as funny as Oliver painted it. But he also had to admit Oliver's story was funny the way he told it.

After a short time, Luke knew he had to turn the conversation to a more serious place. "Natalia, I am so happy for you. Getting to know your parents has been wonderful." He paused because he didn't want to hurt Natalia's feelings. "But, how are you going to keep them here undetected?"

Natalia opened her mouth to say something, but then closed it. She gave a slight shrug. "I haven't gotten that far. I've just been enjoying the moment."

Luke nodded. "That's very understandable, Natalia. Yet . . . " He glanced at everyone in the room. "We have to start making plans. It seems the Illumi-Alliance is already trying to target immunes." He pointed at Dr. Liwei. "Just look at what happened at the Aerospace Center in Hohhot."

Natalia nodded, but had a worried look on her face.

Xiaofeng took Natalia's hand. "Honey, I knew we would not be able to stay indefinitely. We'll have to go into hiding somewhere."

Natalia's eyes widened. "But where?"

Luke leaned forward. "Jeremy, how would you like to open another restaurant?"

Jeremy turned to Luke with a puzzled look. "I've barely gotten the one in Paris off the ground."

Luke nodded. "But it's going well, right?"

Jeremy gave a slight shrug. "Well, yeah, but I have investors to consider also."

Oliver became excited and shook his index finger. "I think I know where Luke's going here." He turned to Jeremy. "It can be a front for our own secret organization. Matteo and Xiaofeng can run it."

"What?" Natalia put her hand to her mouth as if realizing she said it more loudly than she intended. "I mean, they've just been taken out of danger, and we want to put them back into danger again?"

Matteo waved his hand. "Hold on, Natalia. Let's hear them out."

Her eyes widened. "You mean you want to do this?"

Matteo shrugged. "I want to be useful. This may be a way to do that."

Natalia sat back and shook her head but remained silent.

Luke gave a small nod to Matteo and turned back to Oliver. "It's more than a secret organization, Oliver. I agree Natalia's parents can run it, if you supply them with new identities, but we need a lab to create an antidote to the Invocation wafer. A new restaurant can be the front for that."

Jeremy's eyes widened. "But, Luke, hiding a lab? That's very difficult."

Luke shook his head. "Jeremy, think bigger."

Jeremy cocked his head and squinted.

Luke opened his arms. "You use a lab now, right?"

Jeremy nodded. "Yes, of course. I utilize a company to try out new flavorings and reactions."

Sarah grabbed Luke's arm. "I get it." She turned to Jeremy. "Why do you need to work with another company? Start your own lab."

Jeremy started to speak, but closed his mouth, twisting the corner of it as if in thought.

Natalia gave a slight chuckle. "Well, that would certainly be the news to get the investors interested. The labor would be cheaper in China, and we could see the lab and restaurant as a package deal. We would state that the lab would support all the restaurants."

Xiaofeng took Matteo's hand. "We could definitely run it for you."

Matteo nodded. "It would give us something to do to help and give you and Natalia a reason to visit." He looked over to Natalia and smiled. She gave a resigned sigh and shook her head. Then she returned his smile.

Oliver sat back. "You can sell that idea and still provide a front for making the antidote." He shrugged. "Who's going to question what goes on there since you will be testing many different chemical reactions and compounds?"

Jeremy looked at Natalia with raised eyebrows. "What do you say? Care to tackle another building?"

She smiled. "I can if you can tackle another nebula."

Jeremy cocked his head. "The investors will need something totally different and awe-inspiring to fork over more money."

Natalia gave a slight smirk. "Awe-inspiring is all I know to do."

Jeremy grinned. He then turned somber again. "In what city should we put this?"

"Shanghai." Everyone turned to Xiaofeng. "Matteo and I have always talked about living there. Plus, it's a city very accepting of new, modern, and bold."

Matteo nodded.

Natalia shrugged. "OK. I'll start drafting up plans tomorrow."

Sarah's jaw dropped slightly. "You can make plans that fast?"

Natalia chuckled. "My mind is always thinking of new designs. I think I have something, or the beginning of something, that just might go over with our major investors."

Luke smiled. "That's great." He pressed his lips together. "Just be sure the lab is the first to get built and up and going. I have a sinking feeling we may need it sooner rather than later."

Natalia nodded.

Sarah leaned back as though suddenly anxious. "But how long will all of this take? Do we have the time for this?"

Natalia put her fingers to her lips for a moment before answering. "Well, it will take time. Fortunately, one of our investors lives in Shanghai. I'll approach him tomorrow to see if he can speed anything up for us."

Sarah nodded, but didn't look convinced. Luke had to side with her. This was not the speed with which he wanted things to go. Dr. Mercure would be ahead of them—and in some ways this might put them even more behind.

"Luke."

Luke turned to Jeremy.

"I see you have that pensive look again," Jeremy said.

Luke shook his head. “Sorry. I just feel we’re losing time we don’t have.”

“We have to start somewhere.”

Luke nodded. “I know.”

Natalia reached over and patted Luke’s knee. “Don’t worry. The design I have in mind will allow us to get the lab up and running first. We can build the restaurant around it.”

Xiaofeng smiled. “And Matteo and I have old connections there I think we can exploit. We can have a workforce ready as soon as the place is ready.”

Luke gave a weak smile. That was at least comforting. He wasn’t sure why he had such a bad feeling about all of this, but he couldn’t seem to make it go away. “Well, at least we have a plan. That’s more than we had a little while ago.”

Oliver looked at each of them. “Why the long faces? This is exciting. I feel we’ve just reached the next chapter in our journey.”

THIRTY

Hôtel du Louvre

Luke looked at Sarah and smiled. She had fallen asleep while reading, and her head hung toward her chest. He gently repositioned Sarah with her head resting on his shoulder. She stirred slightly and then settled back into rhythmic breathing.

He didn't tell her, but he had almost not made this flight. Scott, wary about having to pull another marathon shift, finally relented after Luke promised to do some of the work while away. He was unsure when he would have the time to do that, so it likely meant he would have some late nights. With the five-hour delay, it could give him time to get work done before it reached Scott. Luke looked at his watch. He still had about three hours before the plane would land. He laid his head back, closed his eyes, and tried to get some sleep.

Luke woke with a start when the plane hit an air pocket. He looked over and saw Sarah wiping her hands with a washcloth.

She looked over and smiled, handing one to him. "I didn't want to wake you until the last minute. You seemed in such deep sleep. We should be landing shortly."

He smiled and took the washcloth, still warm, and wiped

his face. The warmth felt good as well as the sweat he was able to wipe off his face. The whole process served to wake him up.

Luke put his seat in its upright position and stretched. "Oh, being in business class really makes a big difference. My legs don't feel cramped as they usually do on such a trip." He handed the washcloth back to the flight attendant and looked back at Sarah. "How did you get business class anyway?"

She shrugged. "It's our department's policy. I'm sorry you had to foot the upgrade yourself."

Luke was too. But it was also worth it. Not only being with Sarah, but having the leg room made a huge difference. "Don't worry. I'll get Larry back somehow."

Sarah chuckled. "That may not be the wisest course of action."

"Any openings in your department?"

"Actually, yes."

Luke raised his eyebrows in a hopeful gesture.

"But I don't think you'd like it."

"Why?"

"I can't picture you going from an astrophysicist to a nurse's aide collecting urine and excrement for testing."

Luke scrunched his nose and shook his head. "On second thought, paying for the upgrade doesn't seem so bad."

Sarah laughed and patted his arm. "I thought that would be your response."

The plane landed, they gathered their luggage, and took a taxi to their hotel.

* * * * *

The Hôtel du Louvre, a beautiful five-story hotel, had large light tan stones for the first four floors. The fifth floor, covered in gray tiles around its decorative windows, also served as the roof of the hotel. Inside, the lobby looked both plush and ornate. Luke felt as though he had stepped back in time. He was quite happy with his room, as it was more up to date. He had a standard room while Sarah had a small suite, which had a sitting area separate from the bedroom. Both of their rooms had a view of a large fountain across the street. To his surprise, his room adjoined that of Sarah's.

After checking in, Luke knocked on the door that joined their rooms. He heard a muffled question. "Yes? Who's there?"

Luke smiled. "Sarah, it's me. Luke. Unlock your side."

He heard the door unlock and he opened it. Sarah had a surprised look on her face. "Luke?" She peaked around him. "Is that your room?"

He nodded. "Fortuitous, no?"

Sarah laughed and nodded. She invited Luke in to go over plans. Her room looked elegant with light lavender walls and dark gray chairs and sofa. The hotel supplied an assortment of tea cookies and Sarah had prepared tea before he arrived. He sat in one of the chairs, grabbed a cookie, and Sarah poured tea.

"Nice room, Sarah."

She sat on the sofa next to him while taking a bite of cookie. "Isn't it?"

"So, what's the plan?"

"I think the meeting will occur in the Matisse Room of the hotel."

Luke cocked his head. "Why do you think that?"

"When I was in Jason's office, I saw a brochure of the hotel on his desk. It had that particular conference room circled."

Luke nodded. "OK, but how are we going to monitor their meeting? Most of them already know our faces."

"That's why Oliver and Viktoria are coming."

Luke sat his cup down. "But doesn't Rosencrantz know

Oliver?"

Sarah shook her head. "According to Oliver, they've never met."

Luke raised his eyebrows. "I guess that makes sense. I'm sure there are many employees Rosencrantz wouldn't know even though they work for him. But that still doesn't answer the question of how are we going to know what goes on at their meeting."

"Viktoria will get herself assigned to the meeting, and Oliver will be a waiter for the event."

Luke gave a slight laugh. "And how did they manage that?"

"Apparently, once Viktoria got assigned, she was responsible for which personnel would be allowed into the meeting."

They heard a knock at the door. When Sarah answered, both Oliver and Viktoria entered.

Luke stood. "Well, speak of the devil."

Oliver smiled. "That sounded ominous."

After greetings, Sarah gestured for both of them to sit. "We were just discussing how you would monitor the meeting."

Oliver shrugged. "I have experience doing all sorts of jobs. Being a waiter is one of them."

Luke chuckled. "Well, I don't doubt that. But, wasn't there some type of vetting process?"

Viktoria shook her head. "Just me. Rosencrantz wants to ensure all waiters do not understand French. Therefore, getting waiters who don't live here is essential. So Oliver not being known by the hotel staff will not be an issue."

Oliver pulled out a small case and gave an earwig to both Luke and Sarah. "Sarah, I know you understand French well, so you'll hear what I hear. I should hear most of what they say as the hotel staff will bring up the food to Viktoria, and I'll serve it."

Luke gave an approving nod. "So, we just sit here and listen?"

Oliver nodded. "Pretty much. I'll try and establish a video feed as well, but I'm not yet sure if I can get that established undetected. I'll send you word if I get it up and running."

Viktoria leaned in. "Since likely all of The Six will be staying here, we need to keep a low profile and not be seen together. Once Oliver and I leave, we won't be in direct contact until this is all over. The meeting starts at 10 a.m. tomorrow. Most will arrive for a dinner tonight. This will be a get-together with little business, so we won't worry about tonight."

Luke looked at Sarah. They both nodded.

Luke smiled. "Looks like we get to order in."

THIRTY-ONE

THE STEPS

Luke whistled as he took a shower. Being able to spend a lot of alone time with Sarah made him happy. After drying off and donning jeans and a pullover, he looked at his watch: 17:45. He was to meet her at 18:00 for dinner in her sitting room. That gave him just enough time to finish getting ready.

He knocked on the door between their rooms and then entered. "Sarah?"

"In here," came the answer. She had a pleasant tone.

Sarah smiled at him as he entered the sitting room. Room service had already been delivered and she had dinner ready for him. There seemed to be soup, an entrée, and some type of dessert with fruit and chocolate.

"I hope you don't mind. I went ahead and ordered for both of us."

Luke shook his head as he sat down. "It smells delicious."

After a few minutes of eating in silence, Sarah brought out her phone. "I hope you don't mind, but I wanted to go over some of the things Xiaofeng told us a few weeks ago. Things have been so hectic, I haven't had a chance to talk with you about them. Have you had a chance to mull over her comments?"

Luke shook his head as he took a sip of tea. "Not really. She sure gave us a lot to think about, though."

Sarah nodded. "You may have to re-explain it all to me. She lost me at gluons."

Luke almost choked on a piece of meat he was in the process of swallowing at the same time he laughed at her comment.

"Are you OK?"

Luke nodded as he continued to cough. "Yeah. Laughing and swallowing don't really go together." He cleared his throat. "Anyway, I think her point was that what God created would yield something about him. Sort of like leaving a fingerprint behind."

Sarah nodded. "I sort of got that. I can understand God would need to be a unique being to show his superiority over us, and that he is worthy of worship."

Luke sipped some water. "I guess where I get hung up is about the sin thing."

Sarah cocked her head. "What do you mean?"

"Well, I can understand most of the Ten Commandments and see how many of our laws relate to that." He gave a slight shrug. "After all, killing people for no reason is a little counterproductive."

Sarah gave a short laugh. "Yeah, I would think so."

He smiled. "But it seems some things are just *nature*. I don't see what's wrong with sex of any kind. It's just fulfilling a natural desire. After all, if God made us, didn't he instill the instinct?"

Sarah set her fork down. "I get where you're going, but I think it has more to do with control and respect."

Luke turned his head. "What do you mean?"

"I just mean, animals act on instinct. Humans have the capacity to act on reason. The Scriptures I've read seem to place a value on the giving of oneself, one's body, as a sacred gift. In that sense, it should be given once and to only one person."

Luke sat back in thought. "That certainly elevates it to another level." He shook his head. "But that seems like a tall order."

"I think that was the other point Xiaofeng made. We can't do it without him. It seems that is why the Holy Spirit was given—so he could work with us and through us."

Luke nodded. "That's right. She talked about God being three in one."

Sarah laughed. "Yeah, that's when she started talking about gluons."

Luke thought about what she had said. It made some sense. As he sat there contemplating, he heard Sarah trying to talk to him.

" . . . Earth to Luke. Come in, please."

"What?" Luke shook his head and smiled. "Oh, sorry. I was just starting to put some of what she said together."

Sarah's eyes widened. "Please, do tell."

Luke sat back and thought how to cohesively put his thoughts in a logical order since they were pretty chaotic in his mind at the moment. "So, just as the Holy Spirit ties the three parts of God all into a cohesive entity, yet they function separately, it seems his purpose is to also bind us to him in a similar manner. But we remain separate as well."

"She talked about the strong force."

Luke nodded. "Yeah, even though protons would naturally repel each other because they have the same charge, once they get close enough, the strong nuclear force becomes stronger than their repulsion."

Sarah's eyes lit up. "Oh, I think I understand. While we don't naturally gravitate to God, once we come to him, his love—or strong force—overcomes our repulsion and we remain with him. That's the purpose of the Holy Spirit, to bind us to him."

Luke nodded. "Yeah, I think that sums it up pretty well. So, the three . . . " Luke collapsed backward on his seat. He tapped his head with his hand. "That's it." He looked at Sarah. "That's it."

"*What* is it? You've discovered something. What? Tell me."

Luke was now extremely excited. "That piece of paper. Remember that piece of paper I brought back from the prison?"

"The one that had the four letters, *F-S-H-S*?"

Luke nodded. "Think back to what Xiaofeng said. She said God was made of three parts."

Sarah nodded, but looked quite confused.

"What were they?" Luke asked.

"She called them God the Father, God the Son, and God the Holy Spirit."

Luke nodded excitedly. "Now put them together without the word 'God' in front of them."

Sarah paused and looked deep in thought. Her eyes lit up. "*F-S-H-S*. Father, Son, and Holy Spirit."

"That's it."

"So, the first step was to find the Bible and the second step was to understand who God is."

Luke nodded. "Those seem to be the steps."

Sarah leaned forward. "This is kind of exciting. So, what do we do now?"

"Well, Xiaofeng mentioned to me it isn't enough to just know *about* God. One needs to experience him."

"And we do that by receiving the Holy Spirit into our lives?"

"That would seem to be the logical step."

"How do we do that?"

Luke gestured toward Sarah's phone. "You were reading in John about Nicodemus and the Messiah talking. What did he say?"

Sarah reached for her phone. Luke went and sat next to her. She opened the Scripture app Oliver had sent her and found the passage. "It states, 'God loved the world and sent his son to save the world. All we have to do is believe in him and what he did.'" She looked over at Luke. "Is that what you want to do?"

Luke leaned forward, closer to Sarah. "I think so. That seems to be the next logical step."

"Do you know how to do that?"

Luke gave a slight shrug. "I think we just ask."

Sarah took his hand. "OK. Let's do it."

Luke nodded. He tightened his grip on her hand and bowed his head. "Dear God, this is all new to me, so I ask you to be patient with my lack of understanding. I do know you came to Earth out of your love for us to pay the penalty your justice demanded. I don't fully understand all of that, but I do now believe in you and in what you have done for me—and everyone. I trust in you alone for my future as I realize nothing I do can ever live up to your standards."

Sarah squeezed his hand. "Yes, and I ask your forgiveness of my sins as well. I, too, don't fully understand all that entails, but I trust you and ask you to send your Holy Spirit to guide us and bind us to yourself. Give us wisdom to better understand your Scriptures. I don't know how you do this, but I trust you to do it, and thank you in advance."

"Absolutely." Luke opened his eyes and looked into Sarah's. They looked more vivid than he remembered. "Do you feel anything—feel anything different?"

Sarah was still for a moment. "Yes and no. I feel excited, like I just made a great discovery, but I still feel like me."

Luke nodded. "Same here. I guess that's what Xiaofeng

meant by accepting by faith. It isn't a visible or automatic change."

"I think as we understand more, we will change our perspective more."

Luke gave her a hug and a kiss. "I really feel like celebrating."

"Well, it's a good thing I ordered dessert."

THIRTY-TWO

NEW PERSPECTIVE

Luke's phone sounded. Sarah's picture appeared.

"Hi, Sarah. Good morning."

"Good morning, Luke." She sounded happy. "I hope I didn't wake you."

"No. I've been up for a while. I couldn't sleep long this morning."

She gave a short laugh. "Same here. Listen, I've ordered breakfast, if you want to come over."

"Oh, that sounds great." He opened the door and walked into her room while still on the phone.

She sat in a chair with the vantage point of seeing him enter. She laughed and hung up her phone. "I guess 'over' was the wrong word."

Luke laughed. "Right word, just a short distance."

She motioned to the coffee table in front of her. "Well, breakfast is served."

Luke sat in front of the food. "I could get used to being spoiled like this."

Sarah took the cover off his plate and handed it to him.

"Well, don't get too used to it. I'm not sure my department head is going to understand why I ordered room service so many times."

Luke raised his eyebrows. "Oh, I get it. You're saying, 'Pony up.'"

Sarah smiled. "Maybe. We'll see." She sat up and took a bite of her eggs. "Anyway, how was your morning?"

Luke nodded, swallowing a bite of food. "Very good. Once I woke up, I had this urge to pray and read."

Sarah held her fork midair and looked at him. "Well, that's a first. I never heard you say that before."

Luke smiled. "That's because it's never happened before." He took a sip of tea. "I started reading John and couldn't stop."

Sarah's eyebrows raised. "You mean you read the whole book?"

Luke nodded. "Yeah. Like I said, this has never happened before. And the funny thing is, it all made so much more sense. I was really connecting to the story, and in many places I felt like God was really speaking to me personally." He waved his knife and fork slightly. "Never had that happen before." He smiled. "I really enjoyed it, though." He pointed his knife toward her. "You?"

"Well, I've never had the problem of not reading, but yeah, everything was clearer this morning." She nodded. "And it did seem to resonate with me a lot more than before."

"I think our perspectives are starting to change already."

She smiled. "The Holy Spirit."

He nodded. "I think so. The strong force has done its work."

Sarah suddenly looked at her watch. "Oh, what time is it?" She reached for the small case with the earwigs. "Here, put this in. I bet Oliver and Viktoria are already on."

Sure enough, as soon as they inserted the devices and turned them on, Luke heard Oliver's voice.

"Luke. Sarah. Are you *there*?"

"Hi, Oliver. This is Luke."

"And this is Sarah."

"Well, good morning, sleepyheads. I was beginning to think Viktoria and I were on our own this morning."

Luke looked at his watch: 9:15. "Oh, don't get melodramatic. We've both been up for some time. The meeting doesn't start until ten."

"Yes, but once it starts, I probably won't be able to communicate with you. Sarah, I sent you a secure app. Download it and you should be able to view what will be going on. I've put a small camera within the tea service on the back table. If they project anything, you should be able to see it."

Sarah reached for her tablet. "OK, Oliver. I'm setting it up now."

Viktoria's voice came online. "Oliver, here comes the food—and Rosencrantz."

"Roger that."

"Ms. Komcova, I'm glad to see you're already in position. Here is the roster of who should be coming. I want you to verify each and every person, even if you think you recognize them."

"Yes, sir."

"And you can vouch for this waiter?"

"He has the experience and doesn't speak or understand French—just the basic French words most people know."

"Good. Carry on. I'll return shortly."

Luke heard a knock and then someone spoke English with a heavy French accent. The hotel waiter accompanying Rosencrantz with the food was apparently talking to Oliver about all that was being provided for service.

Sarah got the app downloaded and pulled up the camera online. "Oliver, I have the picture streaming now. I can see the table and the screen."

Luke laughed. "Yeah, and you look good in all white."

"Very funny. Not to be rude, but let's cut the chatter down to only what is critical."

Victoria interjected. "Guests arriving."

Luke sat next to Sarah; she positioned her tablet so both of them could see.

Luke pointed as three people entered the room. "There's the two Mauchard brothers and Dr. Mercure."

"You know, I'm beginning to wonder if there isn't something between Philippe and Simone."

Luke turned to Sarah with raised eyebrows.

Sarah shrugged. "They just always seem to be together." She pointed. "Did you see that? Philippe put his hand to her back to guide her toward the table for a seat."

"Interesting." It seemed there was more than just business going on between these two.

More people came in and milled about. As they passed across the path of the camera, Sarah and Luke tried to identify them.

Luke pointed again. "I see our boss, Rosencrantz, is back. And there's Dr. Li from Hong Kong."

"And there's Meriwether from Australia and Cortêz from Brazil."

As they kept watching, another batch of people entered.

Luke leaned forward. "Whoa. I only expected one more. I see the Supreme Oracle entered, but who are the other four people?"

Sarah shook her head. "I don't know, but they look military."

"And serious. Look at the woman. She looks like she could kill you just by looking at you."

Sarah slapped his arm. "Stop kidding."

Luke shrugged. “Who’s kidding? Look at her. Have you ever seen anyone more serious-looking?”

Sarah rolled her eyes, but smiled.

Luke tried to hear what some of them were saying, but it proved too difficult for him to understand. His French being not that good, and with everyone speaking at the same time, it all sounded like gibberish.

He looked over toward Sarah. “Can you make out any of the conversations?”

She shook her head. “No. With everyone speaking, it’s hard to pick anything out. Plus, it seems like everything is just pleasantries at the moment.”

After a few minutes, all began taking their seats. They could see Oliver begin serving brunch.

THIRTY-THREE

STUNNING NEWS

Rosencrantz stood. All attention turned to him.

"Thank you all for coming. This is a very important meeting, and we have a lot to discuss. Let's first talk about the Mars mission. Lieutenant Beyer, I'll turn the floor over to you for an update."

Sarah tried to interpret as fast as she could so Luke could keep up with the conversation. He could make out only a few words, but couldn't process them fast enough to keep up on his own.

Rosencrantz sat and the serious-faced woman stood. "Thank you, Mr. Rosencrantz. I have to say, all is on schedule." She smiled. Well, that's what her facial expression was supposed to be. In Luke's opinion, her face went from serious to less serious. If he didn't know it was supposed to be a smile, he would have missed it entirely.

"Explain the strategy." This statement came from Dr. Mercure.

Lt. Beyer's gaze turned to Rosencrantz. He nodded and handed her a remote. An image came on screen. Both Luke and Sarah leaned in toward the tablet and squinted to get a better look at what she had displayed.

As if reading their minds, Beyer continued. "This is a diagram of the new space station, which has been under construction for the last two decades. As you can see, the plan was to have six completed spaceships that can carry a large contingent to Mars."

Sarah and Luke looked at each other, mouths agape. They looked back at the screen without saying anything.

Beyer displayed another picture. "And this is an image of the space station from one of our satellites."

There was an audible gasp from around the room. Both Luke and Sarah did the same.

"As you can see, we are approximately three-fourths complete. Five of the six are already able to travel through space. Yet there are many interworking components that still need to be completed. I expect the sixth ship will be travel-worthy within the next month or so."

Luke looked at Sarah. "How did they accomplish this—and so secretively?"

Sarah sat back. "Well, think about it. Think about how much money you donate every month. Multiply that by twelve and then by about a billion—and that's ballparking on the low side. That's a lot of money pouring in to pay for something like this. Then, if you're sending up materials and people from six different continents, no one knows what is really going on."

"Except those who work there."

Sarah gave a smirk.

"What? What am I missing?" Luke asked.

"Ever heard of altering one's memory?"

Luke's eyes widened. He suddenly felt like an idiot. "Of course. No wonder it's never leaked out."

Sarah nodded. "Exactly. Best scam on earth."

They heard clapping from around the table. Someone asked, "So, when is the launch day?" Luke couldn't tell who asked the question.

René turned and stated, "It hasn't changed. July 14 of next year."

Philippe chimed in. "Bastille Day, 2090."

"But that's only nine months away." That sounded like a nervous reply from Simone.

Rosencrantz raised his eyebrows. "Is there something wrong with that date, Ms. Mercure?"

Simone shook her head. "No. No. It's just . . . we still have a lot of work to do."

"Indeed." Rosencrantz swept his hand across the table. "That's why this meeting is so important. We all need to realize the goal is now at our doorstep. We can't falter now. We're too close." He turned back to the speaker. "Thank you, Lieutenant Beyer."

Beyer sat down. Rosencrantz remained standing. "Now, we need to discuss the lottery." He gestured to René Mauchard.

René stood, walked to the front of the room, and paced. He did this for several seconds, as if in thought. He looked up and smiled. "Ladies and gentlemen, as you know, my father had a great vision for mankind reaching Mars and the stars beyond. We are about to embark on the first part of his vision. Soon, we will have a large colony on Mars, and within the next century, who knows where we will be in our galaxy or universe?"

Everyone around the table clapped. René's smiled broadened.

"Now, what some of you know, some of you believe, and . . ." He paused. " . . . some of you doubt, is my father's quest to prolong mankind's future undeterred."

Luke looked at Sarah. "Any idea what he's talking about?"

Sarah shook her head.

"My great-grandfather was a very religious man. He believed the Bible to be true and literal."

There were a few snickers in the audience.

René nodded. "I see we have some doubters here. My father doubted as well. Yet he took precautionary measures, instituted the Invocation wafer so he could control what people would remember, took all religion out of society, removed those immune to the effects of the wafer, and established the oracles and their teaching of Community."

"The prisons." Luke didn't realize he had said it out loud—until Sarah looked at him and nodded.

"Many of you have probably never read the Bible." René smiled. "And that is as it should be. Yet it speaks of one some call 'Messiah' and others 'God,' one who will take those who believe in him out of this world, and then all sorts of apocalyptic events will occur here on this earth."

More laughter was heard.

René again nodded. "Yes, it sounds preposterous. But it is important to understand the consequences. My father felt controlling memories and sending those immune to Mars would prevent such a prophecy from occurring, even if it happened to be true. If not true, then we have a large group of people to serve those on Mars."

A few clapped and laughed.

René smiled. "I think his plan was ingenious. Those who remain won't remember to pray for such an event—and those who can won't be on earth for it to occur."

More enthusiastic clapping erupted.

René held up his hands. "Now for some sobering news. Since the almost sixty years from my father's actions, some additional immunes have arisen. Our biostatistician's analysis indicates there may be up to one hundred thousand immunes who have been born since all were initially removed."

Gasps could be heard around the room.

"Now we have a couple of options. Each ship can carry approximately two thousand people in hyperstasis and about another five hundred fully awake. That gives us fifteen thousand individuals who can take this journey. That means we can't take all of the immunes, so we either have to find a compound to make them susceptible to memory reprogramming or we have to increase our rate of Mercy Farewells."

Cortês raised her hand halfway. "Excuse me, Mr. Mauchard. But how do you plan to support fifteen thousand individuals on Mars?"

René gestured back to Beyer. She stood and cleared her throat. "In spite of popular belief, this will not be our first visit to Mars."

This seemed to have caught everyone off guard as all looked around to see if anyone else was aware of this. Apparently, they weren't. Luke looked at Sarah. She, like him, was wide-eyed.

Beyer held up her hands. "I know this is surprising, but we had to be sure this current mission was a success. Two other voyages have landed on Mars and established a facility that can hold and sustain about fifty thousand individuals. Hydroponics are already established and functioning well. A large underground water supply, although frozen, has been found. Sustainability seems to be extremely possible. Once the colony is established, terraforming will be the next main goal."

René returned to standing in front of the room. "Thank you, lieutenant." Beyer sat back down.

"I know some of you are disappointed you were not in this loop," René said. "But this was an important step to achieve before you were brought in. As you can see, we are on the verge of a revolutionary breakthrough in the evolution of mankind, and you are all a part of it and important to its success." René then spent much time discussing details of what already existed on Mars, what this mission would add, what was the projected timing of future missions, and how Mars would one day become almost a second Earth. Afterward, he fielded some general questions, but seemed to not want to answer any specific ones. All of his comments were general in nature. Luke assumed he was leaving all his options open. As some kept asking the same question in different ways, he ended the discussion by giving a broad smile and replying, "Now, enjoy the rest of your brunch. Further assignments will be given for us to reach our goal in the time frame established."

More rounds of applause followed. Conversation on top of conversation began. Luke knew Sarah would be unable to follow any further discussion.

THIRTY-FOUR

On God's Side

Luke heard a knock on Sarah's door. They both looked up from their reading and then at each other.

Luke stood. "I'll see who it is."

He went to the door and looked through the peephole. It was Oliver and Viktoria. He opened the door, and both entered quickly.

Sarah spoke first. "Oliver, Viktoria, anything wrong? I thought we were not supposed to meet until all of this was over."

Oliver shrugged. "Technically, it is over." He looked at Viktoria. "We wanted to get your take on what went down at the meeting."

Viktoria nodded. "I filled Oliver in as best as I could based on what I heard. But I wasn't in the room. I was outside the door most of the time."

Sarah gestured for them to sit. "Our take is probably the same as yours. It was quite the bombshell. So, all of this was to satisfy someone trying to prevent some type of biblical prophecy?"

Luke shrugged. "Sounds like a mixture of paranoia and desiring control." He looked at each of them. "We should get Matteo's thoughts on all of this."

Oliver nodded. "Good idea."

Sarah raised her eyebrows. "Anything else to convey?"

Oliver shook his head. "No, except this: Philippe seemed just as surprised at the news of previous Mars missions as everyone else."

Luke raised his eyebrows. "Really? Any way to exploit that?"

Oliver shook his head. "Not that I know of. But it's clear he and René are not equals in all of this."

Sarah poured tea for everyone. "What are our next steps?"

Oliver took a sip and sat back. "Jeremy's antidote is more critical than ever."

Viktoria nodded. "Where is he with getting the lab up and running?"

Luke shook his head. "I'm not sure. But speaking of Jeremy, I'm surprised we haven't heard anything from him. I guess he's still in Shanghai."

Oliver nodded. "He should be. He was going to do his best to get everything up and running as fast as possible. We should head there before going home. Can you two cut your time here short?"

Sarah cocked her head. "Well, I can't leave until after tomorrow. My official reason for coming here was to meet with Anton and go over eligibility requirements for folks to go on the Mars mission."

Oliver gave a slight nod. "And to see what he may know about all of this."

Sarah's eyes widened a bit. "Yes, that too. I'm just not sure how to go about that. I just hope he gives something away unintentionally. I can't really ask any direct questions."

"I know." Oliver took another sip of tea. "But you can ask some probing questions, like: Has he met with Dr. Mercure? Or, what is his involvement at the prison?"

Sarah gave a hard sigh. "Those seem rather direct than indirect to me." She cocked her head. "I'll do what I can."

Oliver nodded. "In the meantime, Viktoria and I will head to Shanghai and meet you there."

"Oliver." Everyone's attention turned to Luke. "I want you and Viktoria to know the decision Sarah and I made last night."

Oliver raised his eyebrows and gave a sly smile. "You propose or something?"

Luke opened his mouth to say something—but Oliver's comments had thrown him totally off. "Uh, no, that's not the direction I was going."

Viktoria shook her head. "Too bad."

Luke felt heat rising to his cheeks. He glanced at Sarah. She displayed a shy smile. He felt trapped. "Well, we haven't had that discussion yet." Luke paused. "Uh, I was wondering. Have you made a decision about what you've read in the Bible?"

"Oh, the Bible." Oliver looked at Viktoria. "No, we're still sort of digesting." He looked back at Luke and then at Sarah. "I guess you two have found something?"

Sarah nodded. "We took the next step and prayed to God. We accepted what his Word says about him coming to earth and paying the ransom needed for our sin."

Oliver's eyes widened. "Really? And?"

Luke turned up his brow. "And *what*?"

Oliver opened his arms slightly. "I mean, what happened?"

Luke shook his head. "Nothing earth-shattering, if that is what you mean. It was kind of exhilarating, though, and this morning I had a desire to pray and read more Scripture. I connected to it more than I ever had before."

Sarah nodded. "I feel I have a different perspective on life.

Although the doubt of what will happen is still there, I have a sense of surety everything will be OK in the end—no matter what happens."

Viktoria leaned in. "Really? That's what you achieved?" She glanced at Oliver. "That's what I have always wanted to have. My life has been filled with so much uncertainty for so long, I really want to have that kind of assurance."

Sarah put her hand on Viktoria's knee. "You can, Viktoria. If it worked for me, there's no reason it won't work for you."

Viktoria shook her head slightly. "What do I do?"

"Just do what Luke and I did, and what the Messiah told Nicodemus to do. Believe in what he came to do for the world. He paid the price God required for mankind's disobedience. The rest is to just trust your future to him. We cannot do anything on our own."

Viktoria swallowed hard. "It seems too simple. Is that really all you did?"

Luke and Sarah took the next half hour or so to go over all that Matteo and Xiaofeng had told them about proteins, gluons, the strong force, and how that related back to God. It seemed to take a lot more explanation to help Oliver and Natalia understand as the two of them were not scientists, and likely not initially familiar with either the concepts or the terminology. Luke could see the understanding start to sink in.

Viktoria looked at Oliver. "What do you think?"

Oliver laughed. "I can't believe I'm saying this, but all that makes sense." He gave a half-shrug. "I think we should do it. What I've been reading has been interesting. If doing this helps me to really understand it deeper, I'm all for it."

Viktoria smiled. She took Oliver's hand and they each bowed their heads.

Luke felt their prayers were nearly verbatim to what he and Sarah had prayed the day before. In just a couple of minutes, they were done. They all looked at each other. There was silence for a minute or two.

Luke laughed slightly. "Well?"

Oliver smiled. "It's like you said. I don't feel different, yet there is a sense of exhilaration."

Viktoria nodded. "I just have a sense I have done the right thing. There is a sense of peace that now fills me. It wasn't there before."

Sarah came over and gave Viktoria a hug. "I'm so happy for you—for all of us."

Luke nodded. "Xiaofeng and Matteo will be happy to hear their explanations have made a difference."

Oliver smiled. "I'll be sure and tell them." He laughed and shook his head.

Luke just stared at him. "What's so funny?"

"Not really funny. Just ironic."

Luke cocked his head. He had no idea what Oliver was referring to.

"You're the one who was so negative in the beginning while we were all gung ho. Yet here you are the first one to take this step of accepting what the Bible said to do."

Luke smiled. Yes, it did seem fairly ironic. Looking back, he could see the progression which led him to this step. He could no longer believe everything that had occurred was purely coincidence. "I guess God knew what was needed to turn me around."

Oliver nodded. "I guess God knew you were a harder case—and so worked on you first."

Luke gave Oliver a smirk, but then thought about this possibility. Maybe it was truer than he cared to admit.

Oliver laughed. "It will be interesting to see how things go now that we have gotten on God's side."

THIRTY-FIVE

BAD MEMORIES

Luke pressed the elevator button to head to the lobby. He had been trying to get his taxi app to work in Paris. He wasn't finding success.

Sarah grabbed his arm. He looked up at her. She had a wild expression. "What's wrong, Sarah?"

"Simone!" she whispered. "She's heading toward the elevator."

Luke glanced up and saw Simone approaching. She looked absorbed in something she was reading and didn't pay attention to anything else. She came up beside them, glanced at the elevator buttons, and went back to reading.

Sarah looked at Luke with raised eyebrows. She turned toward Simone and displayed an adorable smile. "Simone. Hey, fancy meeting you here!"

Simone gave a slightly startled look before recognition settled in. "Sarah. What . . . what are you doing here? I mean, it's just a surprise. How are you?"

"I'm fine. I'm on my way to see Anton—about the Mars mission."

Simone squinted as if she wasn't completely understanding. Suddenly, the light dawned. "Oh, about the physical requirements of those traveling. Yes, of course."

The elevator doors opened and they entered. Luke pressed the button for the lobby. "Simone, you must have had a meeting here, I guess."

Simone smiled, but Luke could tell it was forced. "Yes, I could have commuted, but it was just easier to stay here for the meeting."

Sarah nodded. "I totally get it. I would have done the same thing."

"But what about you? I'm surprised your company would pay for such a hotel."

This time Sarah gave the forced smile. "Well, we don't get to Paris often, so we upgraded. It costs us a little personally, but it's worth it to ensure a good stay here. Paris is so beautiful. We really wanted to enjoy it."

Simone nodded. "Of course—and you should."

They exited the elevator. Sarah gave Simone a hug. Simone did the kiss-the-air technique as she hugged both sides. Simone waved and exited the hotel. Luke and Sarah walked to the concierge desk.

"Taxi, please."

The man behind the desk looked up and smiled. "Certainly, sir. There's one waiting outside. For the future, I can recommend an app you can install."

Luke held up his phone. "I already have one, but it doesn't seem to work here."

The man cocked his head. "Really?" He held out his palm. "May I?"

He took Luke's phone and brought up the app. "Since the upgrade, the city feature is not too obvious. Go to menu, press 'other,' then 'travel,' then 'city.' That puts it in the city mode going forward. Just do it again for each city."

Luke took his phone back. "Thanks. I never would have figured that out."

The man smiled and nodded. "I know. Many have complained about it. Hopefully, they'll make it more intuitive during the next upgrade."

Luke thanked the man and he and Sarah made their way to the waiting taxi. Sarah gave the destination to the taxi in French.

On the way to the Neuroscience Center, Sarah put her head on Luke's shoulder. "Thanks for being here with me. I don't think I would be up to all of this—and meeting Simone—without your support."

Luke gave her a slight squeeze. "Anything for you. You know that."

* * * * *

Everything looked the same as they entered the center. Luke stayed downstairs in the waiting area as Sarah went upstairs to meet with Anton in his office. After about half an hour, Luke went to find the restroom. After a few minutes of looking, he remembered seeing one upstairs, so he took the elevator to the second floor.

As the elevator doors opened, he stepped out and looked over the railing to the floor below. It brought back memories of their first visit, when Sarah discovered the lobby area was in the shape of a brain, and then realized the squiggly lines were actually defining the folds in the brain. He tried to remember what they were called. *Gyri. That's it.* He smiled while remembering Sarah's giggle at this discovery.

It was then that he heard someone approaching. It was Sarah—coming down the hall quickly. "All finished?"

She had a panicked look on her face.

"Sarah, what's wrong?"

She grabbed his arm and kept her voice low. "It was him. Luke, it was him."

Luke forced her to look at him to calm her down. "Sarah, look at me. Try and calm down. Explain what you mean."

Sarah closed her eyes and took several deep breaths. "Anton was the one who injected me with the compound that took away my memory."

Luke's eyes widened. "Really? What made you remember?"

She shook her head slightly. "We were talking about the inoculations needed for those going on the mission. I don't remember exactly what he said, but all of a sudden the vision of him injecting me and making a similar comment came to me. I excused myself to go to the restroom." She glanced down the hallway toward Anton's office and then back to Luke. "I can't go back." She shook her head. "I just can't."

"Does he know you know?"

"I . . . I don't think so."

"OK. Go to the restroom and collect yourself. Go downstairs and appear to be on the phone. I'll go to his office and tell him you got a call and we have to leave. I'll tell him you will follow up with other details via teleconference."

As Luke held her, he could feel Sarah shaking. Whatever the memory, it seemed to have really unnerved her. He kissed her forehead and she went into the restroom. Luke headed into LaMarre's office.

He gave a knock on the doorframe since the door was already open.

Anton looked up. "Luke. Hi. I didn't realize you were here. Are you looking for Sarah? She just stepped out for a restroom break."

Luke shook his head. "No. Actually, I just ran into her.

Apparently, she received an important phone call and has to address an issue back at work. She's downstairs now waiting for me. I just wanted to let you know she regrets leaving so suddenly, but she will follow up with you via teleconference."

Anton cocked his head. "Oh, I'm sorry to hear that." He gave a slight shrug. "Well, we were able to get the major details worked out, so teleconference will probably work."

Luke nodded and turned to leave.

"Tell her I hope her issue gets resolved satisfactorily."

"Thanks. I'll be sure and tell her."

Luke took the elevator back downstairs. He was a bit surprised at Anton's seeming indifference. Anton's words were correct, but his body language didn't match. No wonder Sarah freaked out.

Once Luke got Sarah back to her hotel room, she was still badly shaken. He had her lie down and checked on her periodically. While she seemed to rest, she obviously had a very fitful sleep. She was lying in a different position every time he checked on her.

An unusual thought came to Luke. He felt as though he should pray. He did. He prayed for Sarah's recovery, wisdom for him to know what to do, and for all of them on the best way to move forward. Luke felt better afterward. He felt as if he had accomplished something even though it wasn't anything tangible.

Sarah slept until dinnertime. He decided they would eat downstairs as they had been cooped up in their rooms for so long. A beautiful restaurant lay on one side of the lobby; it was enclosed entirely by glass, allowing diners to see the outdoors. The sun had set and the fountain across the way displayed multiple colors in the water as it sprayed up and flowed over its tiered edges. Luke found it mesmerizing, beautiful. Apparently Sarah did too, as both of them sat in silence for some time. Sarah would periodically break off a piece of bread and eat it. Luke did the same as he waited for their entrées to arrive.

Although he was reluctant to bring up the topic, he thought Sarah should talk through it. "Sarah, care to talk about what happened when you went with Oliver and Viktoria to the prison and they rescued Matteo?"

She looked at him with a weak smile. "No, but I probably should."

He raised his eyebrows. "So, what happened?"

She cocked her head as if bringing up memories. "I was surprised to learn Anton spent time at the prison. But then I thought that would be good since I knew him and could quickly engage him in conversation. We talked a while about his job there and how it tied into the Neuroscience Center."

She paused as the waiter brought their entrées and filled their wine glasses with a chardonnay.

Sarah continued. "According to Anton, the prison had reached out to him as some of their clients . . . " She gave a half laugh. " . . . He never called them prisoners. Always 'clients.' Anyway, that they needed some psychiatric evaluations. So he would spend time there monitoring their behavior to see what kind of treatment they needed."

"Was that true?"

Sarah's eyebrows raised. "Is the sky red?"

Luke laughed. "I get you."

"Anyway, the discussion kept him distracted from the monitors. I saw Oliver and Viktoria get Matteo out of his prison cell. Then I tried to find a way to leave gracefully but quickly. But I think I slipped up."

"Why? What happened?"

"He asked why I really came. I mentioned I had heard he spent time there and was just curious about his work."

"I take it he didn't buy it."

She shook her head. "No. He kept pressuring me how I knew about him there and how I knew about the prison. I don't really remember what excuse I gave, but I do remember him hitting a button which locked the door so I couldn't escape. He bound me to a chair and injected me with something. That was the last thing I remembered before I woke up in my apartment back in Houston."

"What do you think he really suspects?"

She shook her head. "I don't really know. I think he just thought I was being nosey. Since I was alone—or at least he thought so—and they haven't made any more moves, I think we are safe. But my quick exit today may raise his suspicions more."

Luke nodded. "So the faster Jeremy finds an antidote, the better."

THIRTY-SIX

SHANGHAI

The plane's wheels hit the runway—hard. Luke saw Sarah jerk awake, discombobulated.

Luke laughed and rubbed her upper arm. "Hey, sleepyhead."

"What was that jolt? Did we land?"

Luke smiled. "We landed all right. The pilot must be inexperienced."

Sarah put her belongings back into her tote bag. Once at the gate, Luke pulled their carry-ons down from the overhead bin. They shuffled behind the long line of folks disembarking and going through customs. Once cleared, they saw Oliver and Viktoria waiting for them.

Sarah gave each of them a hug. "Thanks for meeting us, but we could have gotten a taxi."

Oliver shrugged and took Sarah's bag. "I know. But we thought this would be faster. Besides, Jeremy and Natalia want you to see the new place."

Before Luke could respond, Viktoria added, "You won't believe how much work has been done. Natalia outdid herself this time."

Sarah laughed. "Well, it must be truly spectacular. I thought what she did in Paris was wonderful."

Oliver led them to a waiting limousine. Luke's eyes went wide. "Traveling in style these days, are you?"

Oliver smiled. "If it was up to me, I would have picked you up on a motorcycle, but Jeremy had other ideas."

"Good thing I have more than one friend, then."

Oliver laughed and helped place the luggage in the trunk. They all got in and Oliver gave the destination to the limo and sat back next to Viktoria.

"So, we're not allowed to go to the hotel first?"

Oliver gave a mischievous smile. "Luke, Jeremy cancelled your hotel reservations."

Luke thought that odd, but didn't say anything. He didn't want to play into Oliver's ruse, or whatever he was planning. After all, this was all on Jeremy's dime, so he decided to just enjoy the ride. He gave Oliver a shrug instead. Sarah gave him a concerned look. He patted her arm. "Don't worry. I'm sure Jeremy will explain."

The sun was setting and the city's lights were coming on. Shanghai seemed to be coming to life. In some ways, it looked like a very modern city with skyscrapers with various unique designs. The lights highlighting various buildings cast colorful shadows. Yet there were parts of the city that looked traditional with buildings displaying characteristic pointed eaves and pagoda-styled structures and archways.

In the distance, Luke saw a glowing nebula. It looked ethereal with hints of lavender and maroon colors that seemed to be in constant motion. He put his face closer to the window for a better look. He grabbed Sarah's hand and pulled her to the window. "Sarah, look."

She gasped. "It's beautiful." She turned to Oliver. "How did they get it done so quickly?"

Oliver shrugged. "A question for Jeremy."

Viktoria smiled. "I told you a lot of work has already been done. They have crews working 24/7."

Sarah gave a slight nod with raised eyebrows, then turned back to the window. "Luke, this is nothing short of a miracle."

Luke gave a slight nod. Perhaps their Shanghai investor was more thrilled with the idea than anyone could have hoped.

The limo rolled to a stop. They all exited. Luke couldn't believe his eyes. He stood staring at the building, which appeared to be all glass and looked round, at least from this perspective. The Pangea symbol and logo were already over the entrance, along with a banner in Chinese.

Luke turned to Sarah. "What does the banner say?"

"Opening soon." She turned to Oliver. "Is it completed?"

Oliver shook his head. "Not yet, but they're pretty close."

Inside, the atrium/lobby area looked similar to the one in Paris. But that was as far as the similarity went. Immediately past this ran a moving walkway.

Oliver gestured. "Care to take a tour before we meet the others?"

They all took a spot on the walkway. They found out the building was indeed circular, and the moving walkway took them in a circle all the way around the building. The ceiling, also of glass, allowed the nebula to be seen from the inside. Luke couldn't help but envision being on a date with Sarah with the lights down low, the light from the nebula yielding a romantic glow throughout the restaurant. Being an open-floor plan, a divider was positioned every so often as they traveled the full circle of the walkway. There were workmen in almost every section.

Luke pointed to a divider. "I assume these are what partition the restaurant into the different continents?"

Oliver nodded.

Viktoria pointed to one of the large projections in the back of one of the sections workmen were installing. "Natalia said these projections will produce the hologram to give the continent of each section. The décor of each section will be the color assigned to that specific continent."

Sarah grabbed Luke's hand. "This is beyond anything I would have imagined."

Oliver stepped off the walkway toward the center of the building. All three followed.

Luke looked around. "The bar area, I presume."

Oliver nodded. "Impressed yet?"

Luke looked at him with eyes wide. "That's an understatement."

Oliver laughed. "I thought so." He nodded toward the interior. "There's an elevator in the middle of the bar. Let's go down a floor."

They walked around equipment and workmen to get to the center. A sign read "Restrooms" in both English and Chinese. When they entered, a hallway, past the entrance to the restrooms, led to a door. It said "Employees Only," again in both English and Chinese. Along each wall were a series of screens with various pictures of Shanghai; these then alternated with various landmarks from around the world.

Oliver nodded to Luke. "Put your thumb on the screen to your right."

Luke did so and the door unlocked. They all walked through, and the door closed behind them as an overhead light came on.

"Now, use your thumbprint and your code on the panel on the wall in front of you."

He did so, entering the numerical code he always used in the elevator to get to Jeremy's Houston penthouse, and the elevator door opened. They all stepped in and the elevator began descending.

Luke gave a short laugh. "I feel like I'm part of a mystery novel."

Oliver put his hand on his shoulder. "Hasn't it sunk in yet, Luke? You are."

Luke gave a slight nod. Oliver was right. Ever since the day he picked up that first piece of confetti with *T-H-B* on it, his life had indeed turned into a kind of mystery novel. The problem was, the mystery never seemed to end. *What would the final chapter look like?*

The elevator door opened. Luke couldn't believe his eyes. He stepped out into a most impressive laboratory. There looked to be four different labs, each divided with clear glass. Construction looked complete here. Chemists seemed hard at work. He spotted Matteo in the lab next to the one they were in. When Matteo turned and saw them, he waved and made his way over.

"Luke! Sarah! Welcome! Welcome." He gave each of them a hug and included a kiss on the cheek for Sarah. He waved his hand toward the lab before them. "What do you think?"

Luke shook his head. "Matteo, this is beyond what I expected."

Sarah nodded. "And how did you get it up and running so quickly?"

Matteo smiled. "Between Natalia's connections and ours, it all seemed to come together much faster than we hoped." He motioned for them to follow.

They went to the end of the lab, through a door, and then down some stairs to a large living area. Xiaofeng sat on a long sofa talking to someone on the phone. She looked up and smiled, giving a slight wave. Sarah waved and smiled in return.

Xiaofeng ended her conversation and came to greet them. She gave each of them a hug and a kiss on the cheek. "It's so good to see both of you again." She gestured toward the sofa and chairs. "Please come in and sit. You must be tired from your long flight."

Everyone took a seat. Matteo brought over tea and coffee. Xiaofeng passed around a plate of cheese, crackers, and fruit. "Please, help yourself," she said, sitting back. "Jeremy and Natalia will be here shortly."

Matteo nodded. "They've been working nonstop ever since we started this project." He looked at Luke. "He took your words to heart. As you can see, the lab is up and running before the restaurant."

Luke gave a slight nod. "How did you get everything done so quickly?"

Matteo smiled. "I really believe God orchestrated the whole thing." He paused, looking at Luke as if waiting for a response.

Luke raised his eyebrows. "Oh, I believe you."

"A miracle is not beyond your belief anymore?"

Luke smiled and shook his head. "Not anymore."

Matteo gave a nod. "Good. I am glad to hear that."

Xiaofeng chimed in. "The investor Natalia reached out to had just demolished a building on this site and had the debris cleared. It was very fortuitous, but she still had to do a lot of convincing to get him to agree to let them build a restaurant here. He had his heart set on an apartment building."

Luke smiled. "I assume Natalia made him an offer he couldn't refuse?"

Xiaofeng laughed. "Something like that. They let the investor have twenty-five percent of the restaurant's profits, but the lab was Jeremy's first priority."

"So, how do you get the workers for the lab here without them going through the restaurant?" Luke asked.

"Jeremy bought the building next door. The workers enter that building, then go down an elevator which joins the lab. They don't really know this is below the restaurant unless they really stop and think about it, which most don't."

Luke nodded. "Pretty clever."

Xiaofeng smiled. "And he will turn all the floors except for the first three into apartments. Restaurant and lab supplies are stored on those floors." Xiaofeng cocked her head. "He did concede to the investor getting seventy-five percent of the apartment profits."

Luke knew giving in like that was not Jeremy's traditional path for business. "That seems like a lot of compromise for him."

Xiaofeng shrugged. "I'm not sure how he has worked in the past, but speed was his main concern here. That seemed the fastest way to break ground and build. He did get approval for the lab and has sole ownership of it. I think that was why he conceded so much on the apartments, as that was the investor's main interest."

Matteo laughed. "But Jeremy and Natalia did get another penthouse out of the deal."

Luke chuckled. "Now that sounds like Jeremy."

Everyone laughed.

"Am I the butt of another joke?"

All turned to see Jeremy coming down the stairs with Natalia. There were more hugs and kisses before everyone settled into their seats.

"Jeremy, it's all so fantastic," Luke said. "You really came through on this one."

"Thanks, Luke. You were right. Getting the lab up and going was critical to our mission. But I owe you even more, now."

Luke turned up his brow, and a sly grin came across his face. "You mean you've finally realized how hard it's been for me to put up with you all of these years?"

Jeremy gave a slight laugh. "Something like that, I guess."

Jeremy's statement took Luke back. He expected a retort, but didn't get one. "What's wrong, Jeremy? You do look tired, buddy."

Jeremy shook his head. "Tired? Yes. But that's not it. You started the cascade, Luke."

Luke felt bewildered. He scrunched his forehead and shook his head; he just didn't follow Jeremy's train of thought. "What do you mean?"

"Out of all of us, you were the one who was the most resistant to reading a banned religious book. Yet you were the first to follow its instructions. You helped Oliver and Viktoria follow you. They helped Natalia and myself do the same."

Matteo's eyes watered. "Luke, you accomplished what Xiaofeng and I could not. You've given our daughter to us for eternity. Thank you."

Stunned, Luke wasn't sure what to say. "Uh . . . " He gave a short laugh. "This was unexpected. I . . . uh . . . don't know what to say." He shrugged. "You're welcome." He smiled. "I guess if anyone as stubborn and hardheaded as me can understand it, anyone can."

Jeremy laughed. "That must be it, buddy. You helped us realize God can reach anybody."

Luke gave a smirk. That was the Jeremy he knew.

THIRTY-SEVEN

CONTEMPLATION

Luke awoke and looked at the clock next to his bed: 05:04. He sat up and yawned. He knew Scott and Brian would be leaving work soon and likely had a lot for him to do, so he decided to get it done as soon as possible so they would be able to focus on their mission undeterred tomorrow. He donned some jeans and a pullover, combed his hair, and headed toward the kitchen.

As he walked down the small hallway composed of six bedrooms, he realized he and Sarah were the only ones staying in this enclave who were not married. Should he try and correct that? The thought had been popping into his head a good bit lately. He shook his head. He had to keep from thinking about that right now. He had to focus on work, and wanted to do that before everyone got up.

Luke had been amazed the night before when he learned there were six bedrooms underneath the lab, and that this is where Matteo and Xiaofeng were now living. Natalia and Jeremy were staying here also, until the completion of their penthouse, which would still be some time from now. It was the next project after the restaurant.

The kitchen was part of the living area, separated from it by a long counter. Luke made himself coffee and created a small work area for himself as he sat at the counter. He pulled his tablet from his satchel, logged into his virtual computer, and looked to see the work that awaited him. His eyes widened. It seemed that between Scott, Brian, and Larry, they weren't giving him much slack for being away. It would take, likely, four hours to complete everything they had assigned to him. He got to work. After a couple of hours, he heard someone coming down the hallway.

Luke jerked his head back slightly. "Liwei. Hi. I wasn't expecting you."

Liwei smiled. "Hello, Luke. Good to see you." He came over and shook Luke's hand. His accent was heavy, but Luke realized he could understand him perfectly.

"Your English is improving." Luke held up the coffee pot from the trivet next to him. "Care for some?"

Liwei nodded and retrieved a cup. "Thank you."

"I didn't know you were staying here."

Liwei took a large gulp of coffee and nodded. "Yes. I stay here until apartment complex done. Xiaofeng and Matteo very nice to me." He smiled. "Also, give me job."

Luke held up his cup and toasted with Liwei. "Congratulations, Liwei. I'm very happy everything worked out for you."

Liwei smiled and gave a slight bow. "Me too." He finished his cup. "Excuse, please. I get dressed and go to work."

Luke smiled back. "Have a good day, Liwei."

Liwei turned and headed back to his room. "You too, Luke."

Luke turned back to his work and didn't even notice Liwei coming back through until he saw him walking upstairs to the lab. Luke smiled. He was happy things were working out for

Liwei. He paused and put his hand to his chin. He wondered if Liwei had family back in Hohhot. If so, he had sacrificed a lot. Luke shook his head and turned back to his work.

Around 08:30, Matteo and Xiaofeng came into the living area. Luke looked up and smiled.

Xiaofeng came over. "You're up early. I thought you'd sleep in. You should, you know."

Luke shook his head. "Couldn't today. I have work to get done so folks can continue when they get to the office in Houston tomorrow."

Xiaofeng patted his shoulder. "Well, we'll leave you to it. Matteo and I are going upstairs to ensure everyone gets started on their projects. We'll be back down around lunchtime."

Luke nodded. Matteo gave a slight wave as he and Xiaofeng headed up. Luke smiled to himself. It seemed being here was really rejuvenating both of them. He couldn't be happier for them—or for Natalia.

Luke finished his work a little after nine o'clock. He sent Scott, Brian, and Larry an email explaining what he had done and provided the links they needed to get to the projects. As he closed his computer, Jeremy walked in.

"You're the early bird, I see."

Luke laughed. "Unfortunately, yes. I had some work I had to get done. Just finished." He held up the coffee pot. "Want some?" Luke put his hand on the pot. It felt lukewarm. "On second thought, you'd better make more. This isn't very hot anymore."

Jeremy grinned. "No problem. I'm used to redoing your work."

"Ha ha. You're a riot in the morning. You should start your own show."

Jeremy laughed and threw a bag of cinnamon rolls on the counter. "Here. Have one as I make a fresh pot of coffee."

Luke opened the package and took a big bite of a roll. “Mmm. Thanks.” He took another bite and asked Jeremy a question—with his mouth full.

Jeremy turned and looked at him. “What, what, what, what, what?”

Luke laughed as he swallowed hard. “I said, What are your plans today?”

Jeremy chuckled as he poured himself a cup of coffee. He turned and refilled Luke’s as well. “It looks like I’ll be upstairs all day.” He glanced at his watch. “The workers of the next shift will be here around ten this morning.”

“Anything I can do?”

Jeremy shook his head as he sat across from Luke. “Not really. I’m just supervising—ensuring they put stuff where it belongs.” He shrugged. “Not hard, but very busy as it seems I’m answering one question after another all day long.” He grinned. “And I used to think your questions were annoying.”

Luke chuckled. “Glad I was good practice for you. How’s the lab going?”

Jeremy nodded as he took another swallow of coffee and fished for a cinnamon roll. “Natalia’s parents have been awesome. I really don’t think we would be nearly as far along without them.” He took a bite of roll. “They really know their way around a lab. They both have a group of scientists doing tissue and transporter work with compounds being made.”

Luke raised his eyebrows. “Impressive. Any leads yet?”

Jeremy shook his head. “They’ve only started. But I’m hopeful. With us having experienced scientists and Simone only graduate students, our progress can be faster than hers.”

Luke nodded. “I sure hope so.”

They sat in silence for a couple of minutes. Luke then looked up. “Jeremy, why so many bedrooms?”

Jeremy took his last bite of roll. “Well, I knew Natalia and

I needed a place to stay until we made other arrangements. Then, if any of you visited, you would have a place to stay." He paused. "But the main reason was a request from Matteo."

Luke cocked his head. "What was that?"

"He wanted a safe house for people transitioning."

"Transitioning? You mean like Liwei?"

Jeremy nodded. "He's expecting many to be in a similar position."

Luke nodded. "He's probably right." He shrugged. "We may all be in such a position before this is all over."

"If what Oliver told me is true, it would seem 'over' may mean us being on Mars."

"Maybe." Luke laughed. "You could have the first Martian restaurant."

"On that note, I'm going to get dressed for work."

Luke laughed as Jeremy left. He gave a big yawn. Apparently, coffee wasn't going to get him through. He realized he needed more sleep. He headed back to his bedroom.

THIRTY-EIGHT

FAMILY FEUD

Philippe looked up as the door to his office opened and René walked in unannounced. “Well, please do come in,” Philippe said dryly.

René walked over and threw a document on his desk.

Philippe looked up. “What’s this?”

“We got two refunds on your Granted Fantasy account.”

Philippe cocked his head. “I thought that would make you happy. That’s a savings of a couple thousand credits.”

René crossed his arms. “I know you, Philippe. You’re getting it somewhere. I can only assume it’s from Dr. Mercure.”

Philippe sat back. He could feel heat rising through his face. He picked up the report and threw it back at René. It fell to the floor. “Mind your own business, René.”

“What do you think I’m doing?” He bent down and picked up the report. “She’s very ambitious, Philippe. What if she pulls information out of you that you didn’t intend to give?” He cocked his head. “I’m only looking out for you.”

Philippe flew to his feet. “Oh, are you? Well, at least I’m interested in someone who has ambition and a brain in her head." He pointed at the report René was holding. "That's why I've moved on. I want something more fulfilling."

"Is she the right one? Her work is so critical. You have to be able to supply the right amount of pressure—and she can't afford to get distracted."

Philippe could feel his face getting hotter. *How dare he be condescending.* "I can do my job. You just worry about you."

René stiffened. "What is that supposed to mean?"

"Well, at least I've been open about my indiscretions. Unlike you, who bounce between the blonde bombshell in accounting and the guy built like Ajax in the IT department."

René just stood there looking at him.

"Oh, so you thought no one knew?"

"Mind your own business, Philippe."

Philippe crossed his arms with a short laugh. "Oh, so it's no one's business if it's you, but it's your business if it's me?" He took a few steps away from René and turned. "Don't think because your office is one meter longer than mine you are superior. Dad left equal shares of this company to both of us." He gave René a hard stare. "You can't do anything without me."

René shook his head and walked over to the yellow sofa and sat. His tone softened. "I don't want to do anything without you."

"Humph." Philippe wasn't buying the change in tone. He was still angry. "Oh yeah, we're a team." He pointed toward the conference room. "How are we a team when you withhold information from me? Why didn't you ever tell me about the elevator that goes to the inner vault, or that we've already funded two Mars missions?" He threw his arms in the air. "What else don't I know?" He turned away from René, then turned back. "Apparently, we're only a team when you feel it's expedient for you." He crossed his arms again. "I'm not buying your act."

René's eyes watered. He shook his head. He glanced up at Philippe. "We all have needs, Philippe. I needed something without any pressure. Surely, you can understand that. They're fun to be with, and we just have a good time together. I can just turn my mind off for a while."

Philippe sighed. "René, what you're doing has more risk. Your guard is down. I know I have to be on my toes all the time." He sat down next to René. "If you want to turn your mind off, then you need to go to a spa or read. Sex is definitely a stress release, but you can't turn your mind off."

René gave a slight nod. Philippe felt almost sorry for him. Being in charge was a big burden, but he couldn't go soft on him.

"René, if you want to work as a team, you have to be totally open with me. You can't act like Dad did and be a lone wolf—if you want me involved. This has to be a partnership—or nothing."

René nodded. "You're right, Philippe. I promise. No more secrets."

Philippe ran his hand over his chin. René seemed extremely stressed. Philippe put his hand on René's shoulder. "There's a spa I sometimes go to. I'm going to have Sonja make you an appointment for this afternoon. You go, OK?"

René nodded. "Yeah, that sounds good."

"I'll text you the address so you can give it to the limo."

René stood, nodding his head. "Thanks, Philippe." He headed back to his office through the conference room.

Philippe returned to his desk. He phoned Sonja to make the spa appointment for René. He then sat back in his chair. Now came the critical moment. Was he going to be supportive for René, or use this as his opportunity to become the head honcho? He reasoned that, after all, René was his brother. He could probably be more influential *not* being the point person.

Now that he understood René's weakness of insecurity, maybe he could make things go his way while letting René field the criticisms and repercussions.

As Philippe sat there buried in his thoughts, the conference door opened. René stuck his head in once again. Philippe raised his eyebrows.

René entered and handed another electronic pad to Philippe. "I told you I'd keep you informed."

Philippe took the report. "So, what's this?"

"That is the list of all those currently in our Paris prison."

Philippe turned up his brow. "And I need to know this, why?"

René shook his head. "Not *who* is there, but the *number* there."

Philippe scrolled to the last page. He looked back up at René. "Two thousand."

René nodded. "The number to put into hyperstasis."

Philippe looked back at the document and scrolled through it. "Why not just put these in hyperstasis? These are the ones Dad had identified for that purpose, aren't they?"

René gave a short laugh and pointed to the document. "Yes, but that was almost sixty years ago. Look at the ages of most of those there. We can't send them to Mars."

Philippe scanned through the list again. "They're not all old, though."

René shrugged. "Well, we can't take everyone who qualifies anyway. I vote to clean shop and start over. It'll be easier to know when we're ready."

Philippe slowly nodded. René's rationale was becoming clear. "When the prison is full, then we have all the immunes we need for transport."

René pointed his finger at Philippe. "As long as we have a compound to alter their memories. The last thing we would need is a riot after getting them to Mars."

Philippe knew where René was going with this. Simone needed to get results, and time was running out. He nodded. "I understand, René."

René nodded and headed back toward his office. He turned when he got to the conference room door. "Inform Dr. LaMarre to start Mercy Farewell for all those in the Paris prison."

Philippe nodded.

"And stay on top of Dr. Mercure." He smiled. "And I don't mean that literally."

Philippe gave a smirk.

René chuckled as he exited.

Philippe drummed his fingers on his desk. Was René trying to stay true to his word, or trying to show he was still in charge? Either way, René was right about this. The earlier he got Anton started, the better.

THIRTY-NINE

Lab Intrusion

"Wait a minute. You mean you want me to stay here another week?" Luke couldn't believe what Larry was saying.

"It's worked out great so far. When Scott and Brian leave for work, you either QC their work or complete what they did. Then, when they come to work, what you've done is already waiting for them. I think we've already done twice the amount of work we could have if you were here. In another week, I think we can get this done and allow the pilots and crew to do full flight simulations, including landing and takeoff."

It was odd hearing Larry allowing him—*encouraging* him—to be elsewhere. More time with Sarah would be great.

"While there, I need you to go back to Hohhot and get them back on schedule. With Dr. Liwei's disappearance, they are behind. Your goal is to get them back on schedule."

"OK, Larry. That will probably take me another week."

"No problem. Once we've completed this assignment, I don't mind you taking the extra time to get them up to speed."

Luke smiled to himself. With Dr. Liwei here, understanding what needed to get done should not be a problem. This would make things go much faster.

"Now for some good news."

Luke laughed. "You mean, what you just told me was the bad news?"

Larry chuckled. "Well, it depends, I guess. I need you to stop by Hawaii on your way back."

Luke's head jerked back slightly. "Hawaii? Really?"

"We have to start preparing for terraforming techniques. You need to find the right asteroids that can be used to bombard Mars and get water vapor into the atmosphere. Dr. Cohen at the Mauna Kea Observatory has been gathering data on a number of asteroids. You need to see which ones are ideal for harvesting to be used for the terraforming project."

Luke was extremely excited to get this assignment. Getting back to the astronomy side of his work would be great. Larry paused, then went on.

"Luke, is Dr. Morgan there with you?"

Luke waved to Sarah and motioned for her to come over. She had a confused look. She mouthed, "What?"

He handed her the phone and shrugged.

"Hello? Oh. Hi, Ken." She grimaced, glancing back at Luke. "OK. Yes, I completely understand." She nodded her head. "Yes, I can leave before the end of the week." She ended the call and handed the phone back to Luke.

Luke's eyes widened. "You have to leave?"

Sarah twisted the corner of her mouth and nodded. "I'm afraid so. My supervisor, Ken Wilson, wants me back before the start of next week."

Luke's shoulders drooped. All his plans with Sarah had just evaporated. "Well, let's go up and tell Jeremy and Natalia."

Oliver appeared from the bedroom hallway and poured himself a cup of coffee.

Luke laughed. "Well, good morning, sleepyhead. It's unlike

you to sleep in."

Oliver shook his head. "I was up all night looking for Viktoria."

"Did you find her?" Luke couldn't help but have panic in his own voice.

Oliver shook his head. "No."

Luke gave a nervous look at Sarah and turned back to Oliver. "That can't be good. What happened?"

Oliver took several swigs of his coffee. "I woke up in the middle of the night and she wasn't there. I went looking for her, but didn't find her."

Sarah walked toward Oliver. "Why do you think she left?"

He shrugged. "She must have received a call and left without waking me."

Sarah looked from Oliver to Luke. "What if they're on to us?"

Luke shook his head. "How?"

Sarah shrugged. "I don't know, but it makes me nervous."

Luke headed for the stairs and motioned for the others to follow. "Well, let's go tell Jeremy. He has a right to know."

Once up the stairs, they saw the labs in full swing. Jeremy was with Matteo in the adjacent lab, looking over his father-in-law's shoulder at something. Dr. Liwei was showing something else to Xiaofeng and Natalia. All three of them walked over.

Jeremy looked up and smiled. "Come to see how the antidote work is going?"

Luke shook his head. "Viktoria is missing."

Jeremy shot a concerned looked at Luke and then turned to Oliver. "You don't know where she went?"

Oliver shook his head.

Suddenly, all the lab walls went opaque.

Luke turned, wondering what happened. He looked toward

Jeremy. "What's happening?"

"Unauthorized entry." Jeremy took Matteo's arm. "Dad, you and mom get downstairs now." He motioned for Liwei to follow them.

Rather than exiting the current lab and running back to the stairs Luke and the others had come up on, they each went to one of the nearest cabinet doors in the lab, opened them, and walked in. Before Matteo left the lab bench, he pressed something underneath and that section of the benchtop went underneath and another portion of the lab bench extended in its place.

Before Luke could understand what was happening, he heard that familiar . . . *click, click, click* sound coming toward him. He whirled and saw Viktoria approaching—with Caine and Abel at her heels.

Caine gave a wicked grin. "Well, well, well. Dr. Loughton, it seems you are always around where trouble lies."

"I haven't noticed any trouble until *you* arrive."

Caine gave a chuckle. "You're always the funny man."

Jeremy stepped forward. "Why are you here?"

Viktoria walked around the lab with her superior Illumi-Alliance air, slowly looking at what was on the lab benches. "We have reason to believe you're doing something covert here."

Jeremy's face reddened and he clinched his fists. "The only thing covert here is your paranoia. I have all the legal permits for this lab and all the permits needed for this restaurant."

Viktoria gave a slight smirk. "It's highly unusual for a restaurant to have a lab such as this."

Jeremy's face reddened even more. He looked like he would blow a gasket. "And what other restaurant owner has a reputation like mine? The reason people come to my restaurants is they know they will have wonderful food, they will be entertained, and the quality will be top-notch. That doesn't come by being a 'me too' restaurant. This . . . " He swept his hand, gesturing toward the lab. " . . . This is how I stay ahead of the competition."

"And where do you stay?"

Jeremy's head jerked back slightly. "What?" She seemed to have taken him off guard.

Viktoria walked up to him. "You're a very prominent man, Mr. Pangea. Yet, there is no record of you staying in any hotel in Shanghai."

"Oh, Natalia and I stay here."

Viktoria's eyebrows raised. "A prominent man like you lives in a lab?"

"It's temporary until our penthouse is completed." He pointed to the lab office in the corner of the lab. "There's a sofa in there. And a cot. Between the lab and getting the restaurant up and running, there's little time for anything but sleep and work anyway."

Viktoria nodded her head in a perfunctory manner. She glanced over at Natalia. "Your wife looks pretty fresh from sleeping on a sofa and taking sponge baths."

Jeremy looked over at Natalia and back to Viktoria. "My wife is a remarkable woman and looks good no matter what."

Natalia smiled, but didn't say anything.

"Besides, we've used the showers in the employee locker room." He pointed back the way Viktoria had entered. "You passed it on your way here." He raised his eyebrows. "Shall I show you?"

Viktoria shook her head, turned, and walked around the lab bench. She picked up a beaker and swirled it. The liquid turned from clear to cobalt blue and back to clear. She sat it back down. "Very impressive." She gave him a hard stare. "Why build a lab here?"

Jeremy shrugged. “Why not? I cut out the middle man, get answers faster, get five chemists here for the price of one in the States, and they have skills not found in the rest of the world.” He gave a forced smile. “It’s good business.” He pointed to Viktoria, Caine, and Abel. “You three, however, are not good for business.”

Viktoria nodded toward Caine. “Check the cabinets.” She then pointed to Abel. “See if he’s here.”

Jeremy looked from one of them to the other. “If *who’s* here?”

No one answered Jeremy’s question. Caine smiled and headed for the same cabinets Matteo, Xiaofeng, and Liwei had entered. Luke’s muscles stiffened. *Things could fall apart quickly.*

Both cabinets appeared locked. They didn’t open. Luke thought that odd. They had opened freely before.

Viktoria looked at Jeremy. “Open them.”

He went over and unlocked them. Caine pushed him back and opened the cabinets. Only glassware and lab equipment were visible. Caine turned to Viktoria wide-eyed and gave a shrug.

Viktoria turned to Jeremy. “Why were these locked?”

Jeremy gave a half smile. “I told you: I am a good businessman. The chemists here are top-notch, but pilfering and selling is likely a better source of income for many. We keep tight control on our equipment. Only lab supervisors have access to supplies.”

Viktoria pointed to the other cabinets. “Check all of them.”

Caine made Jeremy go with them.

Sarah stayed with Natalia. Luke could tell both were extremely nervous.

Viktoria went into the adjacent lab; Luke and Oliver followed. She looked around. Her gaze focused on the door at the far end. "Where does that door lead?"

"More supplies."

She stared at Oliver. "Open it."

Oliver locked eyes with her. "I have two words for you."

Viktoria gave her threatening grin. "And what would those be?"

"Coconut River."

"What?" Viktoria stood transfixed, staring at Oliver. "What did you say?" Her words came out as barely a whisper.

"Coconut River," Oliver repeated.

Viktoria blinked a couple of times and shook her head. She stumbled backward a couple of steps, then caught herself. Her demeanor changed. Her eyes went from being cold to pleasant.

Caine and Abel walked in with Jeremy. Natalia and Sarah walked in from the other lab.

Caine stepped forward. "Only supplies, ma'am."

Abel shook his head. "He's not here." He then pointed at the far door. "What about the door?"

Luke saw Viktoria give a slight nod to Oliver.

Viktoria looked at Abel. "Let's find out." She motioned to Jeremy to come over toward her. "Open it."

Caine and Abel walked over with him. Viktoria motioned them back. "Stay here and keep an eye on the rest of them." She scanned each of them. "I'm not sure I trust them."

Jeremy walked to the door and opened it. Viktoria went in. After a few minutes, she came back out.

"Well?" Caine looked at Viktoria.

Viktoria shook her head. "Supplies."

Abel sighed. "So, it's all a bust?"

"We had false intel. Let's go."

Caine walked up to Luke. "Maybe we should take this one, just for good measure."

Luke looked into Caine's eyes and just stared at him.

"Stand down, Detective Caine. We've accomplished our mission."

Caine sighed and stepped back.

But then, in a flash, Viktoria whipped out her gun and pointed it at Oliver. "Maybe we should take this one."

Caine pointed at Oliver. "Why him?"

Viktoria gave a wicked grin and a slight shrug. "I don't know. Maybe I don't like the way he looks." She put the gun into his chest and pushed him back.

Oliver raised his palms and stepped backward. He had fear on his face. Was it an act, or had he lost control of her again? Viktoria kept pushing him back with her gun all the way to the wall. They stood immobile for several seconds. Still with the gun in Oliver's chest, she reached forward and . . . kissed him—passionate and prolonged. She holstered her gun and turned. With a wicked grin on her face, she motioned for Caine and Abel to follow.

Luke saw Caine give Abel a curious look. Evidently, Viktoria saw it also as Luke saw her give a shrug and heard her state, "I like to keep them guessing. They'll be even more wary of us next time." She walked out of the lab.

Caine and Abel looked at each other, shrugged, and followed her out.

Everyone gave a sigh of relief.

Oliver grinned. "That's my girl."

Luke shook his head. "Oliver, like I have always said: you two are one scary couple."

Oliver threw his head back and laughed.

FORTY

More Plans

Once Viktoria and the two agents had left the lab, Natalia quickly headed downstairs. Everyone followed. Luke heard her call for her parents as he followed her down.

"Mom? Dad?"

Both looked up from where they were sitting on the sofa. Xiaofeng stood. "We're OK, Natalia."

Natalia walked over and gave each a hug. "I was so worried for you. What did Viktoria say when she came down?"

Xiaofeng patted Natalia's hand. "It's OK, dear. She just said she was sorry for the intrusion and everything would be all right."

Everyone else walked over and sat down.

"I have a more basic question." All eyes turned to Luke. "How do those cabinets work?" He looked at Jeremy. "They were not locked when Natalia's parents and Dr. Liwei used them, but then they were later. First they appeared empty, but then full of supplies."

Jeremy smiled. "You liked that, did you? That was actually Matteo's idea."

Luke's eyes widened as he looked at Matteo. "How did that work?"

Matteo chuckled. "Xiaofeng and I anticipated this would happen at some point. When the doors are activated by thumbprint, the shelves slide and form an opening for a doorway that leads us downstairs. If not activated, the cabinets' contents are displayed."

Luke smiled. "Well, that's pretty ingenious. I assume the handles are activated only by your prints?"

Matteo nodded. "Mine and Xiaofeng's."

Sarah turned to Oliver. "Will that happen often?"

Oliver gave a slight shrug. "I hope not. Viktoria and I will have to work out a more careful strategy so we're not caught off guard and she's not left in the dark."

Sarah shifted in her seat. "Well, it was very unnerving."

Oliver nodded. "I'm sure she'll be back soon and make an official apology."

Xiaofeng waived her hand. "Oh, that's not necessary. Poor thing. I can't imagine living in her shoes. What our world has done to her . . . " She shook her head.

Oliver gave her a slight smile. "That's very kind of you, Mrs. Mancini."

Xiaofeng held up her palms. "Please, Oliver, call me Xiaofeng. And kindness has nothing to do with it. We're very grateful to have someone like the two of you on our side." She smiled. "Most of the time, anyway."

Oliver laughed and nodded his head.

Xiaofeng stood. "Let me get us all some tea and coffee."

Natalia got up to help her. "So, what's our plans from here?" she asked.

Sarah sighed. "I have to head back to Houston. Ken, my supervisor, wants me back. They're apparently shorthanded—something about prescreening everyone at work for the upcoming lottery."

Jeremy turned up his brow. "Prescreening? How is it a lottery if only certain ones can get in?"

Sarah shrugged. "Well, it does make sense. You can't have people with a propensity for health issues going. The medical needs in such an environment would be overwhelming."

Jeremy bobbed his head. "Yeah, I guess that makes sense." He looked at Luke. "You heading back too?"

Luke shook his head. "I have to go back to Hohhot and help them get up to speed." He turned to Dr. Liwei and smiled. "It seems your disappearance has put them behind. I will likely need your help in knowing what to do to get them back on schedule."

Dr. Liwei laughed. "Good to know my work made a difference. Sure. I'll make a list of what I know needs to get done."

Luke nodded. "Thanks. That should make things go faster. Although . . . " He looked at Sarah. "Losing my interpreter may slow things down a little. I then have to go to Hawaii and do some asteroid gazing."

"Hawaii?" Sarah's shoulders drooped. "Of all times."

Luke twisted the corner of his mouth. "I know. It would have been nice to combine this business trip with pleasure."

Xiaofeng and Natalia brought over drinks and handed them to the group.

Luke took a swallow of tea. "Jeremy, what about you and Natalia? Heading back to Houston anytime soon?"

Jeremy shook his head. "It will be at least several more weeks. I can't leave now until I get the restaurant in running order." He shrugged. "Yet everything seems to be on schedule. With crews working 24/7, it may go faster than expected. I interview chefs starting tomorrow."

Natalia sat down next to Jeremy and patted his thigh. "We. *We* interview chefs starting tomorrow."

Jeremy laughed. “Yeah. I screen them for talent. Natalia screens them for meeting the restaurant standards.”

Natalia nodded. “Chefs can be quite temperamental—and spoiled.”

Luke chuckled. “Sounds like the voice of experience.”

“Hey.” Jeremy shook his finger at Luke. “I resemble that remark.”

Luke threw his head back and laughed. “Yes. Yes, you do.”

Natalia patted Jeremy’s leg again and smiled.

Someone was walking down the stairs. They all looked up and saw Viktoria. She came over and sat next to Oliver. She glanced at each of them. “I guess ‘sorry’ is the wrong response?”

Xiaofeng waved her hands. “Viktoria, no apology is necessary.”

She shook her head. “No, Oliver and I need to work out a better system so this doesn’t happen again—especially unchecked. I hate to think what would have happened if Oliver had not been here.”

“It all happened as God planned.” Everyone looked at Matteo. “Now there will be less pressure for the Illumi-Alliance to come back here anytime soon. This gives us a good window of opportunity to get things done and find an antidote.”

Viktoria smiled. “Thanks, Matteo. You’re always so positive. I hope I can get there one day.”

Matteo nodded. “You will, my dear. You will. One day. One day we’ll all be there.”

Luke thought about that. He would at some point have to quiz Matteo about this statement. He had taken the first step of relying on God for his future. But he realized he really didn’t know what that future was like. Maybe he would do some reading tonight and get Matteo’s thoughts on it tomorrow.

Jeremy stood. "I have a new recipe I want to try out on you guys. Anyone game?"

Luke held up his hand. "If it's food, I'm in."

Jeremy chuckled. "What a surprise." He waved Luke over. "Come help."

"You mean you want a taster? I'm good at that. Remember?"

Jeremy smiled. "I remember you were good at complaining."

Luke bumped Jeremy with his shoulder. "I only complain when you don't do your job well."

Matteo got up. "I think the kitchen will need supervision."

Natalia looked at Oliver. "You aren't going to join them?"

Oliver's eyes widened. "In the kitchen?" He shook his head. "Trust me. That's the last place you want me." He yelled over his shoulder. "I'll wait and critique."

Luke gave a retort. "Yeah. You're all talk and no do."

Oliver's mouth fell open. "What did you say?"

Luke laughed. Everyone let out an "Ooh."

"Challenge on." Oliver followed Matteo into the kitchen.

Natalia laughed. "Girls, we will either have a good meal, or we're facing death and mayhem in the kitchen." The women laughed together.

FORTY-ONE

MEETING MAHER

Luke exited the pool and passed several string bikini-clad bodies to get to his lounger. He smiled to himself. Maybe Sarah not being with him here in Hilo was good. Otherwise, he would have to keep apologizing for being wide-eyed all the time. He laid back and let the heat of the sun dry his body. The warm sun felt excellent. He glanced at his watch as he had to time his stay in the direct sun. It had been awhile since he had been outside like this. He knew sunscreen could only protect so much.

He flipped over onto his stomach. As he did so, he caught a glimpse of someone who reminded him of Sarah. He had to do a double take, but quickly realized it wasn't her. The hair looked similar, but Sarah was far more gorgeous than this woman, who was wearing a hot pink bikini. He closed his eyes and let the sun's rays do their magic. His mind drifted to Sarah. He wondered what she was doing right now. What he would give to have her in the lounger next to him. That would have made such a perfect addition to this assignment. He wasn't complaining about the assignment, but he was definitely undergoing Sarah withdrawal. Tomorrow should take his mind off his forlorn state. By this time tomorrow, he knew, he should be halfway up the Mauna Kea summit.

Luke turned over onto his back once more. He had about all of the sun he could handle for the day. He contemplated one more dip in the pool before heading back in for dinner. Then his phone beeped. He didn't recognize the number, but it looked local, so it was probably work-related.

"Hello, this is Dr. Luke Loughton."

"Hello, Dr. Loughton, this is Dr. Mahershalalhashbaz Cohen."

"Who?" Luke almost hung up. Was it a crank call? *Is that even a name?*

"Dr. Loughton, I'm the head of the Mauna Kea Observatory."

"Dr. Cohen?"

"Yes."

"Sorry. All I heard was 'Maher-something' and my mind didn't hear the rest."

Luke heard laughter from the other end of the phone. "I get that a lot. Sorry about that. Listen, I'm in town this evening and thought I'd stop by for dinner. That is, if you're free."

Luke sat up straighter. "Oh, that would be perfect." After some discussion, they settled on a nearby restaurant. Luke said he would meet Cohen there by 18:00.

* * * * *

Once at the restaurant, he found Dr. Cohen easy to spot; he was the only one reading an astronomy magazine. Luke thought that a little odd since electronic versions of magazines were now more common. Also, Dr. Cohen didn't look much older than Luke, although his skin, hair, and eyes were much darker. Luke assumed him to be of Middle Eastern descent.

The waiter took him to Dr. Cohen's table.

Dr. Cohen looked up from his magazine. He smiled and stood, holding out his hand. "Dr. Loughton, I presume."

Luke nodded and smiled. "Please, call me Luke. Thanks for agreeing to meet with me."

Dr. Cohen gestured for Luke to sit. "Please. Have a seat. You can call me Mahershalalhashbaz."

Luke, caught off guard with that statement, wasn't sure what to say or how to respond.

Dr. Cohen paused, then laughed. "Just call me Maher. I don't expect you to use my full name."

Luke chuckled. "Well, I appreciate that. Otherwise, you'd have to settle for 'hey, you.'"

Dr. Cohen threw his head back and laughed even harder. "Believe me, I've responded to far worse."

The waiter soon came by with a bottle of wine and poured each of them a glass. The waiter smiled. "Compliments from the owner for all guests tonight."

Luke looked at Maher with raised eyebrows. "You picked a good place, Maher."

Maher gave an approving lift of his eyebrows. "Evidently." He looked at the waiter. "Thank you."

The waiter smiled, nodded, and headed to the next table.

Luke contemplated whether to ask his nagging question—then went ahead and did so. "Forgive me for asking, but how did you get such a complicated name?"

Dr. Cohen smiled. "I come from a very Hebrew-centric lineage. It took longer for Israel to conform to the Community philosophy. Even today, their version of Community is slightly different than those here."

Luke scrunched his brow and turned his head. "Why is that?" He had never heard of other countries accepting different standards—even slightly different.

Maher shrugged. "I can't tell you why—just that we are taken into Community when we reach thirteen years of age, not ten."

Luke's head jerked back slightly. He had never heard of any other country doing this. "That's interesting. And how does that relate to your name?"

Maher smiled. "My family was more traditional than most. My father wanted me to have a unique name."

Luke smiled. "Well, I think he succeeded there."

Maher nodded. "Indeed. Yet, I've grown to like it." He chuckled. "I've never been confused with anyone else."

Luke gave a mock surprised look. "You don't say?" Luke turned more serious. "Is it a family name or something?"

Maher shook his head. "No, the name was given as a sign to mark a significant event in the Jewish nation's early history. My father stated he wanted my life to become a significant event in our future."

Luke gave an approving nod. He held up his glass. "To being significant."

Maher lifted his glass and took a sip. He developed a faraway look in his eyes.

"Maher, is everything OK?"

Maher glanced up. "What? Oh, yes, everything's fine. I was just thinking about that statement. It reminded me that my father never visited me after being taken to Community. I always wondered why." He shrugged and gave a slight smile. "Anyway, it's all a distant memory now. I guess the why isn't really important anymore."

Luke wanted to tell Maher it was likely that his father's memory of him had been wiped. Yet, he didn't know Maher well enough to be that open with him—at least at this point.

Maher chuckled again. "I used to laugh about my father telling of his marrying my mother."

Luke cocked his head. "Oh? Why?"

The waiter then brought their entrées. Maher paused until they were alone again. While eating, Maher continued.

He waved his hands with knife and fork in his grip. "This probably won't come across as funny as it was since you would have to really understand my mother's personality. She was quite feisty."

Luke smiled. He didn't know where Maher was going with the story, but he was certainly intrigued.

"My father and mother had an arranged marriage . . . "

Luke almost dropped his fork. "What? That still happens?"

Maher laughed. "Well, not now." He cocked his head. "I guess even then it was quite uncommon." His voice got lower. "I guess, practically impossible these days." He waved his hands again. "Anyway, after their engagement, my father stuck to the tradition of him deciding when the marriage would occur. My mother had to be patient and wait until my father decided. She had to be prepared for any day and any time of the day."

Luke's eyes widened. "I've never heard of such a thing."

Maher smiled. "In very olden days, it was quite common. The groom prepared a place for him and his bride. The groom's father decided on a date, and the groom and his groomsmen would have a shofar—"

Luke gave a blank stare. *"A what?"*

"Oh, uh, something like a trumpet. He would have it sound as they approached the bride's house. All of the bridesmaids would then scurry about getting the bride ready before the groom arrived. He would come, the priest would perform the marriage, he would take his bride to his home, and they would have the wedding feast."

Luke shook his head. "Wow. That's quite the story. So, why were you laughing about it earlier?"

Maher smiled. "My mother ruled the roost, so to speak, thereafter. That was the one and only time she let my father have the upper hand. She took control after that."

Luke laughed and nodded his head. "Oh, I see." After laughing a few minutes, he looked at Maher. "So, did you do the same thing?"

Maher turned solemn and shook his head. "I haven't married yet. I don't think any woman today would stand for such a wedding."

Luke raised his eyebrows and cocked his head. "You never know. There may be a few romantics still out there."

"Maybe." Maher shook his head. "Oh, it's just an old custom anyway."

Luke could tell not seeing his family after being taken to Community still affected Maher. Suddenly, the realization that Maher could remember such detail made him wonder if he was actually immune. Could an extra three years make the difference? After eating in silence for a few minutes, Luke looked back at Maher. "How does the Invocation wafer taste to you?"

Maher's focus shot to Luke. Now it was his turn to be confused. "What?"

It dawned on Luke that asking this question likely came across as a very odd inquiry of another person. Nevertheless, he plunged ahead. "The Invocation wafer. I'm just wondering how it tastes to you. Is it sweet or bitter?"

Maher squinted. "Why do you want to know?"

Luke realized he had backed himself into a corner. He had to somehow save face and not look like an idiot. "Oh, just wondering. A friend of mine just created a new one, so I was wondering how you think it tastes."

Maher shrugged. "I think it tastes very bitter. But we just got the new wafer last Invocation. It tasted much better." Maher smiled. “So good, in fact, I went to Invocation two weeks in a row.” He laughed. “I’ve never done that before.”

Luke laughed. Maher’s response made him think Maher may be an immune after all, especially since he also remembered so much about his childhood. Hopefully, Luke would have time to further explore that with Maher before he had to leave for Houston. “I’ll be sure and tell Jeremy. He’s the one who developed the new wafer. It’ll make his day.”

Maher stopped chewing. “Jeremy? You mean Jeremy Pangea?” He stared at Luke for a second. “You know Jeremy Pangea?”

Luke nodded. “Yeah, we actually went to college together.”

“I traveled to Paris a few weeks ago and ate at his restaurant. It was some of the best food, and one of the best experiences, I have ever had.”

Luke smiled. “That’s Jeremy for you.”

Maher pointed his fork at Luke. “You’ll have to introduce me sometime.”

Luke nodded. “Sure. It would be my pleasure.”

The waiter came and dropped off a dessert menu. Luke scanned it, but passed, ordering a coffee instead. Maher ordered a brandy.

Once the waiter left, Maher looked at Luke. “Before dinner is completely over, let me go over your assent to Mauna Kea.”

Luke nodded. “Yes, please. I can’t wait to get to the top and see what you’ve done so far.”

Maher smiled. “I’ve got some special asteroids to show you.”

FORTY-TWO

MAUNA KEA

Luke, glad Maher agreed to take him to the top of Mauna Kea, found Maher waiting for him when he got to the front of the hotel. Maher invited Luke into his car, if one could call it that. "Maher, what kind of a vehicle is this?"

His new friend smiled. "This is a gift from the observatory for me to use in ascending and descending the mountain. I call it EA-4. It's an enhanced automated 4-wheel drive vehicle."

Luke noticed it responded to voice commands like a taxi. But it looked nothing like a taxi. It had a full 360-degree view and only had room for two passengers. It reminded him of one of the UFOs he had seen on the old TV show channel, except this one had wheels that would expand for extra traction as needed. Maher had him strap in, and the vehicle headed down the road.

"I'm going to take our trip more slowly than normal so you can acclimate better," Maher said. "Plus, there are many spectacular views along the way worth seeing since this is your first trip."

Luke nodded that he was fine with all that—until they actually headed up the mountain. He found it a little unnerving. "Uh, Maher. Will this glass dome really protect us if we would have a mishap?"

Maher grinned. "Nervous, are we?"

Luke gave a weak smile. "A little."

Maher patted his shoulder. "Don't worry. It's actually bulletproof—not that anyone will shoot at us. But it won't shatter if we do happen to turn over."

Luke's eyes went wide. Maher laughed. "Don't worry. It's never happened . . . " He gave a sly smile. " . . . yet."

Luke's mouth suddenly went dry. He found himself licking his lips. "Well, don't set any firsts on my account."

Maher laughed. As the vehicle continued to climb, Maher kept looking at his watch.

"Anything wrong, Maher?"

He shook his head. "No. I just want to get to the first destination with morning sun." He smiled. "You'll see why."

After a short period of time, the car pulled off the main road and soon rolled to a stop. They got out and walked to an overlook area. Luke was stunned by what he saw—and let out a low whistle. He saw a beautiful waterfall, about twenty meters in height, which flowed into a pool surrounded by lush vegetation. The mist refracted the sunlight, forming a large rainbow across the falls.

"Maher, this is beautiful."

He smiled. "This is known as Rainbow Falls. Quite appropriate, don't you think?"

Luke nodded. He stood there and looked at the mesmerizing falls. After a time, Maher tapped his arm and they headed back to the EA-4.

As the EA-4 traveled farther up the mountain, Maher pointed to the peak. "The peak is 4,205 meters above sea level. We'll travel through almost every ecosystem Earth has as we ascend: from rainforests to regular forests to grasslands to desert. And we'll pass through clouds and rain."

"Sounds spectacular."

"We'll spend the night at Hale Pōhaku, where all the astronomers stay, which is at 2,800 meters. Then we'll travel to the peak tomorrow."

"I can't wait to view the asteroids. It's been so long since I've done actual astronomy work," Luke said.

Maher laughed. "Don't get too excited."

Luke was confused. "Why?"

"Well, a lot of the astronomy is still looking at data rather than viewing through a telescope."

"Yeah, but I hoped you'd give me extra time on the telescope while I'm here."

Maher patted his shoulder. "Don't worry, Luke. I took care of that for you."

Luke smiled, but also breathed a sigh of relief on the inside.

The changing landscapes they traveled through astounded Luke. While much of the road was paved, that didn't mean it was nonperilous. At times, Luke saw only a large drop-off as he looked out. Although it did no good, he held on so tight at times that his knuckles went white. The sound of the wheels inflating and deflating periodically also was unnerving. Maher would just smile at him. Luke admired Maher as he sat there so calm and collected when it looked like they could fall off the narrow road into a ravine below. Maybe he was that calm because he had ridden this road many times. Luke wondered if he could ever get used to this trek up and down the mountain. While he had been in dangerous situations before, he was the one always in control. Now he was at the mercy of a vehicle of which he had no control—not a comfortable feeling.

As he observed the spectacular views, Luke took the available time to further discuss Maher's background and professional history. It not only helped to pass the time and get to know Maher better, it also helped him focus on something else when the views were ominous rather than spectacular. Maher was at first guarded in his responses, but he began to open up more and more as they headed farther up the mountain. They pulled into Hale Pōhaku just in time for dinner.

Maher showed Luke a small bedroom. He patted Luke's shoulder. "It's not what you're used to, but it serves the need."

Luke smiled. "It's fine, Maher. Thanks."

"I'll see you in the cafeteria in about thirty minutes."

After Maher left, Luke settled in and tried calling Sarah. He missed her so much. He had grown used to having her around. He knew he could no longer take her for granted. He punched in her number and waited. He felt his heart rate increase and his palms become sweaty. He smiled. It felt almost like it always did when he called someone for a first date. After five rings, the line went to voicemail. His shoulders drooped. He tried to sound positive. "Hi, Sarah. This is Luke. Well, I've made it to the base camp on Mauna Kea. If you get this message, give me a call. I miss you." He ended the call and sighed. Luke looked at his watch. Sarah should be home. It was close to midnight there. He sat on the bed and put his head in his hands. He prayed nothing was wrong.

He found Maher sitting by himself at one of the cafeteria tables. He grabbed a sandwich and joined him.

Maher looked up and smiled. "How are you feeling?"

Luke nodded. "A little lightheaded, but otherwise OK."

Maher nodded. "Yeah, the air is thin here. You'll feel better by morning."

After they both ate in silence for several minutes, Luke decided to go deeper with him. "Maher, I mean no disrespect, but I sense you still have strong feelings for your parents."

Maher pressed his lips together, gave a sigh, and looked

down at the food on his plate. "Yeah. Yeah, I guess I do. You probably think that makes me weak."

"What? No. No, absolutely not." Luke looked at Maher, bending his head down to get his attention until Maher looked up at him. "Maher, I totally understand."

Maher stared at him. "All my friends used to tell me I was a traitor to Community." His eyes glistened. "I was supposed to move on and, uh . . . " He cleared his throat. " . . . forget about my parents."

Luke felt sorry for the guy. It seemed both he and Natalia had a stronger bond with their parents than most. Maybe most parents didn't create a strong bond because they knew they would have to give their children up. Evidently others really adored their children. "There was a reason for all of the questions I asked you on the way up here," Luke said.

Maher blinked rapidly, clearing the water from his eyes, and cocked his head.

Luke looked around to ensure there was no one else within listening distance. "I've discovered some things about when we went to Community."

Maher leaned forward. "Luke, what are you talking about?"

Luke held up his hands in front of Maher. "Hold on. I know this may sound strange. But what happened when you went to Community?"

Maher put his hand to his chin in thought. "Well, we had a kind of party. I remember there was a cake . . . " He smiled. "And ice cream." He looked back at Luke. "Our Oracle was there and we had Invocation."

"Exactly. The Invocation wafer contains a chemical that allowed your parents to be susceptible to memory reprogramming."

Maher's jaw went slack. He stared at Luke. "Memory reprogramming?" He shook his head. "I . . . I don't understand."

"Maher, your parents were programmed to not remember you. It's not that they didn't want you, they likely never remembered you . . . or, not until a long time after."

Maher turned up his brow. "That's . . . that's impossible . . . unconscionable." He shook his head. "Wait. I took the wafer, too. Why didn't I lose my memories?"

"You're likely immune to the effects of the wafer."

Maher put his hand to his forehead. "What?" He squinted. "Are you making this up?"

"No, Maher. No. We've found that those who think the Invocation wafer tastes bitter are usually immune to the wafer's effects. Haven't you noticed others have to refer to their notes for work more often, whereas you don't?"

Maher stared ahead, as though looking through Luke. "Well . . . yeah, I guess so. I never thought anything about it." He shrugged. "I just assumed they had a bad memory." His focus turned back to Luke. "Is all that you said really true?"

Luke nodded. "I'm afraid so."

Maher closed his eyes and shook his head slightly. He opened them and looked back at Luke. "But to what purpose?"

Luke bit his bottom lip; he was wondering how much more open he should be with Maher. "It's rather complicated."

Maher's head jerked back slightly. "Complicated? More than what you've already said?" He shook his head. "It's beginning to sound like a blooming conspiracy."

"I'm afraid that is just what it is—and it seems to be tied to the Mars mission."

Maher sat back, his arms hanging at his side. "I'm not sure I'm ready to hear all of this." He waved his hand as though motioning onward. "OK, lay it on me."

Luke gave a slight smile. He was glad Maher wasn't challenging him on this. Yet, anyway. "You mentioned you were Jewish. Did your family read Scripture?"

Maher gave a grimace and shook his head. "No, that was taken away before I was ever born. I only heard the stories Dad used to tell."

"Did you believe in God?"

Maher cocked his head. "God, as in a person up in Heaven looking down on us?"

Luke bobbled his head. "Well, yes—sort of."

Maher shook his head again. "No. They were only stories."

"What if they weren't?" Luke raised his eyebrows with an expectant look.

Maher leaned forward, placing his elbows on the table. "You . . . you've read them?" He spoke with a hushed tone of unbelief.

Luke nodded.

Maher looked worried; he was the one now looking around to be sure no one could overhear this conversation. "How? That's . . . that's forbidden."

Luke took the same hushed tone as Maher. "I know. But it does speak truth."

"Truth? Can one even know it?" Maher scrunched his face once more. "How do you know?"

"I've experienced it."

Maher slightly shook his head. "*It?*"

"The Holy Spirit. He has helped me understand things about God: his love for us, his standard, being willing to pay the price for our not being able to meet that standard, and relying upon his payment of death so I can trust him for my eternal future."

Maher's eyes went wide. He sat back and waved his hands in front of himself. "Now you're just sounding crazy. No one believes that stuff anymore."

"That doesn't mean it isn't true."

Maher curled the corner of his mouth. "Let's just say I'm

skeptical."

Luke smiled. "I felt the same way—for quite a while. Look. The Mauchards engineered the removal of all religion, instituted the Invocation wafer to control everyone, and initiated the Mars mission to take those immune, those who could not be controlled, to Mars."

Maher shook his head. "It all seems so bizarre. I don't know."

Luke nodded. "I know. Just think about it. I have a friend who, I think, can help you locate your parents. If you wish."

Maher put his hand to his chin. "Give me time to think about all of this."

Luke held up his palms. "Of course. I'm not trying to pressure you—just let you know what I know and have experienced." Luke stood. He didn't want Maher to feel any more pressure from him. "I'm going to go and see if I can reach Sarah, my girlfriend. I'll see you in the morning."

Maher nodded. "We'll leave around 13:00, after lunch. Meet me out front."

Luke shook Maher's hand and headed to his room. He hoped tomorrow wouldn't become weird between them.

FORTY-THREE

VIEWING ASTEROIDS

It felt good to sleep in longer than normal. Luke hoped to talk to Sarah before his trip up to the peak. He first called her cell. Again, after five rings, it went to voicemail. Rather than leaving another message, he ended the call.

Luke sat on his bed and sighed. He looked at his watch. It was early afternoon in Mars City, so he tried Sarah's work number. She didn't like Luke to tie up the company line for personal calls, but he had to know everything was fine.

"Medical Center. Debbie speaking."

"Hi, Debbie. This is Dr. Luke Loughton. Could I speak to Dr. Morgan, please?"

"She isn't here right now. Can I give her a message?"

Luke's shoulders drooped. Why was it so hard to reach her? "When do you expect her back?"

"I'm not really sure. She's been in and out."

"Can you look at her schedule?"

"Uh . . . I don't have access. I'm only a temp, and Kathleen Stapleton is on vacation."

Luke sighed. "OK. Thanks, Debbie. Please ask her to give

me a call when she gets in. She has my number."

"OK, Dr. Loughton. I'll put the message in her in-box."

Luke ended the call. At least Debbie had seen Sarah, so she was at work somewhere. He'd just have to be patient.

He went to the cafeteria, had some eggs and fruit, and then went to find Maher. He certainly hoped Maher had thought about what he had told him the night before—and that the rapport they had developed the night before would not change.

Maher stood by the EA-4. "Ready to climb?"

Luke nodded and followed him to the vehicle.

Once inside, Maher looked at Luke and smiled. "Ready for a steeper climb than yesterday?"

Luke's eyes widened. His voice caught in his throat. "Steeper?"

Maher laughed as the EA-4 headed up the road. He acted nonchalant, as if their conversation the day before never happened. "When we get to the top, I'll show you the asteroids we have identified so far, which I think will be helpful." He looked at Luke. "You, of course, have the final say."

Luke smiled, unsure what to say.

"Tonight, I've scheduled time on the Keck telescope to show you some of them."

"Thanks, Maher. I really appreciate this."

Maher nodded. "We'll need to come down each day for sleeping. The air's too thin to stay there too long."

Luke nodded again. That made sense. He grabbed his seat as the vehicle lurched and the tires expanded for greater traction. He glanced at Maher, who seemed be trying to keep from laughing at him.

"So, Luke, what's the whole plan for these asteroids?"

Luke wondered if he was allowed to tell him. Yet the whole thing seemed to be out of the bag anyway. "Well, the thought is, once we colonize Mars, we will start terraforming by bombarding the polar ice caps with specific asteroids to increase water vapor and other chemicals to increase and thicken the atmosphere to start a greenhouse effect."

Maher raised his eyebrows. "Even if that works, the atmosphere won't be breathable."

Luke nodded. "True, but once the surface temperature increases, other chemicals will be released from the surface into the atmosphere. In addition, photosynthetic bacteria will be released to turn the carbon dioxide into oxygen."

Maher turned up one corner of his mouth and raised his eyebrows. "Sounds like a long-term plan."

"Well, there are other plans that will likely occur simultaneously. But, yes, it will take a long time."

Maher gave a small shrug. "At least the assignment for which asteroids to target makes more sense now." He shook his head. "Why couldn't they have just said that?"

Luke looked at Maher. "I'm sure they were just protecting you."

Maher stared at Luke. They both smiled and then laughed. "Oh, you mean giving me plausible deniability?"

Luke grinned. "Or just keeping you in the dark."

Maher pointed at Luke. "Likely the second."

Once at the peak, Luke saw several domes and buildings. They entered the base of the dual-domed Keck telescope observatory. Maher introduced him to a few other astronomers and found a desk and console for Luke to sit and work. Initially, Maher sat with him to explain things and go over how to access the data on the asteroids.

Maher pointed to several of the files. "We used the infrared telescope to help us understand their composition and the optical telescope to take photos. I'll leave you to review these data, and you choose which ones you want to see. If you identify others than the ones already identified, we can get those scheduled for tomorrow night."

Luke nodded.

Maher left, but soon came back with several bottles of water. "It's important to stay hydrated. Drink every so often, even if not thirsty."

"Understood."

After Maher left, Luke looked through file after file of data identifying the best asteroid candidates suitable for Mars terraforming. He couldn't wait to view them after sunset.

Maher returned at sundown with a couple of sandwiches. He handed one to Luke. "Your time for viewing will start in half an hour."

"Great. Where do we go?"

Maher shook his head. "We stay here. The temperature outside is already two degrees Celsius. The telescopes are open to the air. We have to view remotely. The images will appear on the monitor behind you."

Luke turned. He twisted the corner of his mouth. This wasn't the experience he had hoped to have. He looked back at Maher. "How's the image quality?"

"It was just upgraded last year to 3-D. It's just as good as, or better than, the image you would have seen through the telescope itself. Also, you can overlay the infrared view and show the composition of the asteroid via different colors."

Luke raised his eyebrows. "Really? That's great." He handed Maher his list for viewing.

Maher scanned the list and cocked his head. "I'm not sure if we'll get to all of these tonight. We only have a three-hour window."

"Well, let's just do the best we can."

Luke was amazed at how fast the time went as well as the detail the telescope provided. Also, seeing the shape of the asteroids and the others nearby helped him decide the best way to calculate extraction from orbit and the best path to Mars.

Once the hours for viewing were up, Luke rode with Maher back to base camp. Neither man talked much. Although it wasn't that late, Luke felt extremely tired and headed straight to bed. The thin air seemed to have had more of a draining effect on his stamina than he wanted to admit. He fell asleep before he had time to even think over the events of the day.

FORTY-FOUR

Opening Up to Maher

Luke woke to the feeling of being shaken. He stirred and sat up. "What . . . what's wrong?"

Maher stood over him. "Luke, it's almost time to go."

Luke felt extremely confused. "I thought you said we wouldn't leave until 13:00?"

Maher looked at his watch. "Yes, and it's already 12:34."

Luke shook his head to try and wake up. "What?" He looked at his watch and his eyes went wide. "Oh, my." He wiped his hand over his face. "I must have forgotten to set my alarm."

Maher patted his shoulder. "Get dressed and something to eat. I'll meet you at the EA-4."

Luke nodded. Maher left.

Luke, still groggy, washed his face to try and wake up. The thin air was definitely taking its toll, causing him to want to sleep so much. He rushed to get dressed and headed to the cafeteria. Luke glanced at his watch. It was already 13:10, so he settled for a bottle of water, a protein bar, and some yogurt. He took those with him, deciding to eat on the way up to the summit.

Maher waited at the EA-4 as he approached. “Sorry, Maher. I guess my body is having trouble acclimating to the thin air.”

Maher shook his head. “No worries. We’re only fifteen minutes behind schedule.”

As Luke got into the vehicle, he realized he had not called Sarah before he left. He sighed. Maybe he would have time before the day was over. As he ate his protein bar, he decided to try and engage Maher on the conversation they had two days earlier.

“So, Maher, have you had a chance to think more about our conversation the other evening?”

Maher bobbed his head. “Some.” He looked over at Luke. “I don’t want to doubt you, but it just seems so . . . out there.”

Luke smiled. “Yeah, I guess it does. It did to me at first, also.”

“So, what was the tipping point for you?”

Luke paused in eating his yogurt. What was his tipping point? “Well, it was more of a process, I guess. I first had to realize God was real, then I had to come to terms with sin—”

“What do you mean?”

Luke looked at Maher. “Sin?”

Maher nodded.

“Yeah, that was a hard concept for me too.” He took another spoonful of yogurt. “What made sense to me was I couldn’t claim to be perfect. I came to realize God’s standard is perfection.”

“But no one can claim that.”

Luke smiled. “Exactly. That’s the point. Only God can be perfect, but he requires us to reach that standard.”

Maher again turned up his brow. “Really? How?”

“That brings us to the next step. God met the payment for his own requirement.”

Maher cocked his head and shook it.

"I thought you would be able to understand that more than most," Luke said.

"Why is that?"

"Well, you seem to have had a stronger bond with your parents than most. You got to experience—and remember—their love. It seems that's what God did for us. We couldn't meet his standard, so he met it for us because of his love for us."

"Well, when you put it like that, it does sort of make sense. What did he do?"

"There's a verse in Scripture that states, very simply, that sin brings death."

"Because we can't meet the standard?"

Luke nodded. "God is unique, so he set the standard, made the payment for our sin, and now what we have to do is relinquish control of our future to him and what he has done for us."

"That goes against everything I've been taught. We create our own future."

"I think there's two major issues with what we've been taught."

"Oh?"

"Yeah. First, God makes sense when you think about family. And second, we never talk about what happens when we die."

"So, the two pillars of our conditioning and training are false?"

"You tell me. You were deprived of your family and told it wasn't important. You've been told you define your future, but you can't control your life beyond death. Does that sound well thought-out?"

Maher scratched his head. "Wow. That's a lot to digest. Give me some time. OK?"

"Absolutely," Luke replied.

They traveled the rest of the way in silence. Luke said a silent prayer that what he had said to Maher would make sense to him. He was really starting to like the guy.

* * * * *

The evening was almost a mirror of the night before. Luke reviewed the data and photos of the asteroids he saw the previous night, as well as choosing the asteroids to view later that night. He was enthralled to see them with their infrared overlay. The pictures really helped him understand their composition. By the end of the night, he had twenty asteroids chosen as good candidates.

Luke looked up and saw Maher approaching him.

"Hi, Luke. Time on the telescope is up."

"What? Already?" Luke looked at his watch. "How does time go by so fast?"

Maher laughed. "You know the saying: 'Time goes fast when you're having fun.'"

Luke smiled. "Well, it was definitely fun." He shook his head. "I can't believe I have only one more night."

Maher tapped his shoulder in a friendly gesture. "Well, let's go get some sleep."

Luke nodded. Before exiting the building, he put on his parka and gloves and followed Maher to the EA-4. "Man, it's freezing out here," Luke said. "I don't think it's even this cold when I go skiing in the Rockies."

Maher laughed. "Yeah, it can get pretty cold. I think we're at minus-three degrees Celsius currently."

When they got into the EA-4, Luke let out a long "Ahhhh!" He looked over at Maher. "You heated it up for us?"

Maher smiled. "It has a remote-activated heater. I thought you'd like that."

Luke smiled. "It feels wonderful. It would have felt good last night, too."

Maher laughed. "Yeah. Sorry about that. I don't normally use it and forgot about it. But, it's five degrees colder tonight."

"Well, my tush thanks you."

Maher laughed even more heartily.

Luke wanted to pick up where their morning discussion ended, but he didn't want to add pressure. He hoped Maher would bring up the topic, but he didn't.

"So, are you accomplishing what you wanted?"

Luke looked at Maher. "Yeah, I think so. I wanted to identify thirty asteroids. I've identified twenty already. I think I can finish tomorrow night."

Maher nodded. Luke wondered if that was the opening he needed to continue the morning discussion, but he wasn't sure. He waited for Maher to say something else, but his new friend remained quiet.

Once back at base camp, they said good night and went to their rooms. As Luke got ready for bed, he closed his eyes and shook his head. He had gotten so busy that, once again, he forgot to call Sarah. He set his alarm for 05:00. That would make it mid-morning back in Houston. He should be able to catch Sarah at work.

As he laid down, he had a troubled feeling. He just wanted to hear Sarah's voice. That was all he needed. He said a prayer, ensured the alarm was set, and went to sleep.

FORTY-FIVE

Pros and Cons

Luke jerked awake. He looked around, trying to understand the source of the sound. Discombobulated, it took him several seconds to realize his phone was beeping. As he turned off the alarm, the reason for the blaring noise hit him—along with a surge of adrenaline. He dialed.

"Medical Department. Kathleen speaking."

"Hi, Kath—" Luke caught himself in mid-sentence. "Kathleen? Debbie said you were on vacation."

She gave a half-laugh. "Yeah, I wish." Suddenly, she paused. "Wait. Who's Debbie? Who is this?"

"This is Dr. Loughton. I called day before yesterday for Dr. Morgan. Debbie answered the phone."

"Hi, Dr. Loughton. I don't know what happened, but there is no Debbie who works here. I haven't seen Dr. Morgan for several days now."

Luke put his hand on his head. This wasn't making any sense. "Kathleen, I don't understand. Who did I talk to, then?"

"I don't know what to tell you, Dr. Loughton. I don't know who you talked to. Within the week Dr. Morgan got back, she sent me an e-mail stating she had to be out again." Kathleen paused. "I don't mean to be insensitive, but she's making everyone here work overtime. If you reach her, please tell her we need her back here as soon as possible."

"Oh . . . OK, Kathleen. Thanks." Luke disconnected. He let out a long breath. He shook his head. It just didn't make any sense. What could he do from here? *Oliver*. He had to call Oliver. His adrenaline was surging so high his fingers shook, making it difficult to dial.

Luke announced himself even before Oliver said anything. "Oliver, this is Luke."

"Luke? Hey, buddy. Everything OK?"

"Have you talked to Sarah?"

"Well, not since she left China. Why?"

Luke tried to control his voice, but he knew his panic was coming through. "I can't reach her. I left her a message through someone at her work only to now find out that person doesn't work there."

"What? I don't understand."

Luke sighed. He knew he wasn't making much sense, but he had to make Oliver understand the gravity of the situation. "Oliver, someone gave me information Sarah was at work, but I just found out she was only at work for less than a week after she got back. No one at the office knows her whereabouts."

"OK. OK. Calm down. I'll look into it. There's likely a logical explanation."

"Well, you know what happened last time."

"I doubt the same thing has happened again. Just stay positive until you hear back from me. OK?"

Luke took a deep breath. "OK. Sorry. Being so far away makes me feel helpless."

"That's OK, Luke. I totally understand."

Luke knew this was also his chance to come through for

Maher. "Uh, Oliver, one more thing. I met a colleague here in Hawaii who reminds me somewhat of Natalia."

"Really?"

"Well, in the sense that he developed a real attachment with his parents before he was taken to Community. He would really like to find them. Do you think you could see what you can find out about them?"

"Well, I can try. I can't make any promises. What's his last name?"

"Cohen."

"Whew. That could be a hard find. It's such a common name, unless he has an unusual first name."

"How about Mahershalalhashbaz?"

"What?"

"That's his first name. He goes by Maher."

"You're kidding me." Oliver laughed. "Well, that will certainly narrow things down substantially."

"That's what I thought. Let me know what you find—on both counts."

"Will do."

Luke disconnected.

His plan was to talk with Sarah and then go back to sleep. Now, there was no way he would be going back to sleep. He first spent some time in prayer and then headed for the cafeteria.

To his surprise, Maher sat at one of the tables reading something on his tablet. Luke got some coffee and sat across from him.

Maher looked up, his head snapping back slightly. "Well, aren't you the early bird?"

Luke smiled. He didn't want to go into why he was up so early. "Look at you. It looks like you've been up earlier than me. Couldn't sleep?"

Maher gave a slight smile. "I've been going over everything you've said to me. For some reason, I couldn't get it off my mind. I came here and started writing down the pros and cons to believing what you said."

Luke raised his eyebrows. "How scientific of you." He smiled. "Which side is winning?"

"You know, I think what you told me were things I just didn't want my mind to contemplate." He paused. "I'm almost there . . . almost."

Luke laughed. "OK. I won't push."

"Thanks."

Luke stood and patted Maher's shoulder. "I'm going back to my room to try and get some more sleep. But if you want to talk about anything, I'm available."

Maher nodded.

Luke got some yogurt and a protein bar and went back to his room. As he ate, he said a prayer at the same time for Maher—for his parents as well as that his friend would put his faith and his future in the true Messiah.

Luke laid down and tried to clear his mind of worry. It took a while, but he finally drifted into a slumber. He woke about three hours later. He felt more rested, but his heart wasn't really into asteroids today. He shook his head. Never would he have thought that would be the case. He really just wanted to be back home so he could check on Sarah. He got dressed and headed to the cafeteria for lunch. He wasn't really hungry, but knew he needed to eat something and stay hydrated.

As usual, Maher was waiting for him at the EA-4. Not much was said on the way to the summit. Most everything went as the two days before had gone. By the end of the night, Luke had a total of thirty asteroids identified. He was pleased he had met his goal. Hopefully, Larry would be happy as well.

Maher seemed a little more talkative on the way back to

base camp. "Luke, I'm afraid you'll be traveling back down the mountain by yourself tomorrow. You can still use the EA-4, but I have a deadline to meet here."

Luke nodded. "OK. I'll just keep my eyes closed the whole time."

Maher laughed. "It really is safe. You won't have any problems."

"If you say so."

"It's been a pleasure hosting you. You've given me a lot to think about."

"Well, it's been great being here. Thanks for everything." Luke paused. "Also, I just want to let you know I've asked my friend to see if he can track down your parents."

Maher looked at him wide-eyed. "Really?"

Luke held up his palms. "I can't make any promises, but he'll do his best. And . . . he's pretty good."

"Thanks, Luke. I appreciate that."

"Uh, Maher. I would like to send you something."

"OK. What is it?"

"Well, it's something I want you to read. It may help with your pro and con comparison. It's somewhat secretive and will come encrypted. I'll send a decryption code separately, as well as some additional information."

Maher had a nervous look on his face. "Well . . . OK."

Luke held up his palms. "You don't have to read it, and you can even delete it if you want. But I think you'll find it interesting."

"I'll be honest. I'm caught between nervous and intrigued."

Luke smiled. "I completely understand, believe me. I'll let you decide which one wins out."

Maher laughed. "I think you already know."

Luke shrugged. "No, but I'm hopeful."

Maher shook his head. "I'm going to miss you, my friend."

* * * * *

Once back at base camp, they shook hands and gave each other a brief man-hug. Luke went to his room and prepared for bed. He would have an early morning start to catch his plane to California, and then he would take the red-eye flight to Houston. He made a mental note to pick out some Scripture passages to send to Maher that might help him with his decision.

FORTY-SIX

JARED

The flight was called red-eye for a reason. Luke looked at himself in his bathroom mirror. He half-chuckled. He looked like he was coming off a hangover. Well, he was—sort of. A jet-lagged hangover. All he wanted to do was take a shower and fall into bed.

Luke undressed and stepped into the shower. The warm water took off that grungy feel one gets from being on airplanes for nearly eight hours. Amazing what soap and water could do for how one felt. As soon as he got out of the shower and dried off, Luke heard the doorbell. He first sighed; he simply wanted to fall into bed. But the adrenaline kicked in once the thought hit him that this could be Sarah. He quickly donned some sweatpants and a T-shirt and went to the door.

He opened it quickly, without bothering to use the peephole—but it wasn't Sarah.

"Jared." His mind went blank; this was not who he had expected. Jared had never stopped by before. Luke shook his head slightly. "Hi. Come on in."

He instinctively gave Jared a short man-hug and shoulder

pat, but Jared didn't reciprocate. He knew something must be wrong.

"Everything OK?"

Jared turned and stared at Luke. "Where's Jason?"

Luke blinked, his mind again blank. He shook his head. "Jared, what are you talking about?" Seeing Jared's stern look, he gestured to the living area. "Please, come have a seat and tell me what's happened."

Jared sat with a thud. Luke had no idea why he was so mad.

Luke sat on the sofa and faced him. "Jared, you're obviously upset. But I don't know why. Talk to me."

"Don't you?"

Luke shook his head. "I've been out of town for several weeks. I just got back this morning. I took the red-eye, so I'm not sure my mind is totally here. But tell me what's troubling you."

"Jason's gone."

"Gone? What do you mean, gone?"

"Gone. Like, can't be found anywhere."

This seemed too coincidental. *Both Jason and Sarah disappear at the same time?* What could that mean?

"Jared, why don't you start from the beginning?"

Jared sighed and leaned back on the sofa, turning his arm so he could face Luke better. "As you know, Jason has spent a lot of time with Sarah."

Luke nodded. "Yeah. They're good friends."

Now it was Jared nodding. "Yes, but do you know what they were talking about?"

Luke was unsure where this was going. Of course, he would never say that he knew she was pumping Jason for information about Rosencrantz and the Illumi-Alliance. "Various things, I suppose. Why?"

"These past couple of weeks, Jason has been talking nonsense. Going on and on about God, the Holy Spirit, and whether we should be living together." He gave a stern look. "I asked him where he got such crazy ideas. He said it was from what Sarah had been talking with him about." Jason suddenly looked very sad. "I thought I was losing him and would have to have him committed."

Luke almost smiled, but caught himself. That would not come off very well with Jared so in the dark about these topics. No, Luke knew, he had to take things slow. He also knew his mind was quite befuddled from lack of sleep.

Luke gave a slight nod. "Jared, I can't explain his disappearance, but I think I may understand what they were talking about."

Jared looked at him expectantly, eyebrows raised.

"But it's difficult to explain, and I need a clear head to explain it all. My mind is mush from the jet lag. Can you give me a couple of hours so I can sleep? I can then better talk to you about it."

Luke saw Jared's shoulders droop. "When do you want me to come back?" Jared had a deadpan tone.

Luke shook his head. "No, don't go anywhere. Just stay. You can sleep here on the sofa, watch television, eat . . . " He laughed. "If there's anything in the kitchen."

"I've been up most of the night. What I really need is a shower." He suddenly looked crestfallen. "Jason asked me to give back the key to our apartment. I've sort of been living out of the company gym until I figure all of this out."

Luke put his hand on Jared's shoulder. "No need to leave for that. Feel free to take one here. I have sweatpants you can wear, if you like. I also want you to read something on my computer here. I'll be up in a couple of hours, and we can discuss it. OK?"

"Read what?"

Luke went to retrieve his tablet and pulled up the Gospel of John for Jared to read. “It may not make sense yet, but it’s tied to what you just told me.” He handed it to Jared. “Take your time. Do whatever you want in the order you want to do it. I’ll be back out in a couple of hours.”

Jared looked at the tablet screen and then back at Luke. He gave a slight nod. Luke went into his bedroom, keeping the door slightly open in case Jared really did want to take a shower. He fell on his bed and was asleep in a matter of seconds. He woke up once, heard the shower going, turned over, and went back to sleep immediately.

Luke next awoke to the sound of a pan rattling in the kitchen. He turned over and looked at the clock on his ceiling. It was almost 17:00. He immediately sat up. He had been asleep for almost four hours. Before leaving the bedroom, he looked at himself in the mirror and combed his hair to get rid of some of his bedhead.

He trudged to the kitchen and stopped, eyebrows raised.

Jared looked up from mixing something in a bowl. “Oh, sorry. Did I wake you?”

Luke did a slight wave and sat in one of the chairs. “Oh, don’t worry about it. I should have been up hours ago. You should have woke me up.”

Jared laughed. “I think I just did.”

Luke gave a half-laugh. “Yeah, I guess you did.”

“With you having jet lag and not knowing if you would want breakfast or dinner, I thought I’d make some omelets.”

Luke gave a slight smile with eyebrows raised. “Omelets? Wow. Thanks.” He turned up his brow. “But how did you do that? I know there was nothing in my fridge to put together an omelet.”

Jared laughed. “There was nothing in your fridge to accommodate anything, unless you count that science project gone wrong on the bottom shelf." He flicked his hand. "Anyway, I went to the corner grocery and got a few things. Hungry?"

Luke nodded. "You seem in a better mood."

Jared poured the egg mixture into the pan on the stove and held up the spatula. "Yeah. Sorry about that. I was just mad. You were the only available person to take it out on." He poured a cup of coffee and put it in front of Luke and then returned to the pan to complete the omelet.

"Thanks. You're a one-man show here."

Jared held up one hand as he stirred with his other. "Oh, I do this all the time." He paused, his voice low. "Or used to." He gave a shrug and seemed to force a happier attitude. "Comes second nature, I guess." He put the omelets on plates and set them on the table. He got a cup of coffee and sat down opposite Luke.

Luke took a bite. "Oh, this is good. Thanks, buddy."

Jared smiled. "Now, I think you owe me an explanation."

Luke looked up and nodded. "Yes, I guess I do. Did you read what I gave you?"

Jared swallowed and took a sip of coffee. "A good bit of it. Other than the terms 'God' and 'Spirit' being in there, I'm not sure how it's related to what Jason was going on about."

Luke paused and folded his hands while still holding his fork. "Jared, it's all the same thing. From what you told me, it seems Jason has done what chapter three of John talked about."

Jared cocked his head and squinted. "What do you mean?"

"Did Jason say he had the Holy Spirit?"

Jared nodded. "Yeah, and he wanted me to have it, too."

Luke set his fork down. "There are three main steps. One, you have to believe God exists. Then, you have to believe he came to save us. Third, you have to trust in him for your future."

Jared sat back. "Yeah, that's very similar to what Jason said." He shook his head. "But I don't get it. Even if I believed in God, what is he saving me from?"

"Did he mention the term 'sin'?"

Jared gave a slight jerk with his shoulder. "Yeah, I guess. What is that anyway? I'm a . . . " He did air quotes. " . . . sinner, because I'm gay?" He gave a slight shrug while looking sad at the same time. "That's what Jason seemed to be saying." He then looked up and became defensive. "I just know that idea came from Sarah. Maybe . . . " He paused and started to continue, twice, but caught himself each time. He then blurted out what he was thinking. "Maybe Sarah wasn't as much of a friend as I thought."

Luke felt sorry for Jared. He knew Jared was heartbroken and really didn't mean what he said. Luke shook his head. "Jared, it has nothing to do with you being gay."

Jared looked up with a slight smirk, almost daring Luke to defend his statement.

Luke sat back. "Jared, let me ask you a question. Are you perfect?"

Jared looked confused. "What do you mean?"

"Simply that. Are you perfect? Is everything about you perfect? Your speech, your attitude . . . your goodness?"

"Well . . . no. No human can claim that."

Luke gestured to Jared with an open hand. "You've just defined the problem."

Jared shook his head slightly. "What does being perfect have to do with this?"

"It's the reason for the second step we just talked about."

"Sorry, Luke. You're losing me."

Luke leaned forward, putting his elbows on the table. "God can only accept perfection. That's why he made everything perfect in the beginning. We lost our perfection due to disobedience. Since we can't be perfect, God paid the penalty for us that his perfection required. If you remember what you read, it stated that we are condemned. But because God loves us, he paid that penalty. His death did that. It satisfied the justice required with a payment his love could offer. We can therefore trust him for our future so his perfection will be substituted for our imperfection."

Jared turned his head slightly. "I don't know, Luke. That's a lot to swallow." He shook his head. "I know being gay is now accepted by most, but I've heard people all my life say being gay is bad. Now it just sounds like you're saying it makes me imperfect."

"No, Jared. It has nothing to do with that. We're all in the same boat. I could never say anything you do makes you more imperfect than myself. We're both in the same sinking raft. We both need a savior. You may be obsidian black and I'm onyx black. Can I really say you're blacker when the standard is pure white?"

Jared shrugged.

"Plus, God asks us to come to him as we are, not as we hope to be or think we should be. That brings us to the third point. After we come to him and trust him for our future, he gives us his Holy Spirit so we can have a relationship with him and help us become more like him."

Jared sat back. "Whew. I don't know, Luke. I really need to think about all that."

Luke held up his hands. "I totally get it, Jared. It took me quite a while for all of it to sink in before I could accept it." He opened his hands. "Just think about it. I'm open to talk any time."

Jared nodded.

"Can I send what you read to your phone so you can refer to it later?"

Jared shrugged. "Sure. I guess."

Luke smiled. "Great."

They finished eating in silence for several minutes. Jared picked up their plates and put them in the sink. He turned and looked at Luke. "So, you're saying you think Jason took these steps you talked about?"

Luke nodded. "Yes, I think he likely did."

"Well, why did he say we shouldn't be living together?" He gave a shrug. "What is sin anyway?"

Luke thought for a moment. "Our world has defined what is good, right, and legal for so long that the term has been deleted from our vocabulary. Basically, it's anything God decrees is wrong. I can't really say how he does that, and I can't say I totally understand it." He held up his hands once again. "Trust me, it's a new concept to me also, and I'm still wrapping my head around it. But it goes beyond an act to one's actual motivation for the act. A thought can be just as big a sin as an act." Luke gave a smile. "It heightens the imperfect aspect of humans and makes his act of love more profound."

Luke stood up and put his hand on Jared's shoulder. "Jared, don't put the cart before the horse. There is nothing you have to change to accept what God has done for you. I promise, he only wants the best for you."

Jared gave a slight nod. Luke gave Jared's shoulder another pat.

The doorbell rang.

"Excuse me, Jared." Luke was unsure who would be coming by. He opened the door without thinking and then . . . gasped involuntarily. "Sarah."

Sarah smiled and walked into his arms. He wrapped his arms around her and hugged tightly as he closed his eyes; he was just so happy she was OK. He felt the softness of her hair, and her cherry blossom perfume brought back many memories of their times together. When he opened his eyes, he saw Jason standing in the doorway.

"Jason. Hi. Sorry. I didn't see you there. Please come in." He shook his hand and gave him a quick hug.

From the corner of his eye, Luke saw Jared hurrying over. As he turned, he saw Jason and Jared embrace also.

"Jason, I was so worried about you. Are . . . are you OK?"

Jason smiled. "Yes, Jared, I'm fine."

"I didn't know where you were. What happened? Where did you go?"

Jason rubbed the back of his neck. "I'm not really sure. The last couple of days are somewhat blank." He grabbed Jared and hugged him again. "But I'm back now. All is OK. Let's go home."

"Home? Your home?"

Jason looked at him with a funny expression. "My home? Our home, silly."

Jason turned and hugged Sarah. "Thanks, Sarah, for everything."

Jared shook Luke's hand. "Thanks, Luke."

Luke pulled him in close. "Don't forget our conversation."

Jared nodded. He gave a quick hug to Sarah and he and Jason left.

FORTY-SEVEN

Reunited . . . Then Heartbreak

As Luke closed the door, he turned to Sarah and looked at her for several seconds.

Her eyes darted between his. She let out an almost inaudible, "What?"

He shook his head. "I was afraid I would never see you again. I couldn't reach you, and I was so far away."

"I'm here now."

He smiled. "Indeed, you are." He took a step closer, leaned in, and gave her a kiss. She kissed back. He wrapped his arms around her tightly and pressed into her more. She reciprocated. After several seconds, though, she pulled away.

"Luke," she stated in a hushed tone, almost out of breath. "We need to talk."

He smiled and walked with her to the sitting area. He sat on the sofa next to her and turned toward her. "So, what happened? Jared was very concerned—and unhappy with you, by the way."

She gave a sheepish grin. "I thought he might be. I'm glad he had you to turn to. I was going to try and deal with damage control once I got back."

Luke put his hand on hers. "And just where were you?"

She put her other hand on top of his. "Let me start from the beginning."

Luke nodded, looking at her, eyebrows raised.

She looked down as she started, then looked back up at Luke. "During my conversations with Jason and me pumping him for information about Rosencrantz's whereabouts and what big meetings were occurring, I was also talking to him about God and my experience in accepting who he is."

Luke nodded. "Jared was telling me about that. I tried to do the same for him."

Sarah smiled and nodded back. "Good. Good. It probably came across better from you than from me." She shook her head. "It's likely he doesn't trust me right now."

"The impression I got from Jared was that Jason accepted the Messiah for what he did for him and trusted in him for his future."

Sarah nodded and had a weak smile. "Yes."

"But it seems to have caused a schism between them," Luke said.

Sarah sighed. "Yes, Jason became so inquisitive and read a lot after I passed along the Scripture app to him. It was too much change too fast for Jared, I'm afraid."

"OK. I get that, but it doesn't explain why you and he disappeared."

Sarah took a deep breath and let it out slowly. "I was coming to that." She shook her head. "I don't know how, but apparently the Illumi-Alliance knew about Jason's conversion and took him to Paris."

"What?" Luke let go of Sarah's hand and ran his fingers

through his hair. "To Paris? Why?"

Sarah put her hand to her forehead and shook her head. "Maybe he said something to Rosencrantz. I . . . I don't really know." She looked back at Luke. "All I know is I received a panicked phone call from him. He said he thought he was in trouble and asked if I could help. I immediately left for Paris."

Luke put his hands on her shoulders. "Sarah, you left all alone? That was extremely dangerous. What if you were caught?"

Sarah intertwined her fingers and stared at them. "I was, sort of."

Luke sucked in a quick breath. "What . . . what happened?"

She looked back up. "I found Viktoria there since Rosencrantz was there as well. Thankfully, she was her real self at the time." Sarah paused.

"And?"

Sarah put her hand to her chin. Her eyes were watering. "She found Jason had been taken to the same prison you were in."

Luke's eyes got wide. "Why? Jason didn't strike me as being an immune."

Sarah shook her head. "No, he certainly isn't." She took another deep breath. "It gets a little complicated to explain . . . "

"Gets?"

Sarah gave a weak smile. "Yeah, the whole thing is complicated. Still, I met with Anton . . . "

"Anton LaMarre?"

She nodded. "He told me Jason was going to be used as a guinea pig for a new compound Simone had come up with. I—"

Luke grabbed Sarah's hand. "They . . . they already have a test compound?"

"Evidently."

Luke put his hand on his head. This was definitely not good. "I would have thought they had enough test subjects there already." He looked back at her, shaking his head. "Sorry. Go on."

Her eyes began to water again. *Uh-oh. More bad news must be coming,* Luke thought.

"The prison was empty."

Luke's head jerked back. "Empty? What do you mean?"

Sarah looked down and seemed quiet. "I think you know. They were all taken to Mercy Farewell."

Luke's eyes widened. "*All?* The entire prison? Why?"

"The time for them to start gathering immunes has come. They're emptying the current prisons to make room for those they will take on the Mars mission. This is only the first step."

Luke rubbed his hand across his mouth. This was almost too much to take in.

Sarah put her hand on his arm. "Anyway, back to Jason. I think doing the Mercy Farewells really got to Anton and made him more willing to help. I convinced him to convince the others to let the reprogramming test whether someone's memory would return after they had accepted what Scripture stated they should do."

"Sarah, why . . . why would you do that?"

A couple of tears spilled over her eyelids and ran down her cheeks. She didn't bother to wipe them away. "It was either that or let Jason be used for compound testing, which could have destroyed his mind." She looked into Luke's eyes. "Anton said that had happened to a lot of those he tried to reintegrate into society. Xiaofeng was one of the rare exceptions. With Jason not being an immune, I couldn't risk that on him."

Luke reached over and wiped the tears from her cheeks. "You did what you thought was best. I can't challenge that. So, Jason doesn't remember anything about his commitment to

God and receiving the Holy Spirit?"

Sarah shook her head, her eyes still glistening. That information helped Luke better understand why Jason took Jared back so readily. He didn't remember his previous decisions or actions. Luke held Sarah's cheeks and looked into her eyes. "But what about you? Jason doesn't remember, but you do. Anton let you go this time with your memory intact?"

She nodded. "With a warning."

Luke's eyebrows rose.

"He said Simone and Philippe were on the verge of identifying immunes and would collect them with a vengeance. I am one of their top targets."

"Because Simone feels you are a threat to her."

Sarah paused, then nodded. "Likely." She put her hand on his. "But I think Anton is likely ready to hear more. I got the feeling he isn't totally bought in to their agenda. Not anymore, at least. Killing that many people all at once really got to him." She shook her head. "If I can reach him with the truth, I certainly need to try."

"Sarah, that's so dangerous."

She nodded. "I know. But we can't let that stop our mission. God loves him just as much as he loves us."

Her words scared Luke, but also made him admire her all the more. She definitely had the stronger faith between them. He didn't know how he would be able to live without her. He realized that was now his biggest fear. Would he be able to turn that one over to God? He didn't know.

Sarah's brow wrinkled. "You don't think this alters Jason's eternal future, do you?"

"What? Just because he can't remember?"

She nodded as her brow furrowed with worry.

"No, Sarah, no. I don't think so. It's not like the Holy Spirit is taken away. I'm sure he's acting on Jason's behalf even now and will guide Jason back to his previous relationship with God."

Sarah's worried look slowly went away. "I sure hope you are right."

Luke smiled. "Besides, you see him almost every day. You'll be able to see how he's doing."

Sarah smiled back weakly and gave a slight nod. "Yeah, you're right." She looked into his eyes. "Thanks. You're always the more logical one."

Luke gave a short chuckle. "I'll keep your logic grounded as long as you keep my faith grounded."

She smiled, reached over, and gave him a quick kiss. "Deal."

Sarah turned and leaned back into him. He wrapped his arms around her. Having her back in this position made him feel at peace. Luke felt as though he could face anything as long as Sarah was with him.

"At some point, I need to check in with Oliver. He was checking on something for me."

Sarah shot up and turned to face him. "Luke, I'm sorry. I forgot."

"What's the matter? You forgot what?"

"What Oliver told me to tell you."

Luke's eyebrows rose.

"He knew Viktoria was in Paris and told her the parents of the man he was looking for—the man you told him about, I believe—were in the Paris prison. He wanted her to check on them."

Luke turned his head—stunned. "But you said the prison was empty. All had been killed." The reality then hit him. "You mean . . . "

Sarah nodded. "Luke, I'm so, so sorry."

Luke rubbed his hand across his mouth. "Maher talked about his parents the way Natalia talked about hers. He was so looking forward to finding them. I was looking forward to being a part of their reunion." He shook his head. "He's going to be heartbroken."

She turned back around, leaned into him, and pulled his arm across her midsection, kissing his hand in the process. "I'm truly sorry, Luke. Our world is pretty disappointing at times."

FORTY-EIGHT

NEO

The next few weeks sank back into a semblance of order. Both Luke and Sarah returned to work. Sarah somehow made peace with Ken, her supervisor, and with Kathleen. Larry, happy with Luke's findings on the asteroids, put both Scott and Brian on devising plans for extracting them from orbit and getting them to Mars. Luke knew they had already had several meetings with fellow scientists from NASA where both gravity tractors and ion thruster deflection strategies were being explored. Luke was put into a partnership with Dwayne on propulsion. The fuel had to get the six ships to the space station for their launch from there. Luke was first tasked with double-checking all of Dwayne's calculations to ensure nothing had been overlooked.

It felt to Luke as though everything around the Mars mission was speeding up. That would be expected, he guessed. It just seemed too fast in light of everything else going on.

Luke still saw Jared a few days a week in the gym. He seemed somewhat like his old self—just not as talkative and friendly as before. Still, he was willing to give some one-on-

one lessons to help Luke tighten his core. He seemed much more professional than before. Luke wasn't sure if that was due to Jared maturing in his profession, not wanting to mix business with personal life, or just wanting more distance between them.

Luke decided he would find out.

After one evening core-training session, Luke remained around after everyone else had left class. Jared was getting the room ready for the next class.

"Hey, Jared. Have any plans after your next class?"

Jared turned. "No, not really. Jason has to work late tonight to get ready for some type of orientation meeting tomorrow." He furrowed his brow. "Why?"

"I need your advice and wanted to know if I could meet you for dinner somewhere to talk about it." Luke held up his palms. "It doesn't have to be long. I just need your advice on something."

"Is this connected to our previous conversation?"

Luke shook his head. "No, unless you want it to be. This is something totally separate from that."

"Well, I guess so. What about Earth's Garden at 19:00? It's about equal distance between our apartments."

Luke patted Jared on the shoulder. "Sounds good. See you then."

He could feel Jared shooting him a suspicious look as he exited the exercise room, but he didn't look back. This at least told him Jared was now quite skeptical of him. Luke hoped bringing Jared in on his plan would help Jared understand nothing had changed on his side of their friendship.

* * * * *

Once Luke got home, he changed into something a little

more casual and walked to the restaurant. He arrived early and was seated at a table near the front window. This would give him a clear view of Jared arriving. He glanced through the menu as he waited. Almost everything here was considered organic. He chuckled. Earthy food with sky-high prices.

He looked up and saw Jared approaching the restaurant. Jared looked apprehensive. Hopefully, Luke could change that. Once Jared walked in, Luke waved to him. He stood as Jared approached, shook his hand, and gestured for him to sit. The waiter came over almost immediately and brought a large bottle of still water, pouring them each a glass, and then setting the bottle in an ice bucket. Since both were regular customers, they ordered immediately.

"Thanks for coming, Jared. I appreciate it," Luke said when the waiter stepped away.

Jared shrugged. "Sure. No problem. We've never done this before without our partners with us. So, what's up?"

Luke smiled. "I've made a decision, and you're the first to hear about it."

Jared jerked his head back. "You want me to be the first? Why?"

Luke turned his head. "Well, I'm surprised you're surprised. I consider you a good friend. I thought you considered me one, too. At least you used to. I don't want our previous conversation to change that. It certainly doesn't from my point of view."

Luke saw Jared's countenance relax a little. He gave a slight smile. "No, I don't want it to, either. So, what's up? It must be secretive." He laughed. "You planning on proposing or something?"

Jared waited for a response. All Luke could do was look back with raised eyebrows.

"Wait. That's it?" Jared sat up straighter. "You're serious?

You're going to propose to Sarah?" He put his hand over his open mouth. "Oh, that's so awesome. Congratulations."

"Well, I haven't asked yet, and she hasn't said yes yet, but thanks."

"I . . . I feel so honored you would confide in me this way." He turned up his brow. "But why? I mean, why do I need to know before you ask Sarah?"

"I need your advice—and help."

Jared held out his arms with a shrug. "OK. Sure." His arm almost hit the waiter in the leg as he approached. Jared was slightly embarrassed.

The waiter put their plates in front of them, smiled, and left.

As they ate, Luke continued. He pointed to Jared's hand. "Your ring is so unique. Where did you get it?"

Jared swallowed a bite of his panini as he looked at his ring, which exhibited a meshed pattern. "Oh, Jason and I had them designed by a friend of ours." He looked up at Luke. "Oh, you want to specially design a ring for Sarah?"

Luke nodded. "Can you introduce me to your friend?"

Jared nodded enthusiastically. "Oh, absolutely. He has some great ideas and a unique way to figure out what you want. You can mix and match various ideas he has."

"That sounds exactly like what I was looking for. I knew you would come through for me. Thanks, buddy."

Jared's smile broadened. "That's what Neo gets so excited about. He loves creating unique, one-of-a-kind creations." Jared looked at Luke and his expression suddenly turned serious. "Luke, I am really honored you would confide in me this way."

Luke shrugged. "That's what friends do, isn't it?"

Jared nodded. He shook his head. "I wasn't sure if that was what we really were anymore."

"And why would you think that?"

"Well, I haven't taken those steps you talked about. I know they are important to you. I didn't know how you would feel if I didn't take them."

Luke sighed and sat his sandwich down, then wiped his hands with his napkin. "Jared, I do consider them important—extremely important. I care about your future. Yet, I care about you as a person also. I can't force you, only encourage you."

Jared nodded. "Kill me with kindness, is that it?"

Luke laughed. "If that's how you want to put it. No matter what, you're still my friend. I hope you feel the same."

Jared didn't say anything, but gave a slight nod.

"So, how is your relationship with Jason?"

Jared shrugged. "He seems pretty much his usual self. Yet, there are times he seems different, somehow. It's hard to put it into words."

Luke nodded. He assumed the Holy Spirit was still working in Jason's life in spite of his reprogramming. He didn't want to tell Jared about that. Not yet, anyway, as that might freak him out at this time. It wouldn't make sense to Jared until he also took those steps. All Luke could do now was pray and look for opportunities.

"You said there were two reasons for meeting me. What's the second?"

Luke smiled. "I want you and Jason to help me let Sarah know I mean what I tell her."

Jared turned his head, a bit confused. "OK. But what do you mean? How can we help you do that?"

"Well, once I get a yes from her, I'll text you, and I want you to decorate her apartment with flowers, balloons, and candy, letting her know how happy I am about her decision."

Jared's hand went over his mouth again. "That . . . that is

so romantic. I would have just died if Jason had done something like that for me." He smiled. "Count me in." He waved his hands. "Don't even think about it any further. I'll get everything together."

Luke held up his hands. "Now don't go overboard."

Jared just smiled. "Don't worry. I can be tasteful and subtle, but still get the point across in a positive way."

Luke laughed. "OK. I trust you."

Jared turned serious again. "Thanks, Luke. That means a lot."

Their conversation turned more general: work, sports, workouts, and future goals. They both skipped dessert and had after-dinner coffee.

When they got up to leave, Jared shook Luke's hand. "I'll talk to Neo and text you his address. I'm sure he'll be able to help you out."

Luke nodded. "Once I have the ring, I'll let you know the day to get ready."

They walked out of the restaurant together and turned in opposite directions to head to their apartments. Luke hoped he could still be influential with Jared about his decision concerning the Messiah. At least they should now be on better terms moving forward to allow such opportunities.

* * * * *

Luke was surprised when he received Jared's text that same night. Neo also sent him a text. Either they were such good friends that Neo felt obligated, or Neo was desperately in need of business. He hoped it was the first.

The next day at work, Luke received another text from Neo. A cancellation had just occurred and Neo had an open appointment that evening if Luke wanted it. Luke texted back that he would take the slot. He was happy things were progressing quickly.

After work, Luke took a taxi to Unique Engagements. It was a small shop. As Luke looked around, he saw several small cases with rings. It took him a while to realize these were actually holograms and not real rings.

A man with a broad smile entered from the back. Luke nearly laughed. The guy had spiked green hair and a dragon tattoo down his left arm. Luke assumed it went onto his back, but the guy's muscle shirt didn't allow him to see it in full.

Luke walked forward. "Hi, you must be Neo."

Neo shook his hand. "And you must be Luke. Jared said you wanted something rather unique."

Luke nodded.

"Do you have clear expectations, or do you want suggestions?"

"Well, I think I'm in the second category. What do you suggest?"

Neo smiled. "You're not alone. I get many people who want something different from ordinary, but don't really know what that unique something is. I think I can help."

"Great. How do we get started?"

Neo motioned him to the counter. "I've developed several questions that help the program I've developed design what would be unique, but special to your fiancée as well."

Luke raised his eyebrows. "That sounds great."

Neo went through a series of questions. Luke was unsure why Neo asked so many that seemed unrelated to selecting a ring, but if it yielded something wonderful, he was OK with the process.

"OK. Now, based on your responses, I get that you want something very feminine, want a diamond, but not necessarily only a diamond. Sound about right?"

Luke nodded.

"Now, I'm going to show you a series of rings. You don't have to like everything about the rings I show. Just pick out the elements of each ring you like. If you don't like any of them, you can just tell me that as well."

Luke nodded again. This was far more detailed than he had ever dreamed. He spent the next hour going through numerous rings and styles. He picked out what he liked about each one. He had no idea how all of these choices would find their way onto one ring.

Neo smiled. "We're almost done."

Luke laughed. "I've never made so many artistic decisions before."

"You're doing great. I have to say, you're more decisive than some people I've walked through the process."

Luke twisted his neck in both directions, relieving the strain. "OK. What now?"

"The program I have will take all of the choices you've made, group the similarities into effects, and analyze the unique choices." Neo looked at his screen. "It seems the program has put together six potential choices." He held up his palm. "Now, don't think you have to choose one of these. Tell me what you like and we'll go from there."

Luke nodded and took a deep breath. The six choices came up together. There were two he didn't like at all, so Neo eliminated those. Two of them he liked, but he also really liked an element on each of the other two.

Neo nodded. "That's great." He entered a few additional instructions to the program. He looked back at Luke. "OK, we're now down to one. If there is something you don't like about it, we can still edit it, work with it. OK?"

Luke nodded. He couldn't wait to see what came up.

Rather than showing the ring on the computer tablet, this

one was presented as a 3-D hologram within a case. A "wow" escaped Luke's lips. He knew it was the one.

"So, what do you think?"

Luke nodded. "Neo, this is fantastic. The only difference would be, I think the petals of the cherry blossom should be a little pinker."

Neo nodded, made a few keystrokes, and pressed Enter. The hologram shimmered and came back into sharp detail. "How's that?"

Luke nodded. He looked up at Neo. "That is *it*. This is the one I want." Luke looked back at it again. The ring looked delicate, with three small, distinct bands, each of a different color of gold, and each joined at the base of the band. The middle band looped at the top, encasing a teardrop diamond. The tip of the diamond, however, was turned sideways with the point almost touching a cherry blossom, which tied the first and third bands together. The petals of the blossom were iridescent opal with a pink hue. Its leaves, made of jade, supported the blossom underneath and joined the two thin bands at the top next to the diamond. He just knew Sarah would love it.

Neo smiled. "Wonderful. Now we just need to discuss timing."

"And price."

Neo looked at Luke, his smile fading.

"I really love this, Neo, but I need to know if I can afford it." He gestured toward Neo. "So how much is it?"

Neo nodded. "I understand." He wrote down a number and passed the piece of paper to Luke. "If you can make full payment, and not over time, I can give a ten percent discount."

Luke tried to maintain a calm face. It was near the top of his price range. Not what he really wanted to pay, but he could swing it. Besides, Sarah was definitely worth it. "So, when can you have it available?"

"Well, I'm finishing up one order now. I have a policy not to start until full payment is made." He held up his palms. "Don't worry. It is fully guaranteed and comes with a lifetime warranty."

"What if I paid you right now?"

Neo's eyes widened. "Then I would say you're next on my list. I can have it two weeks from this Friday."

"Wonderful." Luke stuck out his hand and shook Neo's.

That night, Luke had a hard time sleeping. He was beyond excited. Two weeks. Wow. In two weeks, he would be engaged to be married to Sarah.

FORTY-NINE

Maher's Parents

Luke's wake-up announcement was persistent. He called "Snooze!" three times, but it then stopped accepting the command, which forced him to get up. All the adrenaline from the night before had definitely dissipated. As he headed to the shower, his phone rang. He had no idea who would be calling this early in the morning.

"Luke. Hi. I hope I didn't wake you."

"Maher. No. I'm up." He glanced at his clock. "It's awfully early there. Everything OK?"

"Well, I'm calling for two reasons. One—and the reason I'm up early—is I received a note from Larry to stop by the Houston Aerospace Engineering Center on my way to a conference in Washington, D.C. Where is the best place to stay there in Mars City? And second, I thought if you had any information about my parents, we could talk about that as well while I'm there."

Luke cringed on the inside. He had meant to talk to Maher before now. Perhaps this was best. He could do it in person.

"Maher, you're more than welcome to stay with me, if you

don't mind a sofa. That will give us a chance to talk as well."

"That sounds great, Luke. Thanks for the hospitality."

"Sure. No problem. If I don't see you, stop by my workstation before you leave."

"OK. I'll see you sometime tomorrow."

Luke disconnected and finished getting ready for work. He waited until lunch to talk with Sarah. He definitely wanted her with him when he gave Maher the news about his family. He looked for her at their usual cafeteria spot. She waved him over.

"Hey, there," she said. "It seems like I haven't seen you in a couple of days. I guess Larry is working you hard again."

Luke nodded. "I've been working with Dwayne in propulsion. It seems everything is speeding up. I guess it's a good thing, but I feel the pressure is getting more intense."

Sarah nodded. "Same for me. We're supposed to prepare for those chosen by the lottery in a week or so. I want to see if I can discover how they're targeting those chosen."

Luke shook his head slightly. "Sarah, please be careful. You know you're under scrutiny. Don't make it easy for them."

Sarah nodded. "I will. Don't worry."

Luke changed the subject. "Are you open tomorrow night? I got a call from Maher, and he will be here sometime tomorrow as he travels through on his way to D.C. He's going to stay at my place, so I thought I'd talk to him about his parents. Can you be there to help me with that?"

Sarah reached over and squeezed his hand. "Sure. That's a big burden to handle alone."

Luke gave a weak smile. "Thanks."

It would be difficult news, so having Sarah with him would be incredibly helpful.

* * * * *

The rest of Luke's day went uneventfully. Since Scott and Brian were working on the asteroid project, they would be hosting Maher in the work environment. They made arrangements for dinner and asked Luke to join them.

Luke didn't get a chance to say hello to Maher until they were at the restaurant. While there, the two of them spoke very little. Scott and Brian monopolized most of the conversation. Luke was OK with that. Maher was there for their project, and they deserved the spotlight. Plus, Maher would be staying at Luke's place for the night, so he would have plenty of opportunity to talk with him.

After dinner was over, Maher took the same taxi as Luke. Maher leaned back in his seat and gave a big sigh.

Luke laughed. "Long day, huh?"

Maher smiled. "Yeah. I'm not used to working during the day."

Luke laughed even harder.

In just ten minutes, they were at Luke's apartment. Sarah was waiting for them.

"Maher, this is my girlfriend, Dr. Sarah Morgan. She's one of the physicians at the Aerospace Engineering Center."

Maher shook her hand and bowed slightly. "Very nice meeting you." He smiled. "You're more beautiful than my mind envisioned based on Luke's description."

Sarah's cheeks blushed as she smiled back.

Luke curled the corner of his mouth. "Thanks, Maher, for pointing out my inadequacy in front of my girlfriend."

Maher smiled, then winked. "Need to work on your creative side."

Luke shook his head and gestured that they all have a seat. Maher sat in the plush chair and Luke sat next to Sarah on the sofa.

Luke jumped in, as difficult as it was. "Maher, I know it's

getting late and you want to know what we found out about your parents. So I thought we'd get right to it."

Maher nodded. "Thanks, Luke." He leaned forward, rubbing his hands together. "So, what did you find out?"

Luke looked at Sarah and then back at Maher.

Maher propped his elbows on his knees. "Uh-oh. That's not a good sign."

Luke shook his head. "There's no good way to say this." Luke paused for one more brief moment, then let it spill out. "Maher, your parents are dead."

Maher dropped his head and slowly shook it. He looked back at Luke. "I knew that was a possibility." He shrugged. "A good possibility." His eyes seemed to moisten, but no tears came. "Any idea what happened and when?"

Luke bit his upper lip. He regretted this part. "Maher, it was very recent. They were actually put through Mercy Farewell."

Maher's eyes widened. "What? That's . . . that's impossible. I should have been notified. They . . . they would need my permission."

Sarah shook her head. "I'm really sorry. But relatives of prisoners don't need to be notified if Community decides they should undergo Mercy Farewell."

Maher looked from one of them to the other. "Prisoners?" He shook his head. "What are you talking about? Why would they be prisoners?"

Now Sarah's eyes began watering. "There's a prison just outside of Paris. This is a place where those immune to the Invocation wafer have, over time, been held. Some were held for decades."

Maher furrowed his brow. "But why were my parents singled out?"

Sarah shook her head. "They weren't."

Maher just stared. "I don't understand."

Luke leaned forward. "Maher, everyone—all two thousand people in the prison—were killed."

Maher's eyes widened. "What? Why?"

"Maher, I was trying to tell you this earlier, back on Mauna Kea. There is a conspiracy going on. Well, it's started. Most of these individuals were elderly. The targeting of free immunes is now starting. They plan to fill the prisons with them—and these will be the ones they send to Mars."

Maher's head jerked back. "But the lottery . . . "

Luke shook his head. "A smoke screen, Maher. A smoke screen."

Maher wiped his mouth with his hand. "This sounds so crazy—so unbelievable. If I didn't know you, I'd call you crazy."

"Maher, it confirms what I talked to you about in Hawaii. We're all in danger now. All three of us are immunes. We have to be careful."

"So, what do you suggest we do?"

"The best thing you can do is accept what I said about God, what he has done for us and how he has provided for our future." Luke slightly opened his hands. "I know that may sound out there, but it's not more out there than what is going on around us."

"You mean this conspiracy?"

Luke nodded. "The Invocation wafer keeps everyone in line, and the Mars mission takes most of those immune and who can question what they do . . . well, it takes them off the planet."

Maher still looked confused. "Do you really believe that?"

"Maher, we have actually heard them say that."

"Them?"

Luke shook his head. "It's going to sound crazy again, but there is an elite group of individuals controlling all of this.

We've overheard them discussing and planning this game plan."

Maher sat back. "Wow. That's a lot to take in. I guess I need to take all that you've said and given me more seriously."

Luke nodded. "Just don't take too long to make that decision."

Maher nodded. "I may have more questions for you later."

"Anytime, Maher. Anytime."

Sarah stood. "Well, I need to get back to my apartment. It's getting late."

Maher stood and shook her hand. "Thanks, Sarah. I appreciate the information."

Sarah gave a small smile and nodded. She then gave him a small hug. Luke walked her to the door. He gave her a quick kiss and she left.

"Maher, there's bedding in the ottoman. Use whatever you need, and if you need anything else, just let me know."

Maher shook his hand. "Thanks, Luke—for everything. I have a late flight tomorrow, so I may sleep in, if that's OK."

"Sure. I'll say my good-bye now, then." He gave Maher a hug. "Don't be a stranger."

As Luke got ready for bed, he prayed Maher would make this important decision—and quickly.

FIFTY

PROPOSAL

Luke started making plans for his proposal to Sarah. He thought about the things that were most important to her and how he could make the occasion extremely special.

Luke knew he needed to talk to Jeremy. He looked at his watch and did the mental calculation in his head. It would be about 08:00 in Shanghai: not too early to call, and yet likely he would reach Jeremy before his day would be in full swing. He made the call.

"Luke, is that you?"

"Hey, Jeremy. I thought you'd be home by now."

Jeremy laughed. "I found out why we got such a property deal here."

"Oh?"

"The restaurant is very near Dishui Lake, a place Shanghai has tried to develop and make popular for some time. Ever since we opened, it seems businesses have clamored to move into this area. Many have begged Natalia to be their architect. It seems we may have another Mars City episode going on. Five housing projects have already started, and their occupancy is already sold out. A man-made beach, a health spa, and more restaurants are already planned for construction."

Luke laughed. "Oh, the pain of being popular."

Jeremy chuckled. "Well, better that than the alternative. So, what's up?"

"Well, this may sound strange, but can I use your penthouse for a night?"

"Sure. But why?"

"You have to promise me you'll keep it secret."

"OK. Sounds ominous."

"Jeremy, I mean it. You can't tell anyone."

"OK. OK. Are you in trouble?"

"What? No, no. Nothing like that."

"Then, what?"

Luke sighed. "I want to propose to Sarah. She loves the nebulae on the city's high-rises. The view from your penthouse is the best in the city."

There was silence. "Jeremy? Are you still there?"

"I'm here, buddy. I just never thought I'd see the day. Congratulations."

"Well, she hasn't said yes yet."

"You don't have any doubts, do you?"

"Well, no. But I'll feel better after it's a sure thing."

Jeremy laughed. "Yeah, I know that feeling. Listen, let me know what evening you want to do this, and I'll have my chef prepare an exquisite meal for the occasion."

"Oh, thanks, Jeremy. That wasn't why I called, though."

"I know, but it's the least I can do. I promise you, it will be a very memorable meal."

"Well, it's this coming Friday night. Is that too soon for you to prepare?"

"Not at all. Don't worry. All you have to do is show up. I'll have the meal served—on the balcony, I presume."

"Yeah, that would be great."

"Once the dessert is served, I'll have everyone leave so you can be totally alone with Sarah."

"You're the best, Jeremy. Thanks."

"I'm going to record that sentence."

"Oh man. I'll never live that one down."

"Absolutely. Never."

"Remember your promise."

"Not even Natalia?"

"I'll text you once Sarah says yes. You can tell her then as she will likely want to talk to Sarah almost immediately. I just don't want anything to leak out."

"Understood. You've got it, buddy. No one knows until I hear back from you."

Luke ended the conversation and sat back with a smile. It was all coming together so well. He got dressed and headed to work. He made up excuses not to see Sarah. He didn't want any of his actions to give anything away. He sent her word to be ready for dinner at Continental Drift on Friday evening, and that he would have to meet her at the restaurant. She knew Larry had him extremely busy, so she would likely not think anything strange of that arrangement.

Luke got off work early on Friday and went to pick up the ring. All sorts of things went through his mind as he neared Unique Engagements: What if it wasn't ready? What if it wasn't the ring he had picked out? What if the design was somehow changed?

He opened the door to the shop with some trepidation. He felt his heart rate increasing and his palms becoming sweaty.

Neo came out with a huge smile. "Today's the day!" he said.

Luke nodded. "Everything ready?"

Neo waved him over to the counter. He reached under it, pulled out a small box, and handed it to Luke. "As you requested."

Luke looked at Neo with a smile. He took the box, sucked in a deep breath, and then opened it. He looked from the ring to Neo. A broad smile came across his face. "Neo, it's gorgeous. It looks even better than the hologram you showed me."

Neo smiled. "Well, I try to make reality better than a simulation."

Luke laughed. "Well, you succeeded."

"I'm so glad you're pleased."

"Oh, very much."

Luke shook Neo's hand, left the shop, and headed for his apartment. All he had to do now was shower, dress, and meet Sarah at the restaurant. He now knew what the proverbial butterflies in the stomach felt like. He had been nervous before, but nothing compared to this. It was a mixture of nervousness, excitement, and apprehension.

When Sarah entered the restaurant's front door, it was almost like the world went into slow motion—to Luke, only she existed. What she wore was so apropos for this night. Her dress was an elegant shade of light pink with a white lace fabric on top. Her dangly earrings were an iridescent opal, and her hair was up in a casual side bun on the back of her head with a few free hair strands on the side opposite the bun creating a balance that highlighted her face.

A bright smile lit up Sarah's face as she saw Luke. He gave her a quick kiss of welcome. "You're absolutely gorgeous."

She didn't say anything, but gave a coy smile. "What floor are we going to tonight?"

Luke smiled. "Top floor." He led her through the bar area.

"Oh, you want a drink first?"

He just kept walking and led her to the elevator in the back.

Her eyes widened. "I didn't know Jeremy and Natalia were back."

Luke didn't say anything. He put in his code and the elevator went to the top floor. Sarah cocked her head slightly when Luke opened the door without knocking, but didn't say anything.

Soft music played as they entered. Sarah looked around as if expecting Jeremy and Natalia to appear. Luke guided her to the balcony. Rather than the usual table with an umbrella, there was a table for two, elegantly decorated with a white tablecloth which had sequins that twinkled from the light of candles lit all around the balcony area.

Sarah looked at Luke with mouth slightly open. "What is this?"

Luke gestured toward the table. "Dinner."

Sarah laughed. "Thanks for the clarification. But why?"

"There's a spectacular view of the city from here, so I thought it would be nice to take advantage of it."

Luke pulled Sarah's chair out and had her sit. A waiter came out with a soup course and set it before them. The waiter pulled the covers off each bowl simultaneously. Steam rose from the bowl, turned a fiery red, and then ignited into actual flame.

Sarah gasped and then giggled. "Wow. That was unexpected."

The waiter bowed and left the balcony.

Sarah took a sip of the soup. Her eyes closed and an "mmm" escaped her lips. "I'm not sure why I'm still awed by these concoctions," she said, "but I am."

Luke nodded. "Jeremy has certainly perfected awe and good taste."

Luke was amazed when the waiter reappeared exactly as they completed the soup course. He returned a minute later with their entrée. Luke looked at Sarah. They both raised their eyebrows. There were medallions of steak around a mound of mashed potatoes looking something like a volcano. On the sides of the "volcano" there looked to be sprinkles of paprika strategically placed to look like areas where lava had flowed downward. Surrounding the outside of the entire dish was a green ring of what looked to be creamed spinach.

After the waiter set their plates before them, he dropped a small pellet of something into the center of the potato "volcano." In a matter of seconds, smoke came out, and then what looked to be a red gravy flowed from the volcano, down the potatoes, and settled between the steak medallions, which now looked like islands in a gravy sea.

The waiter smiled. "Bon appétit." And then he turned and left.

"Luke, this is exquisite. The meat is so tender, and the gravy sets everything off beautifully."

Luke nodded. Jeremy had outdone himself. Seeing all of the nebulae throughout the city as they ate really set the proper mood for the meal—and for the finale he had planned.

Luke kept the conversation light and didn't go into all of the issues they were facing. He wanted this to be a pleasant experience they could both look back on without remembering any negative elements.

When the waiter removed their entrée plates, he brought out tea and then their dessert. It looked to be simple cheesecake, but Luke knew to never think of anything Jeremy did as simple.

The waiter left after he set their dessert before them. A few minutes later, Luke heard the front door close. They were all alone.

Sarah looked at Luke with raised eyebrows. "It hasn't done anything yet. Is it just simple cheesecake?"

Luke laughed. "I don't know. Expect the unexpected."

They both took a bite. Nothing happened, but the texture

was light and creamy. It was truly the best cheesecake Luke had ever tasted. It looked as if Sarah thought so, too, as she closed her eyes after the first bite.

After the second bite, she giggled. "The strawberry sauce is on the inside."

Luke looked at his plate. Sure enough, a red liquid oozed from the cheesecake. It wasn't much, just enough to add a light fruity taste to the cake's creaminess.

After finishing the cheesecake, Sarah dabbed her lips with her napkin. "Luke, this was really a most awesome evening. The food, the ambiance, the view . . . " She shook her head. "I don't think it could have been better. Thank you."

"What if it could?"

Sarah cocked her head slightly as if asking what he meant.

"Be better," Luke said.

Sarah smiled. "Oh, you have something else up your sleeve?"

Luke stood, not taking his eyes off hers. Her eyebrows raised and a smile crept across her face. He came to her side, lowered himself to one knee, and reached into his coat pocket. He pulled out the small case.

Sarah's eyes widened. Her hands went to her mouth, which went agape.

"Sarah, I love you with all of my heart. I can't imagine my life without you in it." He opened the case. "Sarah, will you marry me?"

Sarah gasped. Her eyes watered. "Luke," she said softly. "It's . . . it's beautiful . . . so beautiful."

Luke took the ring, raised her left hand, and placed the ring on her finger. She looked at him as a couple of tears welled over her bottom eyelids and ran down her cheek.

He reached up and wiped them away. "So, what is your answer?"

She looked into his eyes. "Oh, Luke. Yes. My answer is yes."

He wrapped his arms around her and hugged her tightly. He then kissed her passionately, holding her head in his hands, and pressing his lips into hers. He prolonged the kiss. He felt her go slightly weak. She held to him more tightly and pressed herself into him.

After a few moments, their lips separated. "Luke, you really surprised me tonight." She gave a chuckle. "A very good surprise. It couldn't have been better."

He lifted her to her feet and began to dance with her. She put her head on his shoulder and let him guide them across the balcony. After several minutes, they returned to the table. He quickly sent texts to Jared and Jeremy.

Sarah kept looking at her ring. "Luke, this is so unique. How did you come up with it?"

Luke smiled. "I can't give away my secrets now, can I?"

Sarah's smile continued to beam. "I guess not. But I absolutely adore it."

After about another hour of conversation, dancing, kissing, and Sarah admiring her ring, Luke led her to the elevator. She leaned into him, her head on his chest all the way to the ground floor. Once in the taxi, she continued to do the same while looking at her ring at the same time.

"Luke, it picks up the light so brilliantly. It seems to sparkle constantly."

Luke smiled. He was extremely glad she adored it.

He led her to her apartment door. They kissed, once again quite passionately. He smiled. "We can't stay here all night, can we?"

She smiled. "That wouldn't be so bad, would it?"

"We can continue tomorrow. I'll pick you up for breakfast."

"OK." She turned and unlocked her door. She entered, blew him a kiss, and closed it softly.

Luke gave a long, contented sigh. The night went just as he had hoped. He turned to go, but Sarah's door flew open.

"Luke!" Her eyes watered. "This is priceless." She grabbed his arm and pulled him in. "When did you have time to do this?"

He looked around. Jared had done an unbelievable job decorating her apartment so tastefully. There were cherry blossoms in several different vases, there were heart-shaped balloons with "I love you" on them, and regular balloons were everywhere. There was a trail of cherry blossoms that led to the bedroom and were scattered over the bed itself. Above the bed hung a large balloon which said, "You are my life."

"Luke, this night has been absolutely perfect." She leaned in and kissed him—once again quite passionately.

He lost his balance and they landed on the bed with cherry blossoms scattering around them. She didn't stop, and Luke got caught up in the emotion. He felt heat rising within him, his heart raced, and his adrenaline surged. He pulled away from the passionate kiss.

"Sarah, if we don't stop now, I don't know that I can resist."

She put her forehead to his. "Yeah, same for me. Thanks for being the stronger one for us." Her eyes looked into his. "I love you so much."

"That's good, or else I'd have to take back the ring."

She laughed and gave him a hug. "You're stuck with me now."

He whispered in her ear. "Just the place I want to be."

He stood and helped her off the bed. He kissed her once more and left her apartment. He let out a long breath once she closed the door. He couldn't wait to get married. He didn't know if he could continue to control himself in such situations. A cold shower might be in order right now, in fact.

FIFTY-ONE

Wedding Interrupted

Luke stood just outside Sarah's apartment. He raised his hand to knock, but paused. *It did happen last night, right?* It wasn't just a dream that had felt real? A lot of stranger things had happened. Luke shook his head. He had to snap out of it. She surely wouldn't marry him if she thought he was losing his mind. Luke looked at his watch. Ten o'clock, just as he had promised. He knocked; Sarah opened. A bright, adoring smile greeted him. No, it had not been a dream. He couldn't remember her ever looking at him like that.

"So, where do you want to go?"

She pulled him into her apartment. "I made breakfast for you."

"Really?"

"I did. Have a seat."

On his plate were eggs, cheese, strawberries, and a large cinnamon roll.

"Sarah, this is awesome."

Luke dug in. There was nothing special about such a meal, but he couldn't remember anything tasting as wonderful. As they ate, he caught Sarah periodically looking at her ring.

"Still satisfied with it, are you?"

Sarah smiled. "I think I woke up every hour last night adoring it."

Luke laughed. "I guess I did good."

Sarah nodded. "You did good. Natalia said to tell you that as well. I texted her a picture of the ring last night."

Luke raised his eyebrows.

"She called right after I sent the picture."

Luke smiled. "Glad she approves. So, how do you want to proceed from here?"

Sarah tilted her head. "What do you mean?"

"Where and when are we going to get married?"

Sarah put her fork down and pushed her plate away. "What do you want to do?"

"The earlier the better from my standpoint. Our work is going to get crazier the longer we wait. The danger is also likely to increase the closer we get to the Mars launch. If we're together, we can watch over each other better."

Sarah laughed. "Well, that's the logical side of the matter."

Luke cocked his head. "You don't agree?"

Sarah shook her head. "No, I agree. It just sounded so methodical rather than magical."

Luke gave her a smirk. "Don't worry, I can turn methodical into magical. How do you want the wedding to go?"

"I want to incorporate baptism into our wedding."

"Really? Why?"

Sarah shrugged. "Well, we now have the Holy Spirit. I think this is the next step. It would be good to start our lives together doing what Scripture tells us to do."

Luke nodded. "OK, let me think for a minute." Luke thought about all their friends, Natalia's parents, and who could best travel and who couldn't. He thought about baptism, who should help with it, and where it should occur.

Sarah cleared the table while Luke thought through their options.

"OK, here's the game plan." Sarah came back to the table and sat, eyebrows raised in expectation. Luke raised his palms. "Feel free to correct as I go, but here's how I see it."

Sarah nodded. "OK, Mister Methodical, give me the magic."

He smiled. "Picture being on a beach. There are two large white tents for changing. Matteo leads us into the water to baptize us and gives us a blessing. You change into a white wedding dress carrying pink roses. I change into a white tux. We exchange our vows with our friends beside us. We change back into casual clothes and have a party on the beach going into the night."

Sarah gave an approving smile. "That sounds pretty nice. There's only one problem."

"Oh?"

"Matteo can't come back to the States for such a wedding."

Luke nodded. "That's why we're getting married in Shanghai."

Sarah's eyes widened. "Shanghai?" She opened her mouth to say something, then stopped herself. She put her hand to her chin. "Actually, that sounds pretty nice."

Luke smiled. "OK, let's make a short list of who we want to invite. I'll contact Jeremy to help get things set up there. How is a month from today?"

"A month? That doesn't sound like very long."

"Well, considering most people just go to the courthouse on the spur of the moment, or just move in together, it's rather lengthy."

Sarah shrugged. "Well, you have a point. I can have Natalia help me with getting a dress. I'm sure Jeremy will help with catering, so there's not much to actually do, I guess."

"The hardest part will be getting time off. But I have two weeks of vacation left."

Sarah nodded. "Same with me." She laughed. "If I invite Kathleen, then she can't get mad at me."

Luke chuckled. "Strategy is everything."

* * * * *

From that point on, life turned into a blur. Since the wedding would occur on a Saturday, many from work agreed to come for a long weekend. Most extended it even further. Sarah was right. By inviting their bosses, they were not given a hard time with requesting two weeks. Luke and Sarah went to Shanghai a week early to get everything ready. By that point, Jeremy and Natalia had their penthouse completed, so that's where everyone met.

There were hugs all around. Luke noticed the layout of Jeremy's new place looked similar to the one in Houston, but the décor appeared more Asian-themed, and the balcony circled the top of the entire building, not just one side. Matteo and Xiaofeng seemed to look even younger than the last time Luke had seen them. Apparently, working and being with family was sitting well with them. Oliver and Viktoria arrived as well.

After talking and enjoying a few appetizers, the conversation turned to the topic of the wedding. Natalia had everyone come onto the balcony. She pointed toward the east. "The round water area is called Dishui Lake. You can see a new beach has been created. That's where the wedding will occur."

Matteo patted Luke's shoulder. "Natalia gained approval for a private gathering. It's a public beach, but we were able to secure it from 16:00 onward. I'll baptize you there."

Luke wrapped his arm around Matteo's shoulders. "I really

appreciate you doing this for us."

"Oh, it's my pleasure. I'm happy to do it."

Natalia turned to Sarah. "There are two great dress shops downtown. I took the liberty of making a few selections for you to try on. That may save some time." She held up her hands to ensure Sarah didn't feel pressured. "If you don't like them, don't feel obligated."

Sarah laughed. "Natalia, if you like them, I'm sure they are absolutely gorgeous." She gave her a hug. "I really appreciate you taking the time to do that for me."

Natalia smiled. "For you and Lukey?" She shook her head. "It's no trouble at all."

When the evening came to a close, Luke, Sarah, Oliver, and Viktoria accompanied Matteo and Xiaofeng back to the living area under the lab. Everything looked exactly as it had before.

* * * * *

Saturday came faster than expected. The women left around noon to get everything ready inside Sarah's tent. Natalia hired two beauticians to help get Sarah ready after the baptism ceremony. Everyone else got ready beforehand.

Around 17:00, the guys headed to the beach. It wasn't far from Jeremy's high-rise. Luke put his tux and change of clothes in his tent. He thanked everyone who made it to the wedding from work. He thanked Scott, Brian, and Larry for coming. Brian had brought Carmella. She looked more beautiful than he remembered.

When Scott introduced Carmella to Jason and Jared, Luke grabbed Brian's arm. "Hey, buddy, how's it going with Carmella? I didn't know you were bringing her." He raised his eyebrows a couple of times. "Must be getting serious." He nudged him in his side.

Brian laughed. "Maybe. We thought we'd take this opportunity you gave us to turn it into another holiday for us. We've never been to Asia."

Luke smiled. "Glad I could help out."

Kathleen came up and gave him a kiss on his cheek. "I'm happy for you, Luke. You be good to her now, you hear?"

Luke smiled and nodded. He shook Ken's hand. "Thanks for being so accommodating, Ken."

Sarah's boss smiled. "Couldn't pass up a chance to visit Asia, now could I?"

Jason and Jared approached. Luke gave each a heartfelt hug, thanked them for coming, and introduced them to Ken. As they talked, he noticed Maher talking with Jeremy.

He excused himself and walked up and gave a hug to Maher. "Maher, thanks for coming. It really means a lot."

Maher shook his head. "Wouldn't miss it. I'm really happy for you, Luke." He pointed behind Luke. "Here comes your happiness now."

Sarah walked out with Matteo. Luke took her hand and smiled at her. She smiled back. They were both wearing jeans and a pullover. Matteo motioned for everyone to gather in close.

"OK, everyone," Matteo began. "Marriage seems somewhat passé these days. Yet Luke and Sarah have decided to make this day a very special day in their lives. In addition, they have decided to add something else to their special day. Immersion, in olden times, represented purification. Today, they are going to publically demonstrate what the Holy Spirit has done for them on the inside. That is a term that may be foreign to many of you. They will be happy to explain this to you after their ceremony, if you so choose."

Both Sarah and Luke walked with Matteo into the lake. He first turned to Sarah. "Sarah, it has been my honor to get to know you and see what a wonderful person you are. Because of your faith in the one true God, I baptize you in the name of the Father, Son, and Holy Spirit." He then immersed her under the water of the lake, and Sarah stood back up.

Luke reached over and kissed her. The audience clapped. Luke knew most of them didn't understand what they were witnessing. He hoped what they saw would give him a chance to explain it to them later. It was a risk since the government didn't really sanction belief in God. Yet he felt close to everyone, so the risk seemed low.

Sarah then stood while Matteo turned to Luke. "Luke, it has been my honor to get to know you and see how you have matured in spiritual matters. Because of your faith in the one true God, and you now know what *F-S-H-S* means in your life . . . " Luke smiled and nodded. "I baptize you in the name of the Father, Son, and Holy Spirit." Luke felt Matteo submerge him under the water. He stood back up. Sarah reached over and kissed him. He hugged her with a tight squeeze. "Thanks, Sarah," he said. "This was an excellent suggestion."

She whispered, "Now comes the hard part. I have to get beautiful in less than an hour."

He shook his head. "No, that's not hard at all."

He took her by the hand and they waded back to shore. Matteo followed. While Jeremy entertained the guests with drinks and appetizers, Luke and Matteo went to get changed in his tent while Sarah went to change in hers. Natalia, Viktoria, and the beauticians went with her. She blew Luke a kiss. He smiled and blew a kiss back.

Both Luke and Matteo changed into their tuxedos. It didn't take long for Luke to get ready. He helped Matteo with his cummerbund, and Matteo helped put Luke's pink rose boutonniere in place.

"Luke, I'm proud of you for having a ceremony like this. So

many people these days take the easy way out without giving it the proper attention and respect such a step deserves."

"Thanks, Matteo. You and Xiaofeng have been inspirations to me and Sarah."

Matteo smiled. "Well, I'm glad we can be used in such a way."

Both of them left the tent and joined the rest of the wedding party. It took quite a while for Sarah to emerge from her tent. Luke took this time to talk and joke with many in attendance. He felt the time pass relatively quickly.

Natalia came out. She nodded to Matteo. "We're ready."

Matteo went to where two tiki torches were placed in the sand. The poles were decorated with white orchids and pink roses. The wedding party formed a path from Matteo toward Sarah's tent. Luke walked to the tent to retrieve his bride-to-be. Natalia and Viktoria held back the tent flap and Sarah exited.

Luke smiled. "Sarah, you are gorgeous." He meant it—in every way. Her dress, all white and simple in design, looked beautiful at the same time. There were strategically placed sequins that twinkled from the torchlight. The uneven hem at the bottom added a flair of contemporary. Her hair, arranged in ringlets, had a small laced veil woven into her hair at the back, and this draped down her back. She had a small bouquet of pink roses and white orchids.

Sarah looked back at Luke. He couldn't get over her smile, which seemed to show her adoration for him. "You look pretty dapper yourself, Luke. I didn't know white would make your eyes even more blue than normal." She ran her hand through his hair and smiled. The breeze off the water was likely making it look more disheveled than normal.

Luke held out his arm and walked with Sarah to where Matteo stood. The sun was setting and the lake reflected the reds and golds of the sunset.

As he stood there admiring Sarah and thankful for this moment, something caught Luke's eye. It looked like a piece of confetti floating down in a twisting, turning fashion. Another déjà vu moment hit him. *Where did this come from?* One side, apparently metallic, seemed to catch the light of the setting sun and appeared to twinkle. Luke tried to ignore it, but he couldn't help glancing at it. He found he couldn't keep his eyes off it.

Sarah got a curious look on her face. She followed his gaze and she, too, watched this piece of confetti descend. It landed with the nonmetallic side up—on her shoulder. There seemed to be something written on it. Luke retrieved it from her shoulder and looked more closely. There were four letters: *T-U-L-E.*

Sarah gave him a puzzled look. He showed it to her and then put it in his coat pocket. She whispered, "What does it mean?"

Luke shook his head. "More mystery. We'll look at it later."

Luke put that mystery out of his mind and focused on Sarah. He smiled and took her hand in his. Matteo began the ceremony with brief remarks, and within minutes, Luke found himself speaking.

"Sarah, with God as my witness, I choose you as my wife to love and cherish from this day forward no matter what comes our way. I promise to love and support you all of my life." He then placed a tri-gold band on the finger that already held the engagement ring. The golden band matched the other ring perfectly.

Sarah shared a few words, and then did the same for Luke in giving him a tri-gold band. They both turned and faced Matteo.

He held up his hands. "In the sight of Almighty God, you are pronounced husband and wife. May God prosper you and may you glorify him all of your days." He turned to Luke. "Now kiss your bride."

Luke looked into Sarah's eyes, leaned in, and gave a very loving kiss. Not too passionate since they were in public, but passionate enough that Sarah would know his love for her, and one which roused the crowd to applaud.

Everyone joined around them and gave hugs and kisses and congratulations. A couple of bonfires were lit to provide more light. A band started playing. Everyone danced, ate, and talked. This went on for several hours.

Both Luke and Sarah danced with nearly everyone there. As Luke retrieved Sarah from Ken, she looked at him and replied, "Luke, this has to be my last dance."

"Oh, a party pooper already?"

She smiled. "I've found dancing in sand makes my calves hurt." She patted his chest. "I'm willing to still talk with everyone, but let me change into something more beach appropriate."

His eyes lit up. "Oh, putting on the string bikini already?"

She gave a smirk. "Hardly. Maybe some capris and a pullover."

Luke laughed. "All right. I'll be right here."

He watched her head to her tent. Jeremy came up with Oliver and they started talking.

After some time, Natalia approached the three men. "Where's your better half?"

Luke turned his head sideways.

Jeremy laughed. "Get used to it, Luke. From now on you're the worse half."

Natalia pushed Jeremy's shoulder. "Oh stop. It's just a saying."

Luke smiled. "She went to change." He looked at his watch. "But that was some time ago. She should be changed by now."

Jeremy pushed Luke toward the tent. "That's something else to get used to."

Luke laughed. "Let me go see what's taking her so long."

He hesitated at the tent door. "Sarah?" He didn't hear any response. It then dawned on him. He didn't have to wait outside anymore. She was his wife. Waiting was over. He smiled as he entered. "Sarah, need any help?"

He looked around. The tent was empty. *Odd.* Why didn't she come back out to him? Where would she have gone? Maybe someone else saw her. He turned to exit, but then saw the back of the tent blowing in the breeze. He walked over. The tent had been cut. He walked through the back end and frantically looked around, but didn't see anyone. He ran back out to the others.

"Sarah! Sarah's gone!"

Jeremy turned. His smiled quickly faded after seeing Luke's panicked face. He grabbed Luke's shoulders. "Luke, what's wrong?"

"Sarah's gone."

"What?" He squinted. "Are you sure? She's probably here somewhere."

Luke shook his head. "No. I think she's been taken. The back of the tent was ripped."

Jeremy walked back with Luke to the tent. Luke pointed out the large tear in the tent. They walked through. Luke saw a figure in the distance.

"Hey!!"

The man turned and began to run from them.

Luke took off after him. Jeremy followed. The man stumbled in the sand and fell. Luke took the opportunity to gain on him and tackle him as the man stood to run again. They wrestled until Jeremy came up and helped Luke restrain him.

Oliver arrived and helped Jeremy hold the man down while

Luke faced him to get a good look. The man looked familiar.

"Bring him over into the light. I think I know him."

Oliver and Jeremy dragged the man where Luke could get a better look with more light.

"Anton? What are you doing here?"

"I was too late. I warned her. I warned her."

Luke had a tortured look on his face. "What are you talking about?"

"I told her not to marry you. I warned her not to marry you. Now they've taken her."

Oliver wrenched Anton's arm upward. "*Who* took her?"

Anton groaned. "Hurting me won't change anything. I came to warn her they were coming."

Luke grabbed Anton's face with his hand. "Who, Anton!?"

"The Illumi-Alliance."

Luke eyes shot to Oliver, who shook his head.

Luke knew that meant Viktoria wasn't contacted. That also worried him, but he focused back on Anton. "Why do they want her?"

"She's a pure immune. You're a pure immune. They can't have you two together. If you have children, it will destroy their plan."

Luke shook his head. "What? You're not making any sense."

"Immunity comes through the mother. Two perfect immunes will have perfect immune offspring. The two of you will start a cascade of widespread immunity. They can't—they won't—stand for that."

"Where are they taking her, Anton? I know you know!" Luke was in full panic.

"To Mercy Farewell."

READ WHAT HAPPENS NEXT...

And tell us what you think
at *randydockens.com*

Advance orders available at Amazon and Barnes & Noble in June 2018

CAN LUKE AND HIS FRIENDS CONTINUE TO EVADE CAPTURE?

Luke and his friends discover a prophecy that leads them into even further danger. It's a message too important to keep to themselves. But how do they let others know what they have found without being discovered? They try to live their lives as normally as possible—but at the same time to disseminate the information they've discovered to as many people as possible. The question becomes: are their friends true friends when it comes to such sensitive information—information that could put them in prison in a heartbeat, if discovered?

They find themselves in a place they didn't think they would be—and on a mission they never would have believed.

Also check out
questioneveryoneshouldask.com/blog1/

Sample chapter from Book Three of
The Coded Message Trilogy

T-U-L-E

Search for Sarah

Luke's knees went weak and he literally sat in the sand with a thud. He stared at Anton for several seconds. "What? What did you say?"

Anton cleared his throat. "I'm sorry, Luke. I tried to warn her. She didn't tell you anything?"

"She said you gave her a warning that Philippe and Simone were gathering immunes and she was likely at the top of their list because of Simone's jealousy."

Anton's eyes widened. "And that's all she told you?"

Luke nodded.

Anton looked down and shook his head. He looked back up at Luke. "I told her Simone knew she was a pure immune. That made her extremely dangerous in their eyes, and they would do anything to keep her from being with another pure immune." Anton's eyes began to water. "Believe me, I emphasized the word *anything*."

Luke put his hand to his forehead. He couldn't believe this was happening.

"After killing all those people, I told her nothing was past them."

Luke's gaze shot to Anton. "*Them?* Wasn't it you who killed all those people? All those innocent people." Luke pointed his index finger at Anton. "You, Anton. Not them."

"They commanded it." His tone was now extremely defensive.

Luke's anger rose, making his voice louder than he meant it to be. "And you do everything they tell you to do?"

Anton shot a hot gaze back at Luke and shouted, "Yes." Spittle flew from his mouth. He stared in silence for a few seconds and then sighed. Quietly, he replied, "That's the way it works."

Luke shot to his feet and turned several times. "There . . . there has to be something we can do." He pointed at Anton again. "Something *you* can do."

Anton didn't look up, but simply shook his head.

Luke's hands went to his head as he turned in frustration. Suddenly, he stopped. "Wait. They can't do anything without my permission. She's married. They have to have my permission to initiate Mercy Farewell." For a brief moment, he seemed to feel relief. "It's protocol! They can't do it."

Anton looked up at Luke as if sorry for someone who just didn't grasp the gravity of a situation. "Luke, you think they care about protocol now?" He shook his head. "Their minds are made up. There's nothing anyone can do."

Luke was over and on top of Anton in a split-second, holding him up with his hand, squeezing his throat. "Well, you'd better come up with an answer."

"Luke . . . Luke," Anton croaked. "I . . . can't . . . breathe."

Luke let go of Anton and ran his fingers through his own hair. "I can't let this happen." His eyes teared as he looked at Oliver. "Is there anything we can do?"

"Well, we can certainly try."

Ken walked up. "Anything I can do?"

Luke looked from Oliver to Ken. "Do you need Sarah?"

Ken gave a confused look. "Excuse me?"

"I mean, can you complete your work for the Mars mission without her?"

Ken shook his head. "Not very well. She's the one who basically came up with the screening program all by herself."

Luke looked back at Anton. "Do you agree with Ken, or do you think it was all your brilliant idea?"

Anton shook his head and gave Luke a hurtful look. "I'm not heartless, Luke, in spite of what you think. Sarah took my initial idea and developed an efficient protocol for screening who can physically take the strain of the Mars mission. She refined the protocol quite substantially from my original design."

Luke looked between Anton and Ken. "There. Then do you feel you can make a compelling argument?"

Ken nodded, still looking a little confused. "I know I can. If they want this Mars mission to go without a hitch, they need Sarah."

Anton gave a shrug. "Maybe. I'm not disagreeing, mind you. Simone is one tough person to get to change her mind."

Luke put his face right next to Anton's. "Well, maybe you'd better start thinking of how to do just that."

Oliver finally let go of Anton. "Luke, I'll take Anton and Ken with me. If they're unsuccessful, I'll think of something else."

Anton rubbed his wrists and shoulder. "And what do you think you can do?"

Oliver gave Anton a stare. "You just worry about you."

Anton took a step back from Oliver, apparently feeling just as uneasy with Oliver not restraining him as he did when restrained.

Luke nodded. "OK, the four of us will head back to Paris."

Oliver shook his head. "Luke, you should stay here."

Anton nodded. "If you're there, it could make things worse."

Oliver grimaced. "As much as I don't want to agree with this guy, in this instance, I do."

Luke's jaw dropped. "What? You expect me to just stay here while my wife is in severe danger?" He shook his head. "No, I can't—I won't."

Oliver put his hand on Luke's shoulder. "I completely understand, buddy. But it's more about what's best for Sarah right now and her best chances. Anton and Ken are her best chances right now." He looked Luke in the eye. "Believe me, I will do everything in my power to bring her back—no matter their success."

Luke ran his hand over his mouth. He shook his head. "I don't like it." He gave a long sigh. "But if Philippe and Simone see me right now, it will only make them more determined." He threw up his hands. "OK. I concede." His eyes watered again. He grabbed Oliver's shoulder. "If anything happens to her . . . " His throat constricted. Luke could not finish his sentence.

Oliver put his hand over Luke's. "She's family to me, too, Luke. Rest assured, I will not leave family behind."

Luke nodded. Oliver gave him a quick, heartfelt hug and then motioned for Ken and Anton to follow him.

Luke heard Ken say, "Oliver, fill me in," as Viktoria joined the three of them as they left.

Jeremy put his hand on Luke's shoulder until the others had walked out of sight, and then waved for Natalia to come over. "Luke, go with Natalia back to the penthouse. I'll dismiss everyone else for you."

Luke nodded. "Thanks, Jeremy." He turned with Natalia, but then turned back to Jeremy. "Ask Maher up also, will you? He's sort of the odd man out over there."

Jeremy gave a weak smile. "Sure. I'll bring him up with mom and dad."